CW00546669

TRUE CONVICTION

JAMES P. SUMNER

BOTH
barrels
PUBLISHING

TRUE CONVICTION

FOURTH EDITION PUBLISHED IN 2021 BY BOTH BARRELS PUBLISHING LTD.

COPYRIGHT © JAMES P. SUMNER 2015

ISBN: 978-1-914191-04-6 (PAPERBACK)

THIS NOVEL IS A WORK OF FICTION. ALL CHARACTERS, LOCATIONS, SITUATIONS, AND EVENTS ARE EITHER PRODUCTS OF THE AUTHOR'S IMAGINATION OR USED FICTITIOUSLY. ANY RESEMBLANCE TO ANY PERSON, PLACE, OR EVENT IS PURELY COINCIDENTAL.

VISIT THE AUTHOR'S WEBSITE: JAMESPSUMNER.COM

Where it all begins...

TRUE CONVICTION

ADRIAN HELL: BOOK 1

1

The long, straight highway cutting across the unforgiving landscape in front of me is steaming in the afternoon sun.

Holy crap, it's hot.

I can't really complain. I mean, I'm still wearing my leather jacket. I know it isn't helping, but I'm on a job, and you never know who's watching. Reputation is everything in my line of work. For me, it all rests on the image I portray to the people around me. I've become synonymous with this jacket over the years, so I never leave home without it.

Still, I suppose I could've stayed on the air-conditioned bus for the last four miles. But it's been a long day, and I feel like stretching my legs.

I got the call yesterday. I was in Milwaukee, standing on the balcony of a hotel room fifteen floors up. It was early evening. The temperature had been a refreshing sixty-four degrees.

Inside the apartment, lay on the bed, was a dead man. I

had spent three days tracking him. I finally found him holed up inside the hotel. I knocked on his door. When he answered, I kicked it hard, so it flew open and hit him in the face. I assumed the security chain would be fastened and figured the initial force would've been necessary to gain entry. He stumbled backward and fell over, clutching his bleeding nose, which I had broken. His wide eyes had stared up at me, his face a mixture of fear and confusion.

"Sit on the bed," I said to him.

He didn't move at first, but as soon as I drew my gun and aimed it at him, he didn't hesitate a second longer. Once he was on the bed, I had reached into my pocket and pulled out the suppressor. I took my time attaching it, letting him see what was coming... letting him process the realization that it was the last night of his life.

"W-why?" he asked. "What do you want with me?"

Normally, I keep quiet. Silence forces them to start thinking, to jump to their own conclusions, which leads to fear and submission. It's a standard psychological tactic designed to keep your target distracted, so they don't think about resisting.

Plus, it's more entertaining.

Now don't get me wrong. I never take pleasure in doing what I do. If anything, I find it quite monotonous at times. But it pays well and I'm good at it. It's not always easy, but I try to remain detached. To stay out of my own head. It allows me to see things objectively—every angle, every possible outcome.

I operate by relying on my instincts and preparing for anything.

The man clearly had no idea why I was there, though, so I felt compelled to fill in the blanks for him.

I said, "So, here's the thing. You're a piece of shit who's

spent the last few years abusing your wife. Physically. Emotionally. Completely. And that just ain't right."

He quickly reached the conclusion I was going to shoot him. He went through the motions of begging and bargaining, but it was never going to do him any good.

My cell phone had started ringing just as I took aim at the guy's head. I quickly put my Bluetooth earpiece in and answered.

I said, "Hey, man. Just gimme a second, would you?"

Then I put a bullet right between his eyes, causing an instant explosion of crimson and pink to spray across the wall behind him. His body twitched as it fell back, leaving him lying motionless on the bloodstained covers.

I walked out onto the balcony and took a deep, calming breath as I looked at the beautiful city sprawled out below me.

I then took the call from my handler, and he told me about this job. He said it would be a good payout for easy work.

I took it without more than a second thought.

I got an early start this morning. I hopped on the first Greyhound to Minnesota. From there, I flew down to Las Vegas. There were some delays along the way, but nothing major. Plus, the advantage of being in business for yourself is that you rarely have to rush, so I've tried to relax and enjoy the trip.

But by the time I was on the bus heading here, the traveling, the lack of legroom, and the loud, sweaty people were all starting to annoy me. I could feel the beginnings of a headache, and my stress levels were slowly climbing into homicidal territory. So, when we drove past a sign that announced the city limits were only four miles away, I decided to walk it.

The sweat's running down my face and into my eyes, stinging them as I walk beneath the blistering sun. I squint ahead, seeing the steam rise off the blacktop on the horizon. The faint image of the city and mountains beyond is wavy, like a mirage.

My shoulder's aching from the weight of my bag. I always travel light, but fatigue's setting in.

What I wouldn't give right now for an ice-cold beer.

Heaven's Valley is a basin city in the middle of the Nevada desert, about a hundred and fifty miles north of Vegas. Bordering it to the North and the West are mountains. To the South and the East is nothing but sand. Its reputation is well-known. People say it's easy to lose yourself there. It thrives on the sins of the common man. Drugs, money, women... all there for those who want it.

But one man's Heaven can be another man's Hell.

Me? I've made a career out of being invisible and avoiding places like this. But I've developed somewhat of a reputation in certain... unsavory circles, which means I'm more notorious than anonymous nowadays. It also means I sometimes have to travel to places I otherwise wouldn't.

You see, I'm an assassin. Probably the best operating in North America today. Maybe even the world. I don't know. I say that with no ego. It's just a fact. I've honed my craft over the last eleven years, and I take pride in being this good at it.

I was military—first one through the door during Desert Shield. From there, I was recruited to Langley. But since retiring from doing the government's dirty work, I found it difficult to hold down a job that didn't involve shooting people. Old habits, I guess. So, I've worked hard, and with some help, I've become a legend in the criminal fraternity. Nowadays, I'm regarded as the only hitman worth hiring if you want a job done right.

Does that make me sound like a bad person? I like to think not. I'm not an assassin like you see in the movies. I won't ever pull the trigger unless I'm satisfied the target deserves a bullet. In my line of work, you deal with a lot of people who do terrible things, so I don't feel bad saying someone *deserves* to die.

On the other hand, I suppose you could argue that, strictly speaking, I kill people for a living. I'm hardly going to win any humanitarian awards.

But think what you want. I'm going to continue taking money off bad people in return for killing other bad people. Once you've worked for the CIA, it's almost impossible to find your moral compass again, so I just listen to my gut and do what I believe is right. So long as I can look myself in the mirror at the end of the day, I'm happy.

So, who am I?

My name is Adrian Hell.

2

I'm sitting on a stool in the local bar—a small, anonymous place called Charlie's. I'm leaning forward, resting on my crossed arms, nursing a half-empty bottle of Bud. Just to the left of it is a double Johnnie Walker Black, which I like to drink alongside a nice beer. It's just before eight p.m. I'm tired after the walk into town. I headed straight to the first place that looked like it would have a half-decent jukebox and ordered a drink.

A thin layer of dust from the road covers my jeans and boots. The sweat's soaked my white T-shirt through, so I've not removed my brown leather jacket. My shoulder bag is at my feet, resting against my bar stool.

Before sitting down, I'd walked across the bar to the jukebox and cycled through all the crap I've never heard of until I found a couple of good songs to listen to. I'd fed some quarters into the machine, selected my tracks, and then headed back to the bar to order my drinks.

The music isn't too loud, and this place isn't too busy. I close my eyes and listen to the world around me. The clack of the balls on the pool table sounds over my right shoulder, in the dark corner lit only by a neon blue sign advertising a beer I've never heard of. The idle chatter from the table to my left, where three women are discussing work and shopping and men. Two guys are just to the right of me, standing at the bar and exchanging one-line observations about the current state of the government. The bartender is in front of me, wiping down glasses until they squeak.

I open my eyes, examining my reflection in the mirror behind the bar. I take another long pull of my beer and let out a heavy sigh. My ice-blue eyes look like searchlights on the dark landscape of my face, which feels dirty from the hours of traveling. I stroke my chin and throat, feeling the coarse, three-day-old stubble grate on my hand like sandpaper.

I need a shave and a shower.

I rub my hand over my shaved head, briefly massaging my temples. I take a deep breath and feel the strain of a full day on the road slowly leave me.

I smile to myself. I feel comfortable in this bar. Dull lighting, sticky floors, and no pleasantries exchanged between strangers... Just the music and me. If I ever run my own bar, it'll be exactly like this.

I glance outside as the orange glow of the setting sun casts an impressive, picturesque view through the window. Heaven's Valley is a deceptive place. At first glance, it's a bright, opulent city, filled with opportunity. But beneath the surface beats its true, corrupt, dark heart. Gambling, girls, gangsters... This place has one of the highest crime rates on the West Coast. It's definitely some people's idea of a good time, but it's certainly not mine. Unfortunately, in my line of work, the people who like places like this are usually the people who hire me.

It's not easy doing what I do. You need more than just a trained set of skills. You need certain mental attributes as well. Probably the most important is you have to be comfortable taking a life. It's easy to talk about, but when you're in that moment, staring some poor schmuck dead in the eye right before you pull the trigger—that's something else altogether. I've been doing it over half my life, and it's only been recently that I've found myself feeling more at ease with it.

I don't like seeing nice, normal people suffer. Most of the time, the people who hire me are unsavory at best, but the person or people they want me to kill have usually done something that justifies a bullet. Drug dealers, pimps, corrupt cops... you name it. I can easily look myself in the eye after killing anyone who does something that negatively affects regular, innocent people.

The second quality any good contract killer needs is the right attitude. Not just to carry out a job but to make the job work for you. If you play this game just right, your name can put fear in the hearts of every man in the room, even if you're miles away. Look at me... after a decade of doing this, I'm a legend in the criminal underworld. And to the various law enforcement agencies around the country, I'm a myth— a horror story they tell new recruits to scare them. No one believes anyone as ruthless or as skilled as me can really exist.

Suckers.

Fortunate Son by Creedence Clearwater Revival comes on the jukebox. God, I love this song! The soundtrack of the Vietnam War. The conflict might've been a bit before my time, but I appreciate the music that came about as a result of it.

I'm muttering the words quietly to myself when the music suddenly stops. I look up at the barman with a disappointed and confused expression on my face. He's looking behind me with wide, regretful eyes. He looks at me for a second, then lowers his gaze in a silent apology. He puts the glass he was cleaning down and steps slowly away from the bar.

I sigh. I don't need to look behind me to figure out what's coming next. I take another long sip of my well-earned beer and spin around on my seat. I lean back and rest my elbows on the bar behind me, holding the neck of my bottle loosely in my right hand. Walking toward me are two muscle-bound stereotypes wearing suits—one with the jacket on, open, and one wearing just the waistcoat. They're side by side, staring a hole straight through me and looking really pissed off.

I sigh again.

Why me?

They both look similar. The guy on the left is the smaller of the two, but they're both big guys. I'm a shade over six foot, and they both easily have a few inches on me. The smaller guy hasn't shaved in a few days. He's the one in the suit jacket. His shoulders are back, his chest is puffed out, and I haven't seen him blink once. He's clearly been practicing his intimidating persona, and he's giving it everything he's got as he walks toward me. I suspect he's overcompensating for something, which would make him the mouth.

His slightly taller friend in the waistcoat looks more physically impressive and seems more relaxed. He's clean-shaven and easily the more presentable of the two. He's not as tense, and he's blinking more, so I'm guessing he's the muscle—the confident one who doesn't need to pay much attention to the psychological side of conflict like his friend.

What noise there was in the bar has stopped. There's an audible, collective intake of breath as the people around me stop and stare with a mixture of fascination and fear.

It's good that I don't get self-conscious.

The two angry stereotypes stop three feet in front of me.

The guy on my left cracks his neck. He straightens his jacket and clears his throat. "You put that song on?"

I take a sip of my beer and shrug. "Yeah. You not a fan?"

"That song makes my friend here unhappy. Reminds him of someone he knew."

I turn to his friend in the waistcoat and raise my eyebrows. "Is that right?"

It's the first guy who answers me. "Yeah, that's right, and we don't appreciate a stranger walking in here and causing problems like that for us regulars."

I stare at the muscle a moment longer before turning back to the mouth. "I'm just here for a quiet drink. I meant no offense."

"That may be, but offense was caused all the same. Which leaves you in a bad situation."

You can argue this is a flaw of mine, but I love winding people up just before a fight. And let's face it: this is going to end up in a fight. Not much of one, I'll admit, because these two assholes couldn't beat me if I was asleep. But it'll be a fight nevertheless.

I think a bit of trash-talk is a good thing—if you do it right, you can make people so angry that they'll attack you without thinking. This greatly increases the chances of them making a mistake. And all it takes is one mistake and *Bam!* Goodnight, sweetheart.

Plus, it amuses me.

I smile. "Really? Why? I'm sitting in a bar, drinking a beer and relaxing after a long day. Seems like a pretty *good* situation to me. Granted, it'd be better if I didn't have to waste my breath on you two ass-clowns, but I can definitely think of worse things."

Usually, when people their size confront someone, they would expect them to back down or run off. They definitely wouldn't expect anyone to spark up a conversation or openly insult them.

They exchange a bewildered glance, as if asking each other if they can believe I'd have the nerve to speak to them like that.

The mouth points a finger at me. "You got some mouth on you, asshole. You know that?"

I shrug and nod. "I know. Gets me in all sorts of trouble. What's your name?"

He doesn't expect that, either.

He frowns. "Huh? It's... ah... it's Stan."

"Stan?" I point to his friend. "Does that make him Ollie?"

The muscle in the waistcoat cracks his knuckles. I see his cheeks have flushed red with anger. I thought that only happened in cartoons or something.

"No."

I point at him. "Is your surname Dupp?"

"No, it's not, wise-ass."

They're both getting angrier by the second, and I love it. I honestly can't wait for one of them to make a move for me.

Please don't judge me for how I entertain myself.

I turn back to the muscle—whose name *isn't* Oli, apparently. "So, what do they call you? Big and Dumb?"

Before he has chance to answer, Stan lurches forward and throws a big right hand at my face.

Holy shit, *that* did it! Here we go...

Luckily for me, it's possibly the slowest punch ever thrown, and I see it coming a mile away. In one quick movement, I push myself off my stool with my left leg and step through with my right, kicking Stan's front leg away from him. Just a little tap—enough to send him off-balance but not hard enough to break anything.

Because of the weight he put behind the punch, and the fact his leg's now moving uncontrollably away from him, his own momentum sends him crashing forward into the bar. As he goes down, I side-step away and slam my fist into his left temple. He bounces off the bar, and he's out cold by the time he hits the floor.

Using the momentum from the right hand, I continue to turn my body counterclockwise. I bring my left elbow up and swing it behind me, catching ol' Big and Dumb on the side of the chin as he moves in. It's not the most accurate or powerful shot I've ever thrown, but it does the job of sending him staggering backward because he was completely unprepared for it. As he does, I complete the turn and thrust my right fist into his sternum, just below his rib cage. There's a *lot* of power behind it, and it hits him as sweetly as possible.

When you take that kind of shot, your body instinctively doubles over. Because he's already moving backward from the elbow strike, both movements counter one another, and he just slumps straight down. He lands in the fetal position, making an awful rasping noise as he tries to breathe. He rolls around for a moment before giving up and passing out.

I look first at Stan, then his friend, unconscious at my feet. I step back over to the bar and gulp my Johnnie Walker in one. I reach into my pocket and throw down a twenty before picking up my bag and walking out. My footsteps are loud in the stunned silence of the bar. I stand on the sidewalk just outside Charlie's and take a couple of deep breaths, telling my body I no longer need any adrenaline and to slow my heart rate down.

The tops of the buildings are silhouetted against the setting sun in front of me. I look left and right, trying to decide which way will get me to a motel faster. I have absolutely no idea, so I resort to my age-old philosophy: when in doubt, go left.

I set off walking and take out my cell phone. I dial a number from memory. It rings twice before it's answered.

"Adrian! Great to hear from you, boss! How's Heaven's Valley so far?"

The guy on the other end has one of those annoying voices that always sounds happy, regardless of the situation. However, he's one of the few people on this planet I trust, so I let him off.

I met Josh Winters shortly after being recruited by the CIA to lead a black ops unit that was a joint effort between the U.S. and the British. We quickly bonded and became like brothers, so when I got out and decided to work freelance, he was more than happy to come with me. He's been working with me for the past eleven years, making contacts, finding me jobs, and supplying me with information and anything else I might need. My life is in his hands.

I can tell he's smiling down the phone as he speaks. I shake my head and smile to myself. "I've been in this goddamn town half an hour and I've already been in a fight. I don't like it here."

He laughs. "You *do* have a tendency to make a unique first impression, don't you?"

I laugh with him. "Screw you, Josh. We all set for tomorrow?"

"Yeah, you're meeting a guy called Jimmy Manhattan. This guy, and the people he represents... they're old school, Adrian. So, I say this with all the love in the world, but try to avoid being too... *you*, all right?"

I'm almost offended, but I know what he's trying to say. I've worked for guys like these many times, and they take their code seriously. Disrespecting someone like Jimmy Manhattan would bring a lot of unnecessary trouble down on top of me.

"Fear not, my man. I shall be at my most professional."

"That's what I'm worried about! Call me afterward if you need anything."

"Will do."

I hang up and continue my search for a nice motel where I can grab a shower and some sleep. I find myself humming *Fortunate Son*, which I didn't get to finish listening to in Charlie's.

Assholes.

3

I'm walking along a quiet street just off the main strip that runs through the center of the city. The sun is glorious and warm, even at this time in the morning, and it's getting hotter by the minute. A barren, unforgiving desert surrounds Heaven's Valley, so intensely hot sun all year round is commonplace.

I'm meeting Manhattan at nine a.m., so I'm going to get there early and scope the place out. It's an old habit that was drilled into me on the very first day of boot camp—reconnaissance can save your life. Always know where the enemy will come from, and always know how you can get out. Especially in this situation, where I'm meeting someone I don't know or trust. I like to plan my exit strategy long before I make my entrance.

The meeting is in a quaint little family-owned coffee shop called Dimitri's. On the outside, the window frames are a faded brown. The company logo is emblazoned across the glass. To the left is the entrance. There's enough room outside for three sets of tables and chairs, which I imagine are going to be occupied most of the day, given the weather.

I walk inside. I'm surprised at how spacious it is—much bigger than I expected. The layout inside is like a grid, with seating arranged in three rows of three in front of the serving counter that runs almost the full width of the far wall. The rows on the left and right are booths, which seat four people, two facing two. The middle row has round tables with four chairs on each compass point around it.

The café must've just opened. There's an aging guy with short, gray hair setting up the cappuccino machine behind the counter. He turns as I approach and eyes me up and down before turning back to his work. He's probably in his early seventies. His tanned skin is like old leather, and he's got these faded, blue-gray tattoos on his forearms, presumably from time served in the military.

I approach the counter. "Morning. Can I get a coffee, black with two sugars, please?"

He doesn't look around. "Be right over."

I turn and look out at the empty café, trying to decide where would be best to sit and wait. I figure the booth near the window on the right-hand side is best. I walk over and slide across, twisting slightly to my left. I put my back to the wall and rest one knee on the seat, so I can see the entire place in front of me—the entrance, the counter, and the doors behind it, as well as outside through the window. From here, I can see everyone approaching and don't have to worry about anyone coming up behind me. More old habits that have saved my ass more than once.

Some people call me paranoid, but it's not paranoia if the bastards are really after you.

A few minutes pass, then the old guy brings my coffee over.

"You want breakfast?" he asks.

I shake my head. "I'm good, thanks."

He nods once and walks back to the counter. I take a sip of my coffee and gaze around absently. I look out the window and see three men approaching from down the street.

This must be him.

I'm both impressed and concerned that he's prepared enough to show up early like I did. I need to be on my game here.

The door opens and the three men walk in.

Showtime.

The first guy is probably early fifties, wearing what looks like an expensive, light brown three-piece suit. He's a thin, wiry guy but walks with the utmost confidence and grace. He comes across as a man who never rushes to be some-where. He doesn't need to. He's staring at me but not in an aggressive way. It's more like... curiosity.

Hello, Jimmy Manhattan.

The two guys behind him must be the bodyguards. Manhattan doesn't strike me as the kind of guy who needs hired muscle. They might be here more for intimidation than actual protection. Maybe they—

Shit.

I look closer at the bodyguards.

Yeah... they're my two friends from the bar last night.

Both look like they're suffering from a bad hangover. My face betrays nothing, but inside, I can't help but laugh. Only *I* would manage to get into a fight with the security detail of my next employer.

I don't stand, and I certainly don't extend my hand to greet them. I simply pick up my coffee and take another sip.

The old guy walks over to my booth. "You must be Adrian Hell."

His voice is smooth, and his accent is very... East Coast. Brooklyn, maybe? He's a long way from home.

I nod. "Jimmy Manhattan, I presume?"

"At your service. I see your reputation for being thorough and punctual is well deserved."

I shrug. "Well, you know what they say: the early bird gets the... contract, I guess." I smile. "I see you've brought friends..." I look up at them and address each in turn. "Fred... Ginger..." I hold my hands up apologetically. "No hard feelings about yesterday?"

They both glare at me with evil in their eyes and the hint of a snarl on their lips. But neither speaks or even moves a muscle. They just glance at Manhattan and remain still.

I look back at him and smile. "I see you've got the dogs well trained. I'm impressed."

Manhattan lets slip a half-smile but remains unwavering in his cool, confident demeanor. "And I see the reputation about your mouth is accurate too." He looks over his shoulder at Stan. "Give me and Mr. Hell some privacy, would you?"

Stan and his friend walk over to the counter and sit down facing me. I hold their gaze for a second with my best un-blinking, deadpan poker face, then look away. They don't bother me. The only reason either of them is here is to emphasize Jimmy's importance and to intimidate whomever he's meeting. That won't work with me and everyone here knows it.

Manhattan clasps his hands on the table in front of him. "So, Mr. Hell—or can I call you Adrian?"

He's professional and respectful. I suspect his manner is a practiced act to disarm the other person, get them feeling comfortable and relaxed. That's when he'll reel you in. Again, it's never going to work on me, but I appreciate his friendly approach, and I reciprocate.

I shrug. "I've been called worse than both, so feel free."

I quite like *Mr. Hell* though. I might try using that in the future, see if it catches on.

"Adrian it is, then. Now I represent Roberto Pellaggio, and I'm here at his request to offer you a job befitting your particular set of skills."

He produces a brown, letter-sized envelope and slides it across the table to me. I open it and take out a photograph and some papers. It's a black and white eight-by-ten of a man in a suit walking across a road. He's talking on his phone and carrying a briefcase.

Manhattan gestures to the photograph. "This is Ted Jackson. Until recently, we were working with Mr. Jackson on a business deal to secure some land on the outskirts of the city. Mr. Pellaggio is looking to expand his business portfolio by building a casino there."

I don't look up. I'm engrossed in the picture, taking in every detail. "Go on..."

"A few days ago, with no warning or explanation, Mr. Jackson backed out of that deal. He kept the deeds to the land, as well as the money Mr. Pellaggio had already invested into it."

I look up. "And you want me to make him disappear?"

"Mr. Pellaggio is a respected businessman with a—how can I put it?—well known and formidable reputation. A slight of this kind cannot be tolerated under any circumstances. We must send a clear message."

"I understand. Consider it done."

"There's something else. It's also of vital importance that you retrieve the deeds to that land. Mr. Pellaggio is eager to complete this deal and begin construction of the casino, and that paperwork is the key."

"Not a problem."

I'm more than happy to take this job. It's straightforward and easy money—find a businessman, kill him, and steal some paperwork. Give the papers to the mafia and get my money... I can be out of here in a couple of days. I'm not a big fan of this close, desert heat, so the sooner I can get back to somewhere slightly milder, the better.

Manhattan stands, prompting Stan and his friend at the counter to do the same. "I look forward to seeing more of your work, Adrian." He glances over at his bodyguards. "It comes highly recommended."

I laugh. "Thank you."

"We'll speak again when you have completed the job."

Manhattan nods a silent goodbye, then turns and walks out of the café, followed by his bodyguards. As they walk off, Stan turns to me and flips me the finger. I simply smile and wave back.

God, I wish I'd hit him harder.

08:41 PDT

I wait a few minutes after they leave to finish my coffee. I stand, gather the contents of the envelope up, leave a tip on the table, and head back outside. As I open the door, I'm hit by a blast of heat, as if I've opened an oven that's been cooking for three hours. I was only inside maybe a half-hour, but the increase in temperature is staggering.

The sun is pounding down as I make my way along the sidewalk. I'm wearing a white T-shirt and jeans, minus the leather jacket, with black sunglasses and a baseball cap. I cross to the other side of the street, as it's partly shaded, but it does little to cool me down.

I'm in the center of the business district, and it's busy. Maybe it's because I'm not a local and unaccustomed to the climate, but it baffles me how anyone can walk around in a suit when it's this hot.

I take out my cell and dial Josh's number. It rings twice.

"Hey, boss. How did it go with Jimmy the Glove?"

He sounds as sickeningly enthusiastic as always.

I frown. "Is that what people call him?"

"Apparently."

"Do I want to know why?"

He pauses. "Probably not."

"Fair enough. Yeah, the meeting went fine, despite finding out that Manhattan's hired goons were the assholes that started a fight with me last night."

"You're shitting me?" he says, laughing.

"I shit you not, my friend."

"I bet that went down well?"

"It was fine. He seemed to find it quite amusing, to his credit."

"Only you, boss. So, are you happy with the contract?"

"Yeah, it should be straightforward. It's a property deal gone bad. He wants me to take out the target to send a message, then recover the deeds to some land they were intending to buy from him before he screwed them over. It shouldn't take me more than a couple of days. Will be glad to get out of this place and go somewhere slightly colder— this heat is unbearable."

"Surely, the ice in your veins cools you down?"

I shake my head. "Screw you."

He chuckles to himself. "You need anything from me?"

"Not right now, but I know where you are if I need you. I'll be in touch."

Just as I'm about to hang up, I remember one last thing. "Oh, what do you think of 'Mr. Hell' as my business name?"

Josh begins howling with laughter. Exaggerated and loud. I hold the phone away from my ear until he's finished.

"Oh, dear... Heh... Sorry. Are you serious?"

"Yeah, it's how Manhattan addressed me when we were exchanging pleasantries. Kinda liked it."

"Adrian, you know I love you, right?"

I pause. "Yeah..."

"It makes you sound like a professional wrestler. Who's gay."

I remain silent for a few moments, trying to make him feel uneasy. Although, I know that probably won't work. "Josh, you know I love you, right?"

"Yeah..."

"You're a dick."

I hang up and walk on, navigating the increasingly busy streets.

I think I'll do some recon work for the job, get to know the city a little better. According to the information Jimmy Manhattan gave me, Jackson is attending a meeting this morning, which is due to finish any time in the next half-hour. I'll find where he is and tail him on foot for as long as I can. I'll be able to get a look at his car, any colleagues or security he might have—get a feel for his behaviors and routines. I've also got his itinerary for the next twenty-four hours, courtesy of Manhattan's research, so I'll approach when he finishes work to minimize the risk of exposure and attention.

I walk on through the city, taking in the sights around me. The working day is in full swing, with everyone around me dressed for the office and rushing in all directions. People are carrying bags, or papers, or their morning coffee, weaving in and out of the crowds on either side of the street.

The traffic's just as busy. It's mostly taxis—nose to tail, fighting to get through the next set of lights before they change again.

I come to a large junction, where Main Street meets 9th Avenue. I cross over and turn right, which will lead me to Cannon Plaza, where Jackson is currently in his meeting.

After a few minutes, I come upon the plaza. It has a large fountain in the center and lots of people walking across it in every direction. Jackson's in the building at the far end, which is a tall, unmarked, dark glass structure. It's easily twenty stories high, overlooking the plaza below. I fight my way through the bustle of people and sit on the edge of the fountain facing east, so that the entrance to the building is on my left, about fifty feet away.

After a few moments, a young woman with a child in a stroller sits next to me, smiling politely. I smile back and briefly look at the baby as she rummages in her bag. I've never been a particularly broody guy, and children haven't been on my radar at all since I lost my daughter. But I have to admit, it's one cute little kid. It couldn't be more than eight months old. It's got a bubble of spit on its lips and these big, wide brown eyes looking around in awe at everything. It's nice to see that true innocence still exists in this world.

I turn my attention back to the building, looking out for Jackson. I don't have to wait long. After maybe five minutes, I see him walk out of the building. Just like in the photograph, he looks ever the businessman. He's in his late forties and wearing an expensive-looking gray suit. He's talking on his cell phone as he walks purposefully across the plaza. Handcuffed to his left wrist is a brown leather briefcase. That's interesting... You don't normally see that kind of security measure on everyday people. Not unless he's carrying a large amount of money or top-secret documents. But why would he be?

I'm a details guy and I question everything. Sometimes the smallest detail can have the largest impact. I make a mental note of the observation and move on. I'll mention it to Josh later, see what he thinks.

Jackson's walking fast, like he's running late. It looks like he's alone, so I stand and set off following him, keeping a casual distance between—

Oh... hang on a minute.

I stop after a couple of steps when something catches my eye just behind him. I slow down and watch, double-checking to make sure I'm not mistaken. He's not alone. Walking a couple of paces behind, at roughly the same speed, is a bodyguard.

And she's beautiful.

4

She's wearing fitted pants and a low-cut tank top—both are black. She's also wearing a short, tight leather jacket that finishes just above her waist, dark sunglasses, and the brightest red lipstick I've ever seen. Her dyed-blonde hair is resting on her shoulders, bouncing as she walks purposefully, never taking her eyes off Jackson. She's got an amazing body. Because her clothes are so tight, I can see the definition on her arms and long legs.

I have absolutely no idea how she's managing to walk around in this heat dressed like an extra from *The Matrix*—I can barely function wearing a T-shirt!

I get over the initial shock and quickly take my phone out. I take a couple of pictures and send them to Josh, then put my Bluetooth earpiece in and call him. I set off walking after Jackson and the mystery woman. I negotiate my way through the crowds, trying to keep sight of my target while remaining discreet.

He answers. "Yeah?"

"Josh, it's me. Have you got the pictures I just sent you?"

He chuckles. "I sure have! Who's the expensive-looking prostitute?"

"That's what I want you to find out. She's Jackson's bodyguard. And as much as I'm sure you'd love to find out she actually *is* a prostitute, my gut's telling me she's in the business. Maybe not a contractor... A merc, maybe? Find out all you can about her, as well as Jackson and why he's hired her for protection. Also, while you're at it, dig up what you can on Pellaggio, would you? The game's starting to get interesting, and I want to know about all the players on the field."

"You don't ask for much, do you?" He chuckles again. "Leave it with me, Boss Man."

Josh hangs up. I keep a reasonable distance behind them, following them round the corner at the far end of the plaza. As I turn, I see Jackson and his bodyguard approaching a parked limousine. The car's beautiful and high-end. It's a black stretch with a personalized license plate. I look at it approvingly with a well-trained eye, memorizing every detail. I'm familiar with this model. It's armored, with bulletproof, tinted windows and run-flat tires. It's a serious vehicle... Maybe taking this guy out won't be as easy as I first thought.

I take a couple more pictures on my phone and send them to Josh, then hang back as Jackson and his leather-clad protector get in the car. I lean against one of the small trees that line the street on both sides, pretending to talk on the phone as I casually glance over at them.

The woman holds the door open and ushers Jackson inside. She then looks all around the street in every direction—including up, which I find interesting. She glances in my direction. With her glasses on, I can't see her eyes, but I know she won't spot me. I'm practically invisible when I want to be, so there's no way she'll pick me out of the crowd on a standard surveillance run like this.

She finally climbs in after him, slamming the door shut behind her. The limo speeds off, turning left and out of sight at the first set of lights they reach.

Her thoroughness is going to be an issue... She has a level of professionalism you don't normally find in your typical bodyguards. Not many people would think to look up and check for snipers. I'm certain she's highly trained. She might even be in my line of work. I'm not sure yet. But I'm concerned with her presence in the equation.

I turn and casually walk back the way I came. So far, this hasn't quite gone how I expected it to, and it's left me with more questions than answers. This supposedly straightforward job is suddenly a lot more complicated, and I've got a nagging feeling it's not going to get any easier.

10:23 PDT

My recon trip set my spider sense tingling, so I headed back to my motel room to clear my head and plan my next move. It's a standard room. The window overlooks the parking lot, which is empty save for one silver, four-door sedan. There's a flat-screen TV mounted on one wall, above a table with a lamp on it. It's facing the double bed, which is unusually comfortable, given the price of the room. The bathroom has a shower stall, a toilet, and a sink. It's not fancy, but it certainly does the job for a couple days.

I'm not cheap or anything. If I'm honest, I have more money than I know what to do with. I'm just not one for all that luxurious, five-star, A-list crap. I'm more than happy in a generic, anonymous, no-frills motel, away from everyone else.

I'm sitting on the edge of the bed, enjoying the air conditioning, and running everything through my head. Josh insists I keep a laptop with me when I'm traveling, even though I'm far from competent using one. It's next to me, booting up. He texted me earlier to say he's sending me all the information he's found out so far, so I'll look through it all now and see if I can start piecing things together.

Josh Winters is a genius. Sure, we insult each other non-stop, but that's just to get us both through the day. When it all comes down to it, the guy is a legend in so many ways, I've lost count. The things he can do with a computer are mind-blowing. I don't pretend to understand half of what he says or does. But he gets results every time. I need information, Josh gets it. I need a car, a plane, or a gun, Josh arranges it. I need fake documents, Josh makes them for me.

I open up my e-mails and find three, each with multiple attachments. The subject of the first one says *Ted Jackson*. I open it and scan through the information. He's apparently a high-ranking employee of a large, multinational private military corporation called GlobaTech Industries. In addition to having their own army-for-hire, they have numerous subsidiary divisions for weapons development, technological research... even healthcare. They legally own the land Jackson was supposed to sell to Pellaggio.

That explains the extra security measures. In his line of work, I can understand him being cautious. Military contracts are big business. Competition for them is fierce. But even so, handcuffing his briefcase to his wrist for a regular meeting, riding around in a limousine that would make the president jealous, and hiring a hot and probably lethal bodyguard still seems like overkill to me.

Although, having said *that*, he's just screwed over the biggest mob boss in the state. Maybe it's not so surprising that he's upped his personal security.

I turn my attention to the second e-mail, about my employer. Maybe there's something in here that might offer an explanation...

Roberto Pellaggio is a big-time mafia Don who owns half of Heaven's Valley. On the surface, he's opened legitimate businesses all across the city, creating many jobs and generating lots of revenue that he's re-invested into local areas. He owns car dealerships, barbershops, nightclubs, and casinos. All big business. All above board.

But underneath all that respectable businessman crap is where he earns his real money. Drugs, prostitution, extortion... you name it. You go down the list of crimes the mob can commit, and he ticks every box. The money they earn gets laundered through their legitimate businesses, and it disappears back into the city. With the help of some clever accounting, Pellaggio is running a massive, highly profitable empire, and given how much money he's invested in the city, he's popular with local government officials and law enforcement. So, the guy's a pretty big deal and definitely not someone you want as an enemy.

I look through the e-mail and find a news report from a couple of weeks ago. It says Pellaggio has been trying to buy a plot of land near the outskirts of Heaven's Valley. He's looking to expand his empire by building another casino, like Manhattan told me earlier. The land is ideally situated near the city limits, so it holds appeal to people from neighboring towns and cities. In theory, a casino there would service all of the state's gambling needs north of Vegas.

Then, a few days later, another report surfaced in the business section of one of the local papers explaining how the deal apparently fell through. There's a picture of our good friend and future corpse, Ted Jackson. The article goes on to say how Jackson pulled out of the deal for undisclosed reasons, allegedly costing Pellaggio hundreds of millions of dollars in potential earnings.

I guess that's why they called me in. No wonder Pellaggio's pissed.

Okay, so on the surface, it still seems fairly cut and dry. Pellaggio wants to continue his monopoly of Heaven's Valley, but Jackson unscrupulously got in the way of that by canceling the deal. Pellaggio wants to send a clear message and get his business venture back on track, so he hired me to take out Jackson.

But something still doesn't feel right about it all. Jackson would've benefited from the deal as well, making a significant amount of money from selling the land. Plus, while I'm sure there are lots of valid reasons why he would want to pull out of the deal, he's smart enough to know that not explaining himself to the likes of Roberto Pellaggio would end badly for him...

Whenever there is doubt, there is no doubt—that's one of the first things they taught me back in the day. Trust your gut and never pull the trigger until you're satisfied. Some people in my line of work prefer not to know anything—they just turn up, shoot, and disappear with their money. Me? I have to know everything about everything. If you ask a shrink, they'll probably say I have control issues that need addressing. But I simply want to be the smartest guy playing the game. As much as I like getting paid for shooting people, sometimes ignorance isn't bliss. For all I know, the mob is setting me up in some way by hiring me to kill Jackson.

I pick up the phone and call Josh. "Hey, it's me."

"Hey, Cupcake. Whaddaya need now?"

"I'm just thinking out loud here, okay? So, Pellaggio tries to buy the land off Jackson for this casino venture. Both parties are expecting to make a shitload of cash. Then, suddenly, Jackson pulls the plug, costing both himself and Pellaggio a small fortune."

Josh lets out a heavy sigh down the line. "Yeah, seems strange when you say it like that. If you broker business deals with the mafia, you're probably always on the lookout for the big money opportunities and would do whatever it takes to secure them, right?"

"My thoughts exactly. So, there must've been a damn good reason for Jackson to pull a move like this and in such a hurry that he didn't even bother to tell Pellaggio. That's both corporate and *actual* suicide."

"Well, that's why *you're* there, after all."

"Precisely. Do me a favor, would you? Look into Jackson a bit more. Find out what his role is at GlobaTech. Also, see if you can find out if they've got anything in the pipeline that might cause him to switch his priorities in a hurry."

"Good idea. These people work military defense contracts. Could be something big came up that dwarfed the Pellaggio deal?"

"I mean, what's a mob boss gonna do to them if they're working alongside the United States military?"

"Sounds like a good theory. Give me a few minutes, okay?"

The line clicks off. While I'm waiting for him to work more of his magic, I look at the photograph again of Jackson and his bodyguard that I took a couple of hours ago. I've uploaded it to my laptop, and I can see it more clearly now it's on the bigger screen. Then I open up the last e-mail, with nothing in the subject, and skim over the contents. Josh hasn't managed to get a lot of information about the mystery woman, it seems, which actually tells me quite a bit...

He's attached a grainy photograph, allegedly taken four years ago, in what looks like the middle of the jungle. It shows our woman, minus the lipstick and leather, wearing camo fatigues and holding an assault rifle. She's standing between two guys dressed roughly the same way.

Other than that, there's little else to go on. No names or aliases, no known addresses, no reported sightings in the last few years. She's a ghost. And speaking as someone who spends every day trying to stay invisible—it's difficult and expensive to do properly.

Typically, you gain the skills while either serving your country, like I did after a decade of black-ops and covert assassinations, or the military or government directly made you invisible, meaning you're still in active service. Whether she's on somebody's books or not, she's still a factor that I'd rather not have to deal with.

It's human instinct to be wary of the unknown. She's talented and apparently doesn't exist, which is troublesome. Although, it explains why Jackson hired her for protection... Sounds to me like she'll do a damn good job of keeping you alive.

Maybe she's a gun-for-hire, like me...

I shake my head, dismissing the thought as quickly as it came. If she were good enough to be heard of, then I'd know who she is.

Josh added to the bottom of the message that he's running searches through active military and government databases all over the world, which is why it's taking so much time to come through.

My phone rings. It's Josh again.

I answer it and put him on speaker. "What have you got for me?"

He sighs. "Nothing new on GlobaTech. There's nothing in the news and nothing on their website or their local servers."

"So, either there was no pressure on Jackson from GlobaTech, or he's involved in something that's classified and not on the public record?"

"That's about the size of it, yeah."

"Well, either way, it's a dead-end for now..." I stand and start pacing around my motel room, thinking.

After a few moments of silence, I hear Josh laugh on the line. "You're doing that thing where you wear the carpet out trying to think, aren't you?"

I sheepishly sit back down on the bed. "No... I'm just sitting here trying to figure this all out."

Josh scoffs, knowing damn well he was right. "So, what are you gonna do?"

I massage my temples. "I'm going to speak to Jimmy Manhattan again, try to find out what the hell's going on. Either there's more to this than he's letting on, or he's as oblivious as the rest of us about Jackson's true motivations. Either way, it's still probably worth having another conversation."

"Adrian, make sure you don't say or do anything you might regret, okay? Just some friendly advice..."

"If this is any kind of set up, Josh, the bigger concern is that I'll do something *they* regret."

5

Josh tracked down where in the city Jimmy Manhattan
spends his time, so I grabbed a bite to eat before heading
over there. I've changed into a black T-shirt and thrown on
my trusty brown leather jacket. Tucked in the waistband of
my jeans at the back is one of my prized possessions—a
custom Beretta 92A1 handgun. It holds fifteen nine-by-nine-
teen-millimeter Parabellum rounds in its magazine. The 92-
series is the firearm of choice for the United States Armed
Forces. I've always preferred this particular variation to the
96-series, which fires the ten-by-twenty-two-millimeter, .40
caliber Smith and Wesson rounds. The Parabellums have a
higher rate of velocity than their Smith and Wesson coun-
terparts and have a higher penetration depth. Basically, they
cause more damage.

When it comes down to it, I just want to make the
biggest bang.

The barrel is metallic silver, as are the outer edges of the butt. On either side of the grip is an ebony plate with a downward-pointing pentagram engraved in silver. I've always liked the moniker of *Adrian Hell* that I inadvertently acquired several years ago, and I try to play on it as much as I can. Image and reputation are everything in this business, and having an expensive, customized handgun with the Sigil of Baphomet on it really helps both.

I actually have two of them. Usually, when I'm on a job, I wear them both in a custom-made holster at the small of my back. The barrels touch and the butts point out, forming a T-shape which I can easily hide beneath whatever I'm wearing. I'm only taking one with me to meet Manhattan as a precaution. I'd rather have it and not need it than need it and not have it, as the saying goes.

Manhattan works out of one of Pellaggio's nightclubs, called The Pit. It's on the fringe of the city center, surrounded by other popular nighttime destinations. From what Josh has told me, it's your typical hotspot for neon lights, hot girls, and guys looking to either deal drugs or get laid.

I'm not exactly worried about any security he might have with him. A nightclub won't be open for business in the middle of the day, so there will be minimal staff there, and they're unlikely to be threatening. Plus, I've already met two of his bodyguards, and we all know they won't be much use...

But I'm not going looking for a fight—I just want some answers. From what I've put together so far, there's definitely more to it than what Manhattan told me. I intend to ask him, quite politely, if he's trying to set me up in some way for some reason, or if he's just plain stupid.

There's a polite way of asking that, right?

I'm walking around the three blocks that make up the

Neon district. A variety of bars and clubs run down each side of the streets, separated every now and then by a hotel or fast-food restaurant. I can well imagine what this place looks like at night.

The Pit is at the end of the second block, with the main entrance diagonal on the street corner, facing northwest toward the crossroads. The building covers a quarter of the streets running both south and east of the block. Above the small alcove of the entrance is a neon sign that advertises the name of the club. I have no idea what color it lights up at night. I reckon maybe blue and white.

I push the doors gently to see if they open, but they don't budge. On the right-hand wall of the alcove is a large security keypad with a speaker and a buzzer just below it. I press it and wait. After a few moments, the speaker on the keypad crackles into life, and a voice comes through.

"What?"

Hardly an advertisement for world-class customer service, is it?

I lean forward. "I need to speak to Jimmy Manhattan."

"Never heard of him."

The line goes dead.

Well, that was rude!

It was also a lie, and I don't like being lied to. It makes my trigger finger twitch. I press the buzzer again.

"What?"

It's the same voice as before, except this time with slightly less patience. I lean forward again. "At the risk of sounding disrespectful, we both know Jimmy's in there. Now, how about you open the door, so I can talk to him? That way, I don't have to force my way inside, find you, then kick your teeth so far down your throat you'll need to stick a toothbrush up your ass to get at your pearly whites."

It falls silent for a moment, then the buzzer clicks off again. I wait for another minute, then I hear several locks being unfastened within. The right-hand door opens. I expect whoever opened it is standing just behind it, ready to grab me as I walk through, so as I step inside, I shuffle sideways to the left, so I'm facing right. The guy standing there makes no attempt to attack me, however. He simply fixes me with an intense, indignant gaze as he shuts the door and walks back into the club.

He's a lot bigger than I am, in both height and width. He's wearing a muscle shirt and jeans. His arms look like my legs. I'm not small by any means, but this guy dwarfs me. I subconsciously touch the barrel of my gun at my back for reassurance.

Just in case.

He gestures almost imperceptibly with his head for me to follow him, so I set off after him into the club. Inside, it's a nice, big place. The house lights are on, illuminating the main area. It's open-plan and spacious, with the occasional table and chairs positioned around the perimeter. There are different levels and podiums throughout, presumably for dancing on. The bar runs almost the full length of the far wall, surrounded by mirrors and neon blue. Behind the bar are rows of glass shelves that house more liquor than I knew existed. To the right is a red curtain, which presumably leads into a VIP area of some kind.

The big guy is heading for it, but before I can catch up, Jimmy Manhattan appears from behind the curtain. He's wearing a different, equally expensive suit from the one he wore to our meeting this morning. He looks a little more stressed than before as well, but he hides it expertly behind his powerfully calm persona.

He smiles professionally. "Adrian, what an unexpected

surprise. To what do I owe the pleasure? Is there a problem with the job?"

I shrug. "That's depends on your definition of a problem. The job isn't panning out the way you so confidently said it would."

He frowns and shakes his head. "How so?"

"Well, for starters, Ted Jackson has some serious security. He's got an armored limousine and what looks like a highly trained assassin as his personal bodyguard. So, what aren't you telling me?"

"I'm not sure what you're implying, Adrian, but I don't care for your tone."

His voice darkened, the professional courtesy leaving him.

I shrug again. "I couldn't care less what you think of my *tone*, and I'm not implying anything. I'm stating a fact. This guy *you* hired me to kill is clearly not your everyday, run-of-the-mill, working stiff who just so happened to piss off your boss."

In the corner of my eye, I see the big guy move to Manhattan's side, crossing his arms and staring at me. In the proper light, I can get a better look at him. Aside from being built like a goddamn tank, he's a good four inches taller than I am too. He's got muscles in places most people don't have places, as well as a tattoo of a fire ax on his left temple. I feel his gaze burning a hole through me. While I'm completely unfazed by him being there, I can't deny he's an impressive sight. Much better than Stan and Ollie.

Manhattan steps in front of his hired muscle, which I assume is a gesture to defuse any potential confrontation. "Adrian, I can assure you we gave you all the information we had on Ted Jackson. We used one of our best men to tail him."

"Well, after a couple of hours of digging around myself, I've managed to find out that our friend Ted works for a military contractor called GlobaTech Industries. I'm guessing you've heard of them? Your so-called 'best man' failed to mention the target was so well connected."

He remains calm, hiding any shock or frustration well behind his cold, dark eyes. "I have indeed heard of them. If what you say is true—"

"If that's true, then you're asking me to take out a guy who's more protected than the president, which will cost you a hell of a lot more than a hundred grand. You also need to start thinking about *why* he decided not to sell you that land. These people conduct business deals that dwarf your entire operation ten times over daily, so their behavior here strikes me as uncharacteristic. If I carry out the hit on Jackson and take the deeds for you, it won't be the last either of us hear of it."

He can see I have a valid point. He told me that Pellaggio is a businessman above all else, which means he's going to do what's best for his business. Having a global private security firm with ties to the military pissed at you probably doesn't make the list of good corporate strategies.

Manhattan is silent for a few moments, seemingly to choose his words. "For now, I would like you to proceed as you normally would and carry out the contract on Ted Jackson. If you need additional funding, simply name your price. I would like to thank you for bringing these developments to our attention. Rest assured I will speak to Mr. Pellaggio about how he wishes to go ahead. I appreciate your input, but you simply need to do the job we hired you to do and leave the rest to us."

My phone suddenly rings, sounding louder than normal

in the empty, quiet space. I smile apologetically and quickly check the caller ID.

"I'm sorry, but I need to take this…" I answer the phone. "What have you got for me, Josh?"

"I've had a hit on the searches for our mystery woman, boss. I still don't have a name, but there's another file photo. This one is more recent."

I frown. "How recent?"

"Six months ago. It was taken during a routine surveillance operation right there in Heaven's Valley."

"So, what's the story?"

"The photo shows her standing with another man whom you can't see clearly. But the photo isn't the important part. It's where I found the photo that we should worry about."

"Why? Where did you find it?"

"It was on a secure military database on a server housed in the Pentagon. I was lucky to come across it."

I feel my eyes widen a little. "You hacked the Pentagon?"

He chuckles nervously. "Let's… focus on what's important, yeah? The picture was in a folder that relates to an ongoing investigation into something called Dark Rain. Does that name mean anything to you?"

I think for a moment. "Never heard of it. Keep digging though, Josh. That's great work."

"I'll keep you updated." He hangs up.

Manhattan points to the cell. "Is everything all right?"

I'm not sure how much information I should give him. I always try to keep my cards close to my chest, but under the circumstances, I don't have much more information than they do. But I still have too many questions to mess around being discreet.

Screw it, I'll tell him.

"Depends on your point of view. I'm starting to think you've stumbled across something bigger than just the land you wanted to buy."

"What... what do you mean?"

I note that, for the first time since we met, he sounds like he doesn't have a handle on the situation. He looks uncomfortable.

"Jackson's unknown bodyguard appears to have been under surveillance by the U.S. government in the last six months."

"So, what does that have to do with Mr. Pellaggio?"

"Well, Jackson's being protected by another party that isn't his employer. I don't know why, but this is further evidence that this is bigger than just Jackson screwing you over. I would suggest approaching this with more caution than simply sending me in to kill him."

It doesn't take long for Manhattan to see I'm making sense. He glances over his shoulder to his hired muscle and mutters something I can't quite hear. The big guy nods once and walks away, disappearing behind the red curtain.

He turns his attention back to me. "Adrian, it would seem we have underestimated Ted Jackson and his resources. It also appears we have underestimated you. I want to thank you for your vigilance and commitment to this situation and to your job. In light of this development, I would like to extend your contract beyond simply disposing of Ted Jackson. I want you to work with us to see this matter through to its conclusion."

I'm a freelance contract killer. I don't work exclusively with anyone, not even on a temporary basis. I know some people that do, and they prefer it that way—it *does* provide a steady income and a certain amount of security. It's also good if you're just starting out, as it helps establish a reputation for yourself. But it won't benefit me in any way, and I have no desire to associate myself with the mafia any longer than necessary.

I hold my hands up in apology. "I'm flattered, but I have no interest in doing any more of your dirty work than I already am. I'll kill Ted Jackson for you and retrieve whatever he has on his person at the time. But once that's done, I'm gone."

Manhattan nods in a way that suggests he heard what I said but doesn't accept it. "Fine. I'll get a couple of guys on this and leave you to take out Jackson. We'll be in touch."

He turns and walks away, disappearing behind the red curtain and leaving me alone in the empty nightclub.

I glance around. "I'll see myself out, then?"

I open the front door and step back out to the street. I squint while my eyes adjust from the dark nightclub to the bright sunshine. I look up and down the street absently, letting out a sigh of frustration. A motorcycle parked across from me, facing the club's entrance, draws my gaze. It looks like the rider is staring in my direction, but it's hard to tell because the visor is down on their helmet. It's lightning blue with a white trim—a really sweet-looking ride. The rider's wearing black leathers from head to toe. I hold their gaze for a moment. They rev their engine loudly and speed off, out of sight.

How odd.

6

After meeting with Jimmy Manhattan, I headed back to my motel room to change my clothes, then out for a nice walk around the city. I needed to clear my head and assess the current and increasingly complex situation. I'm convinced there's more at stake than just Pellaggio's potential earnings.

After more deliberation than I usually afford my jobs, I think the best thing I can do is kill Ted Jackson and leave town as soon as possible. I *have* to kill him. I don't want word to get around that I've gone back on one of my contracts. That would be bad for business. But I also know how easily I'll involve myself further in whatever's going down. I hate not knowing what's happening.

I know Jackson is working out of his hotel room for the rest of the afternoon; it's on the itinerary that Manhattan gave me yesterday. I've decided to bring my plans forward and take him out right away.

I'm walking down Main Street, heading to the Four

Seasons. It's a lavish, impressive building and covers almost the entire block. Josh, being the hero that he is, has called ahead posing as my personal assistant. You could argue that doesn't require much pretending, but don't tell him I said that. He's told them I need a room on short notice and that I'm meeting one of their guests, Mr. Jackson, for an evening meal to discuss some business. He's explained I'm running late and requested Mr. Jackson's room number, so I can call him from *my* room when I arrive. That wasn't a problem for the helpful member of staff who wanted to make a good impression on two of their richest guests.

I walk through the large revolving doors and into the lobby of the hotel. It's enormous. The floor is polished marble tile with symmetrical patterns on it. To my left is the front desk, where three people are busy talking into their respective telephones. There's a woman with cropped blonde hair who looks to be in her mid-forties, a slightly younger guy with glasses, and a young girl with long, dark hair and too much make-up.

Over on the right is a large dining area, which I'm guessing is their own, very fancy, in-house restaurant. A waiter wearing a tuxedo stands by a podium that has the reservations book and menu on it. In front of me is a row of three elevators, and to either side of them is a large staircase that disappears up, out of sight.

I walk over to the desk and wait for one of the clerks to finish their conversation. The young girl with dark hair hangs up first. She looks at me and smiles. "Good afternoon, sir, and welcome to the Four Seasons. How may I help you today?"

I give her my best boardroom smile. "Good afternoon. I have a reservation with you. The name is Marvin Aday."

You didn't honestly think I'd use my real name, did you?

Josh tends to create my personas for such occasions. He keeps it entertaining by using rock legends as inspiration.

"Thank you, Mr. Aday. Just give me a moment to bring up your room information."

She taps away on her keyboard and programs the keycard for my room. I look around with a practiced nonchalance as I wait. I've changed into a smart casual outfit consisting of a shirt and tie with jeans and shoes. I have a briefcase with me. To the casual observer, I'm just another businessman.

The girl hands me my keycard across the counter. "Here you are, Mr. Aday. You're on the fifteenth floor, room fifteen-twenty-three."

I nod. "That's great. Thank you."

I make my way over to the elevators and get in the first one that appears. I press the relevant button and the doors close. Josh found out that Jackson is staying in the Summer suite, which is roughly in the center of the sixteenth floor. Conveniently, that's directly above my room...

Anyone would think I've done this before.

I ride the elevator to my floor and step out into the hallway. The carpet is a neutral color and looks expensive, with the walls complementing the look by being much the same. Artwork hangs on both sides of the corridor. Nothing I recognize—probably local artists keen for some cheap advertising, or someone dead who is so obscure, it's now deemed fashionable to have their work on display.

I check the brass plaques on the walls to see which direction my room is, then turn right and head along the corridor.

There's no sign of life anywhere. It's too late in the day for the maids to still be cleaning out the rooms of the people who left earlier this morning. I imagine most rooms on the floor will be empty during the day... although, two people are having uncomfortably loud sex in the room I'm passing right now. The woman's putting too much effort into the vocals, so I suspect she's faking it. But judging by the occasional grunt I can hear from the guy, I don't think he cares all that much. Possibly a couple having a torrid affair.

I smile to myself and walk on, soon drawing level with my door on the right. I take a deep breath, calming myself for what lies ahead. I press my keycard against the lock pad just above the handle. It beeps once and I hear the lock slide back. I open the door and step inside, closing it gently behind me.

I walk across the room quickly and place my briefcase on the bed. I remove my tie and roll my sleeves up. After all these years, I still get a buzz of adrenaline when I'm on a job. It's weird to admit, I know, but I love what I do. In a perfectly normal, non-psychopathic kind of way, obviously.

I don't pay much attention to the room. If you've seen one, you've seen them all. I walk over to the TV, turn it on, and scroll through the channels until I find some music. I find VH1, which is in the middle of showing a classic rock Top 100 show. Thin Lizzy are belting out *The Boys Are Back In Town*. I turn the volume up, smile to myself, then move back over to the bed and open my briefcase.

I take out my Bluetooth headset and place it on my ear. I then call Josh, who answers as I'm singing.

To his credit, he sings along immediately.

All together now...

"The boys are back in town! The boys are back in town!"

We laugh.

Nothing ruins a job more than tension and hesitation. The best advice I can give any budding assassin is to relax, clear your head, and just do it. Not methodically but instinctively. Let your hands, mind, and eyes do what they know they need to. Go with the flow, as the saying goes.

"I see preparations are going well," says Josh.

I nod. "As always. Jackson's directly above me now. Is everything in place with the hotel?"

"Sure is. If you ring room service in... four minutes, their afternoon shift will have started. The guy who brings you your food will be roughly your height and build."

"Excellent. And the drill?"

"Should be under your bed, near the window."

"Josh, for all of your annoying habits, you are an absolute genius. How do you do it?"

"C'mon, Adrian. You know a magician never reveals how he does his tricks."

"Yeah, well, I'm not paying a magician. I'm paying you. Take the compliment and spill."

He sighs. "Fine. Well, you know the guy on the front desk?"

"Yeah."

"You're also paying him."

"Am I?"

"Yeah."

"How many more people do I pay that I don't know about?"

I swear, I can hear him smiling down the line. "Now that would be telling!"

"I think I need to hire an accountant. It seems you're spending my fortune on all kinds of things..."

"Adrian, if I were going to screw you out of any money, I'd have done it and gone a long time ago."

"Very true. Right, I'm gonna go do my thing. Call you when it's done."

"Take it easy, Boss Man."

I hang up and use the phone next to the bed to call the front desk and order some room service. Then I move round to the other side, get on my hands and knees, and look underneath the bed. Sure enough, there's a medium-sized industrial drill lying there.

I smile to myself. "Josh, you're a good man."

The drill bit in the end is a quarter-inch wide and close to a foot and a half long. I pick it up, pressing the trigger quickly to check it works. It's surprisingly quiet, which is perfect. I stand up and drag the chair from under the desk near the TV over against the wall nearest the windows. I climb on it and reach up, steady myself, then drill a hole right through the ceiling. This is easily the riskiest part of the job, but the quiet drill coupled with the loud music on my TV should mask most of the noise from the room above. Unless I'm desperately unlucky and Jackson's standing directly on or near where I'm drilling, he shouldn't notice anything.

I break through the ceiling and the floor above. I retract it quickly and wait a moment to see if there's any reaction. I hear nothing. Satisfied I've remained undiscovered, I step back down and retrieve a surveillance camera and monitoring unit from my briefcase. The camera is a thin, flexible cord about three feet long. Attached to it is a small notebook-style computer. The seven-inch monitor shows the live feed from the camera. Where the keyboard would normally be are two joysticks, which control both the camera cord and the lens. I fire it up and step back on the chair, feeding the camera slowly through the hole I've just drilled. The feed transmits to the computer in my left hand. I work the joysticks to look around with the camera.

His suite is huge, which poses a slight issue for me. Jackson is sitting at a desk, resting his head in his hand as he concentrates on whatever he's looking at. To his left are the double doors that lead out to the hall, plus three doors leading off from the main room, which are all closed.

He certainly looks alone...

There's a knock on my door, which distracts me. A voice outside announces itself as room service. I quickly retract the camera and climb down off the chair. I pack the equipment back inside my briefcase and take out one of my guns instead. The weight of my Beretta is always a welcome comfort in my hand. I know that I have complete control of any situation when I'm holding one of my babies.

I move over to the door and quickly glance through the peep hole. I open it, stepping behind it as I do. A guy walks into the room holding a tray with both hands. I push the door shut and step toward him. He turns his head, caught by surprise. Before he can say anything, I slam the butt of my gun into his temple. He slumps to the floor, unconscious. The tray crashes down next to him.

Goodnight, sweetheart.

7

I knock on the door of the Summer suite on the sixteenth floor, directly above my room. The uniform I've borrowed fits reasonably well. I've tucked my gun, which I've equipped with its suppressor, inside the waistband at the back of my pants, covering it with the bottom of my jacket. I'm carrying the tray the waiter dropped on my floor. I hope Jackson isn't genuinely hungry, because I wasn't able to salvage much of the Caesar salad that went flying across my room, and it looks awful.

"Who is it?" asks a frustrated voice from inside the room.

I take a breath. Showtime. "Room service."

There's a brief pause.

"I didn't order anything, and I don't want to be disturbed."

Luckily, I've prepared for this reaction.

"Ah, damn it! Listen, I'm sorry for the mix-up, sir. The

thing is, I need you to sign to say that you refused the delivery before I can return it."

More silence.

"Look, I'm really sorry to bother you with this, sir. It's just if I don't have the correct paperwork, I'm going to get in a lot of trouble. Can you please just quickly sign this? Then I'll be out of your way."

I hear movement inside the room. Bingo! I balance the tray on my left hand and reach behind me, wrapping my right hand around my gun. I hear the bolt unfasten, and a second later, the handle turns.

My plan's simple: drop the tray as soon as the door opens, so the noise masks any sound from my gun as I shoot him between the eyes. Then I'll drag his body into the room and shut the door behind me. I'll search everywhere for any paperwork that relates to the plot of land he's supposed to sell to Pellaggio. Once I've found it, I'll clean the entire scene of any trace I've been there before leaving.

The door opens, but it's not Ted Jackson standing in front of me. It's a tall, gorgeous, blonde woman in tight clothes, holding a gun in a very steady hand and aiming it right between my eyes.

Well, shit!

We stand frozen, staring at each other with poker faces. Each second that passes by feels like an hour, and the silence is deafening. My mind starts racing, desperate to find a solution that doesn't involve me getting shot.

There aren't many.

But the way I figure it, if she wanted me dead, I probably would be by now. Therefore, it's probably best for me to let it play out until I can get in a better position to do something constructive.

Her deadpan expression gives nothing away. "Hi there."

Her accent's hard to pinpoint. It sounds like a blend of different European countries, with a hint of American.

I raise an eyebrow. "Hey…"

"Room service? That's original."

"Well, you know the old saying: if it ain't broke…"

"Send a fixer?"

I shrug. "Something like that."

It actually looks like she's going to smile. Wait for it… and… nope, she doesn't. Her face betrays exactly zero emotion. She's good. And I might've been wrong about the smile. I wasn't really paying much attention to anything besides the end of the gun that's pointing at my face.

She waves the barrel of her gun toward her. "Do come in."

I step inside the suite. It really is huge. I turn in a slow circle, absorbing every detail as quickly as I can—the layout of the room, where the doors and the furniture are… putting it into perspective after seeing it from the floor through a small camera. I glance over at Jackson, who's still sitting at his desk, but has turned around to see what's happening. His face shows more disinterest than concern—clearly a levelheaded guy who's no stranger to dangerous situations. Interesting.

I turn back around to face the woman, who still hasn't moved the gun even a millimeter. She's dressed as she was when I first saw her this morning. Her dyed blonde hair is slightly curly at the end, resting on her shoulders. She has dark green eyes, which would be pretty if not for the fact there was no emotion in them whatsoever.

She's really starting to concern me, simply because she seems so at ease with pointing a gun at me. Most people, even seasoned veterans like me, feel an element of pressure when holding a gun on someone. And don't let anyone tell you different. Also, don't believe what you see on TV. If you have a gun on someone, your whole body's tense. You have to try and stay calm, as the slightest wrong movement could accidentally kill someone. You also have to consider every eventuality around you, such as the person you're pointing your gun at making a move on you. If they do, you have to make sure you keep control over your weapon to avoid it going off in any struggle that might unfold. Finally, you have to prepare yourself for pulling the trigger and being so close to the body that you see the effects. You only learn to accept these things after many years of experience dealing with them. At the moment, this mystery woman is showing she's no stranger to any of it.

She takes a step toward me and leans in close, her face inches from mine. Her lips form a menacing, almost flirtatious smile as she reaches behind me and removes my gun from the waistband of my pants.

"You won't be needing this," she says seductively.

She throws it on the floor without a second thought.

I glance over at it, then look her in the eye. "I want that back. It's special to me."

She raises her eyebrow but says nothing.

I take a deep breath. "I'm gonna put my tray down now, okay? Just letting you know, so you don't shoot me or anything."

She shrugs. "Go for it."

I'm holding the tray in both hands. See, to most people, it's just a tray. But to me it's... actually, it's just a tray to me as well, really. But years of experience have taught me how to find an opportunity for violence in everything. I'll think of something.

I kneel slowly to place it on the floor, keeping eye

contact with her the whole time. The second I look down at the tray, I fling it like a Frisbee into her legs, hitting her just below her knees. It catches her off-guard, and I use the moment of distraction to lunge forward, stepping in close to her and grabbing her right arm by the wrist. I turn into her so my back is against her chest. Keeping her gun under control with my arm and upper body, I jab her twice with my other elbow—once in the stomach and again in her face. She falls backward against the door, stunned but not out of it. She drops her gun, which I quickly bend down to retrieve.

Don't get me wrong—despite what I do for a living, I won't normally tolerate any violence toward women. But she was pointing a gun at me, so as far as I'm concerned, the bitch had it coming.

As I take aim at the woman, I see out the corner of my eye Ted Jackson's cool, calm demeanor slowly leaving the premises. I glance round at him as the color drains from his face, and I stare at the quivering wreck of a man I've been paid to kill. Papers scatter everywhere as he scrambles out of his chair and makes a run for one of the other rooms.

I raise the gun. "Teddy, be cool..."

I fire once, shooting him in the foot with his bodyguard's gun. He stumbles and falls, landing awkwardly. Blood drips all over the expensive carpet. He's screaming, which is understandable, if not a little annoying. I walk over and kick him in the side of the head.

Now he's not screaming.

I look back over at the front door and see the woman slowly getting to her feet, shaking her head to clear the cobwebs. I aim the gun at her again. "Don't do it, sweetheart. I'm better than you are."

She looks like she wants to protest, but I can see her

assessing the situation and realizing that she has no move. She drops back down to one knee and puts her hand to her head where I hit her.

She grimaces. "You're in way over your head."

I shrug. "You might be right. But nevertheless, I've got a few questions I need answers to, and you're going to give them to me."

17:16 PDT

I've secured Jackson and the woman to two of the chairs in the suite using some cable ties I brought with me. I'm now sitting on the sofa facing them, over by the main window, leaning back with my feet on the table in front of me. I was even kind enough to wrap a towel around Ted's bleeding foot. After all, I don't want him passing out or moaning too much before I have chance to speak to him.

Despite my first instinct to just shoot him and walk away, I now find myself in a position where I can find out exactly what the hell is going on around here, and I can't resist. It'll drive me mad otherwise.

The woman hasn't said anything. She's just staring at the floor, almost disinterested. I lean forward and slap Jackson's face to bring him round. Up close, he doesn't look as high and mighty as he did when he was walking with purpose, talking into his cell, and swinging a briefcase around. He groans as consciousness washes over him once again.

I smile at him. "Hey, Ted."

He frowns with what I suspect is a combination of a headache and severe confusion. "Wha-what's happening?"

"Right now? You're tied to a chair in your suite at the

Four Seasons. You have a hole in your foot, which I put there to stop you running off."

He looks like he's really concentrating, trying to make sense of what I'm saying. He turns his head and looks at his female bodyguard sitting next to him, in much the same position. Except she hasn't been shot...

"Don't worry. Your lady friend is here next to you. We'll get to her in due course, but first, I really must get the formalities out of the way."

He snaps back to me. "What formalities? I don't understand."

I hear the fear slowly creeping into his voice, replacing the confusion.

I sit back and gesture casually with the gun. "Sure, you do, Teddy. You agreed to sell some land to a mob boss named Roberto Pellaggio. But you pulled out of the deal and kept his money. He's hired me to ask you really nicely to reconsider your stance on this matter and to let him have the deeds to the land as per your original agreement." I lean forward again. "Say, Ted, I don't suppose you fancy selling my employer the land you just screwed him out of, do you?"

"What? Oh, God! Oh, Jesus!"

His eyes go wide, and the full-blown panic attack that's been slowly brewing beneath the surface finally kicks in.

I figure I'll hammer the point home, for effect.

"Pellaggio is going to pay me a hundred grand to kill you if you don't sell him the land. You shouldn't have screwed him over, Ted. People like him... they don't—*can't* tolerate things like that."

The fear is etched across his face as he looks all around the suite, as if searching for a lifeline. I see his gaze rest on his briefcase, which is standing on the floor next to the desk.

I can see the cogs start turning again, and his desperation changes to opportunity.

He looks back at me. "I have quarter of a million dollars in cash. Let me go right now and it's yours. We can pretend this never happened."

I smile and shake my head. "While that's a generous offer, that's not how I operate. I stand by my contracts, Ted. You can't buy your way out of this."

He leans forward as much as he can, which isn't much. His eyes are watering. "P-p-please... I... I have a family!"

I sigh. "No, you don't."

He holds my gaze a moment longer, realizing that lying and bargaining aren't working. Then he sits back in his chair and sighs heavily with defeat, staring at the floor. A tear rolls down his cheek and splashes on his lap.

I regard him for a few minutes, trying to figure him out. Any confidence he once had has long gone. He looks full of regret and almost... ashamed.

I flick my gaze over to the woman for a second. She still hasn't looked up or changed her expression. I look back at Jackson. "Ted, tell me why you backed out of the deal."

He closes his eyes and swallows. "GlobaTech Industries assigned me to a special project involving the land. I had no choice, I swear!"

I almost feel sorry for him. Almost.

I nod slowly, trying to piece together everything in my head. But little about any of this makes sense to me. "Okay, why do GlobaTech Industries have such an interest in a plot of land in the middle of the Nevada desert?"

He sighs again, pursing his lips together in a subconscious act of defiance. There's obviously a lot more to this than he's telling me, and he seems reluctant to divulge any information. Usually, people will say anything if they think it can save their life. That tells me he's probably under immense pressure from his employer, and whatever deal he's part of must be big. If that's the case, I can see why he walked away from the Pellaggio deal. If it's big enough that he's effectively willing to sacrifice himself for it, he wouldn't have thought twice about turning his back on the mob.

I'll try another approach.

I nod at the woman. "Who's she?"

"She's my personal bodyguard."

I look at her. She's looked up now that the conversation has changed to her. She's staring at us both in turn with a curious detachment, remaining almost stubbornly silent.

"You're being protected by a girl? Jesus, Teddy, is that not emasculating at all to you?"

The woman huffs in disgust at me, which I don't acknowledge. At least I know I can get a reaction. That might be useful later. I simply smile back at her, causing her to roll her eyes and look away. Jackson says nothing, although he clearly wants to. I'm trying to goad him into giving me information, and he probably knows it. But his consistent reluctance is starting to become an issue for me, and I need to put a stop to it.

I look back at him. "She's not exactly your standard security detail. I'm sure you'll agree. So, come on... who is she?"

He looks me right in the eye. I can see his inner torment. He wants to tell me everything. His instinct is to do whatever he can to save his life, but there's still something stopping him. Something he apparently fears more than me.

He should really fear me more.

In one swift movement, I stand and use my free hand to

throw the table in front of me across the room. The spontaneous, violent act takes Jackson by surprise. He gasps in shock. Without warning, I shoot him in his other foot. He screams and blacks out.

I shake my head. "Oh, Teddy... *that's* just embarrassing."

8

Happy that Jackson will be absolutely terrified of me when he wakes up again, I turn my attention to our mystery woman. Despite the commotion, she's remained silent, but shooting Jackson again clearly took her by surprise as well. I can see her thinking... assessing her situation, trying her restraints, looking around the room, and finally coming to the realization that she's screwed. She relaxes back in her chair and looks at me, clearly opting for a different approach to her situation, just like I would.

"I can't believe you hit a woman."

She doesn't sound pissed off—well, no more than anyone else would be after they'd been elbowed in the face. I think she's toying with me, seeing what reaction she can get. I know the tactic well.

I shrug. "Yeah, sorry about that. I... Actually, no, I'm not. You had a gun on me, so you deserved everything you got."

"I only had a gun on you because you were going to try to kill the guy *I'm* supposed to protect."

"Well, I was only going to kill him because he screwed a gangster out of millions of dollars."

"Oh, well, that's all right, then!"

She wrinkles her nose and sticks her tongue out, and I find myself thinking we probably sound like a pair of bickering siblings. To be honest, we sound like Josh and me...

"Why *are* you protecting him anyway? What makes him so special?"

"I'm just following orders, like you."

"I don't follow orders. I don't answer to anyone—a benefit of being self-employed."

"Are you always this argumentative?"

"Are you always this much of a bitch?"

"Oh, your words cut me like a knife..."

"There's no need for sarcasm."

"There's no need to tie me to a chair!"

"You had a gun on me!"

"What, *that* again? Get over it, you pussy."

I sigh. What is it with this woman? I don't particularly want to shoot her, but she's testing the restraint of my trigger finger while pitching her tent on my last nerve.

I sigh. "Enough. You're going to answer my questions, or I'm going to shoot you in the face. Understand?"

She says nothing but raises a quizzical eyebrow—either to show she understands, or to silently call my bluff. I assume it was the former because I don't bluff.

"Good. What's your name?"

She shakes her head slightly. "Does it matter?"

"Yes."

She holds my gaze for a moment. "Fine, my name is Clara Fox."

"Thank you. Okay, Clara, who do you work for?"

"Right now?" She motions with her head to Jackson, who's still slumped in his chair next to her. "Him."

"So, what, are you freelance?"

"I go where I'm told to. I don't ask questions."

"That's a weird answer to a perfectly straightforward question."

"Take it or leave it. I don't care."

"Do you know why you're protecting him?"

"Yes."

"Would you care to elaborate?"

I don't think she's losing patience. I think she's just unhappy. She doesn't strike me as being comfortable when she's not the one asking the questions. I don't know what it is about her, but I kind of like her. Not in *that* way. I just think she's a... kindred spirit.

She sighs. "My assignment was to protect Jackson while he closed a business deal between our respective employers for the sale of a plot of land in Heaven's Valley. We knew that the local mafia had been involved in a previous deal to buy up the land, so we assumed there would be some comeback. I was assigned to Jackson to make sure he remained safe while he finalized the deal."

"Would this deal be with Dark Rain, by any chance?"

She frowns for a split-second, looking both surprised and confused. She clearly wasn't expecting me to know that, and I can see her trying to figure out how I do.

She quickly composes herself again and merely shrugs, as if it's not important information. "Yes."

"And you don't know why the original deal was canceled by Jackson?"

"Don't know, don't care. I do what I'm ordered to do. If I need to know something, I'll be told."

"You're the consummate Army brat, aren't you? Tell me, where are you from? Your accent's very... multicultural."

She smiles, like she's flattered I've noticed. "I was born in Russia. My father was a soldier and died when I was a little girl. My mother was a Swedish nurse, and we moved to America when I was seven."

"Well, you sound great. You should work in a call center or something."

"I'd kill my boss within minutes."

I can't help but smile. "I don't doubt it."

There's a moment's silence, which is interrupted by the groans of a man regaining consciousness after being shot for the second time in the last hour.

Jackson looks groggy. He gazes around the room slowly like he's suffering from a bad hangover. He looks at Clara, who's staring at him curiously. He turns to me. I'm also staring at him, but I have a gun aimed at his head.

I turn to Clara. "Be right with you, honey."

She rolls her eyes and sighs heavily.

I smile, satisfied I've wound her up enough, and turn back to Jackson. "Teddy, so nice of you to join us. Clara and I are just getting acquainted. She's lovely, don't you think?"

He groans, clearly in pain. "What do you... want from me?"

"I want you to answer a few questions, completely and honestly."

"P-please don't sh-shoot me again."

"I can't promise anything, Ted, because you're an asshole. But if you do as I ask, you'll be giving yourself the best chance you can of avoiding a third bullet."

He takes a moment. I can see him weighing up his options in his head, searching for one last Hail Mary plan that will ultimately save him. I watch, somewhat pleased with myself, as the realization of pending defeat finally dawns on him.

He sighs wearily. "What do you want to know?"

"Finally! Okay, first question—why did you revoke your offer to Pellaggio without telling him?"

He hesitates, which isn't a good start.

"Ted, don't even think of lying to me."

"I... I can't tell you. They'll kill me."

He glances at Clara. It's just a quick look, but I spot it.

I look at her. "Are you going to kill him if he talks to me?"

She stares at me blankly, like I'm an idiot. She's really good at looking at me like that... and I don't care for it. "I've *just* finished telling you I'm meant to protect him. Why would I kill him?"

I sigh again. I'm going around in circles here, and I'm starting to lose my patience. I'm wasting time. I maybe need to take a slightly more drastic approach. I stand and walk across the room, picking up my silenced Beretta from where Clara had thrown it earlier. I check the magazine out of habit as I head back over to them and stand behind Jackson. I extend my arm over his shoulder, past his head, so my gun appears in his line of sight. I then fire four bullets at the sofa in front of us. Each one causes a small cloud of white stuffing to erupt from the pillows.

See, when you fire a gun, the barrel gets really hot—a result of the mini explosion that initially propels the bullet out. So, after four shots, the barrel is so hot that you could fry an egg on it.

The shots terrify Jackson, who opens his mouth in a silent scream. Without warning, I place my gun on the side of his neck and hold it there. His silent scream turns into a very loud, guttural one. Out the corner of my eye, I see Clara squirming uncomfortably in her seat at the low hissing of Jackson's flesh smoldering from the heat.

I give it seven seconds before removing my gun. I walk around and crouch down in front of him. "Teddy, I swear to God, I'm going to make you tell me everything I need to know." I gesture to his neck with my gun. The skin has blistered and burst, leaving him with blood and puss oozing down his shoulder and chest. "*That* was nothing compared to what I'm both capable of and willing to do to you."

Jackson starts crying. I put the barrel of my gun near his neck again to give him further incentive.

"Okay, okay! I'll tell you everything!"

"That's the spirit, Teddy." I sit back down on the bullet-ridden sofa. I gesture with my hand for him to speak. "In your own time..."

He sighs and composes himself, occasionally wincing from the pain. "I saw that GlobaTech Industries had this land on their books that they weren't doing anything with. I'd read about Pellaggio's plans for expansion in the area, and I approached him with the deal, so I could make some money on the side. I didn't think for a second that GlobaTech would notice. The land had been purchased for next-to-nothing over seven years ago."

"So, you just wanted to make a bit of cash? Makes sense. But why pull out at the last minute?"

"A few days ago, one of the directors assigned me to a new project, working with a militia organization called Dark Rain. It was off the books, which was why I'd found no record of the land being part of it. The project was being overseen by a small division within GlobaTech that worked outside the standard protocols and operating guidelines. This project required the use of resources found on that land, and it was my job to set things up with Dark Rain. I had no choice but to walk away from Pellaggio's deal. I knew I was causing myself problems with the mob, but I also knew that I'd be protected by this deal, so I went along with it and kept my mouth shut."

I look at Clara, whom I can see already knows some of what Jackson is saying and is either confused or disinterested with the rest. I look back at him. "What did you mean when you said, 'resources found on that land'?"

He sighs, momentarily reluctant to continue but knowing he has no choice. "That land sits on top of the only natural uranium deposit in the United States."

Huh...

Well, I did *not* expect that.

A private military contractor and a militia organization working together, presumably to mine uranium on U.S. soil... what could possibly go wrong there?

For the first time today, words fail me. All except two.

"Holy shit."

9

Silence descends on the room. I'm left reeling from the bombshell Jackson had just dropped.

Perhaps *bombshell* isn't the best choice of words, under the circumstances.

I do my best to gather my senses again. I aim my gun at Clara who looks as shocked as I am.

"Tell me about Dark Rain, now."

She shakes her head absently. "I don't know much about them. They... they only recruited me a couple of years ago."

"What are they planning?"

"I don't know."

I put my gun an inch away from her forehead. "Don't lie to me, Clara."

She remains calm, but her eyes betray her concern. "I honestly have no idea. My mission was to protect Jackson and keep him safe. That's it."

She's very matter-of-fact about it, and my instinct is to

believe her. I've already concluded she's good at her job, but I get the impression she got the short straw assignment because she's relatively new to this Dark Rain outfit. Plus, the look of shock on her face when Jackson mentioned the uranium was genuine.

I turn back to Jackson and put my gun against his forehead. He starts crying again. "Ted, you gotta start talking. Uranium? What's the big picture here?"

"W-we were going to mine it and then process it in one of our labs."

"Process it, how?"

"We were going to use gas centrifuges to enrich the material highly enough that it becomes weapons-grade."

"Weapons-grade? As in, the stuff that goes in nukes?"

"You could use it in nuclear bombs, yeah. Having control of our own deposit meant we could sell it on for a hundred percent profit. GlobaTech approached Dark Rain after learning of the mine's location and proposed the operation."

"So, you were going to sell the land to Dark Rain but do all the mining for them? That doesn't make any sense. If they owned the land, wouldn't they technically own the uranium? Why would GlobaTech offer to sell something on someone else's behalf?"

"The United States and Russia set up a joint program back in '93 to convert all highly enriched uranium into nuclear fuel. Ever since then, practically all weapons-grade material has been disposed of. We saw an opportunity to fill a massive gap in the market."

"That still doesn't explain why you'd give it to Dark Rain."

"Having weapons-grade uranium isn't exactly legal. If they owned the mine, they would have liability."

I nod to myself. "You offered to do all the mining and

processing and selling to make it look like you're doing them a favor—but you were just setting them up to take the fall while you reaped the profits?"

He shrugs. "That was the plan."

"Christ, is there anyone you won't screw over?"

Jackson shrugs again. "It was simply too much money and too good an opportunity to overlook."

"But you essentially gave an underground militia control of a uranium mine! Is the almighty dollar so important that you'd risk the lives of millions?"

He scoffs. "Says the hired assassin?"

"Don't try to lecture me on morals, Teddy. This really isn't the time."

We fall silent. I find myself trying to think of a plan that would allow me to make all this right. It's not my place to get involved, but... think of the consequences if nuclear weapons are manufactured on U.S. soil and sold on the black market. Or worse... imagine if somebody detonated one? If I could've done something to prevent that and didn't, I'd never forgive myself.

I stroke my chin, running everything through my mind. "Has the deal for the land been finalized between Globa-Tech and Dark Rain?"

He sighs heavily. "That's what I'm in town for. I've got all the papers with me. I just need to sign them and the land's sold. Then mining can begin with no liability to GlobaTech."

"And does anyone have any idea what you were intending to do with the land before you were brought on board to broker this deal for GlobaTech?"

"No. I covered my tracks well enough, I think."

"You were just shit outta luck, right?"

He nods at me and smiles humorlessly. "Like you wouldn't believe..."

I walk over to the desk he was working at earlier and pick up his briefcase. The same one handcuffed to him yesterday. There's a combination lock on it. I look over at Jackson. "What's the code for this?"

He hesitates. "Six, eight, seven... three, four, nine."

I place it on the bed, enter the code, and open it. Inside are documents relating to the land purchase resting on top of a quarter million dollars in cash, just as Jackson had said.

I spin it around, so they can both see the contents, and walk over to them. I stand in front of Jackson and aim my gun at his head, then nod over at the briefcase. "Is that everything?"

He nods.

"And I suppose it's too much to ask for you to have any information to hand about Dark Rain?"

"I never dealt with them directly. My only contact with them is through her." He gestures at Clara with his head.

"Okay, fine. Let's recap: GlobaTech is selling land that has a uranium mine underneath it to some militia outfit called Dark Rain. They think you're being really nice by handling all the mining and processing of the material itself. But they have no idea that you're actually setting them up to take the fall for everything, freeing you guys up to sell the material and make loads of money. Am I right so far?"

He shrugs and nods, like a child finally admitting to misbehaving.

"Before all that, however, you were going to sell the land to the mob to make some extra cash. At the time, you had no idea what the land actually was. But now that you do, and your company has charged you with managing this new deal, you've had to back out of the old one. That caused the mob to hire a hitman—that would be me—to kill you for screwing them over. Have I missed anything?"

Jackson lets out a heavy sigh. "Nope, that's pretty much it."

"Excellent."

I pull the trigger and put a bullet directly in the center of his forehead. The bullet itself is roughly ten millimeters in diameter, which is about half that of a dime. The tip is rounded for easier penetration. It travels at an approximate speed of three hundred seventy-five meters per second. As the bullet impacts, the velocity causes the end of the bullet to shoot up to the tip, which means it flattens out to almost double the width. Consequently, the resulting exit wound is much larger than the point of entry.

Jackson's head snaps back violently as the bullet pushes its way through the thick bone at the front of his skull. The recoil of the impact causes his head to hang forward again as the bullet works its way through his brain and out the other side.

A spray of pinkish fluid—a mixture of blood, bone, and brain—explodes over the floor behind him. From my finger squeezing the trigger to the dead weight of his lifeless body sagging against his restraints, just under one second has elapsed.

I let out a taut breath. Job done.

I look at Clara. She seems unfazed, but I can see her thinking of ways to avoid suffering the same fate. I have no intention of shooting her. But it won't do any harm to keep that to myself for the time being.

I walk behind her, careful not to step in the bits of Jackson splashed across the carpet. I remove her restraints and aim the gun at her.

"Okay, Clara. Get up, nice and slow, and move over to the desk."

She does.

"Now ring down to the front desk and tell them Mr. Jackson has decided to extend his stay, so will need the suite for another three nights."

She does.

"Now sit on the bed."

She sits and looks at me, uncertainty and concern evident in her emerald eyes.

"Right. Clara, this is make-or-break time for you. Tell me everything you know about Dark Rain."

She says she's been with them for a couple of years, but given this uranium thing seems as new to her as it is to me, my guess is she's now re-evaluating her association with them.

She looks away for a moment, almost ashamed. "Like I said, I don't actually know much about them. They recruited me a couple years ago after some work I did in Sierra Leone. I met a guy over there who said he was with an organization that had money and plans, and they could do with someone like me. The usual sales pitch, I guess."

I'm actually beginning to feel sorry for her. It's pretty clear she's been blinded by the promise of money and made the rookie error of not finding out who she was going into business with before signing on. And I can tell she's starting to realize that herself.

Her voice is practically a whisper; the confidence and presence she's had throughout all this has gone. "I started out doing a few jobs for them—nothing major. Then a few weeks ago, I was finally introduced to their leader, a former colonel named Roman Ketranovich. He said he was impressed with the work I'd done for them already, and that I'd proven my dedication to their cause."

I frown. "And what *is* their cause, exactly?"

"I'm not sure what their endgame is. But they've got the numbers and the backing to do whatever they want. The colonel is fanatical, and he believes everything he's doing is right—to hell with the consequences. His followers are completely loyal to him and his ideals. They would die for him without hesitation."

"And what about you?"

She shrugs. "I was there for the money. I'm a killer, not a monster."

I smile a little. "I can relate to that…"

"He told me I needed to protect someone for a couple of weeks. Said they were important, and I would be doing Dark Rain a great service. I had no idea they were involved in something that could lead to nuclear weapons. That's more heat than I can be paid to deal with."

I nod. I believe her. "Good. That makes this next part a bit easier."

I walk around the bed toward the briefcase. I take the documents out of it and close it, then throw it over to Clara. It lands next to her. She looks at it, confused, before looking back at me.

I wave the documents in my hand. "I've got what I came for. In that briefcase is a quarter million dollars. Take it and walk away."

She looks shocked, not expecting such kindness after seeing me shoot Jackson in cold blood. I can see her doubts, so I figure I should try to put her mind at ease.

"Jackson was a job, nothing more. The whole thing has obviously got a bit messy, and I'm going to do what I can to sort that. As far as I'm concerned, all this is now *my* problem. I don't see it being yours as well. It sounds to me like you were in the wrong place at the wrong time, and I have no desire to hurt you. But you need to walk away. Now. Take this money—I'm sure you're resourceful enough to put it to good use."

She looks at the case again, then back at me. She smiles. Not her mercenary, ready-to-kill-you smile. As best I can describe, it's a girly smile. But it fades as quickly as it appeared. "I'll never be able to hide from them. The colonel won't allow me to leave. He'll see it as treason, and he'll order me killed if I even try."

"Then help me."

She raises an eyebrow. "What, you can't manage on your own?"

"Well, I've very recently found myself the proud owner of a uranium mine that's wanted by an extremist army that has funding from a private military contractor *and* a powerful mob boss who's determined to build a casino on it —except *he* has no idea it has a uranium mine underneath it. Obviously, this outstanding set of circumstances is nothing I can't handle. It's just nice to have some company, y'know?"

She smiles. Still friendly. "Uh-huh. Sounds like a walk in the park. I'm sure I'd only slow you down..."

I return the gesture. It feels like everything that's just happened has been forgotten.

Hang on a sec...

I don't know what just made me think of it, but earlier today, when I came out of Manhattan's club, there was that leather-clad biker who sped off as soon as they saw me. I know a tail when I see one, and after everything she just said, I assumed it was Clara, but that was *before* I'd found anything out about Dark Rain. If she were following me then, that means they knew who I was all along and why I was there long before I'd heard of them.

How is that possible?

Clara's smile fades as she looks at me, presumably seeing the expression on my face change. I aim my gun at her. "How did you know to tail me this morning?"

Her eyes widen. "I don't know what you're talking about! I wasn't tailing you this morning. I was with Jackson. Besides, I've only just met you."

"Bullshit. You knew I was outside the door before."

"I know, but that's only because I've been expecting an attempt on Jackson ever since I was assigned to protect him. Why else would he *need* protecting? Plus, your bellboy routine was so transparent, it was embarrassing."

"What? No, it wasn't. It... hey, screw you!"

"I'm just saying..."

I lower my gun. "Well, just don't. If it wasn't you following me, then who was it?"

She shrugs. "I don't know. What did they look like?"

"Like you—head to toe in tight clothing, almost certainly a woman. They were on a blue and white motorcycle and wearing a black helmet."

Clara doesn't say anything, but I can tell by the look on her face she's figured something out and isn't happy about it.

"What?"

She lets out a frustrated breath. "Natalia Salikov."

"*Gesundheit.*"

"This isn't a joke! She's one of the colonel's top assassins. If she's on to you, you need to leave town... now. Forget everything you've seen or done and just go."

I raise an eyebrow. This Natalia Salikov seems to have Clara spooked a little. And she doesn't strike me as the kind of woman who scares easily.

I tuck my gun in my waistband and cover it with my jacket. I'm happy there's no threat here now. I step toward her and extended my hand. "Hi. We haven't been formally introduced. I'm Adrian Hell."

She goes quiet for a moment and looks me up and down. Then she bursts out laughing. She holds her stomach as she properly laughs until she's gasping for breath.

I frown, confused. "You know, a guy could develop a complex..."

"*You're* Adrian Hell? *The* Adrian Hell?"

I smile sheepishly and shrug. "You've... heard of me?"

"Yeah, I've heard of you. You're a legend in the killing business. I just didn't expect you to look like, well, like you do."

I stand in silence, feeling my self-confidence nose-dive and crash into a huge ball of fire. "Well, I'm just gonna go right ahead and assume that's a compliment."

Clara rolls her eyes, which I ignore.

"I'm not fazed by a woman on a motorcycle who's *supposedly* a good assassin. I'm going to see this thing through to the end and fix it. I'm not sure how, but I will."

She smiles, softer this time, more genuine and less insulting. "I believe you. I do. But don't underestimate what you're up against."

"I never do. For a start, I need to know how they knew about me before I'd even found out they existed."

"How are you going to do that?"

"I have my ways. But seriously, Clara, get the hell out of here, okay?"

Before she can say anything else, I pick up the keycard to the suite off the desk and put it in my pocket. I take out a handkerchief and wipe down the briefcase and the tray.

Then I walk over and do the same with the table and the sofa. I haven't touched anything else, so I'm confident I'm not leaving any incriminating forensic evidence anywhere. I turn and walk back over to door.

Clara's looking at me somewhat bemused. "Um, Adrian?"

"Yeah?"

She nods at Jackson's corpse, still tied to the chair on the other side of the room. "Aren't you forgetting something?"

"Oh, don't worry about him. He's not going anywhere. I'll sort it later."

I open the door, take the *Do Not Disturb* sign off the inside handle, and place it on the outside one. I step out into the hall and turn back to look at her one last time. "Trust me, I'm a professional."

I wink and close the door, then head quickly toward the elevator.

10

_____

"Uranium! Are you kidding me?"

After I left the Four Seasons, I made my way back to my motel, taking a roundabout route back in case anyone was following me. Once I got there, I had a proper read through all the documents I'd taken from Jackson's briefcase. They were definitely the deeds to the land that Pellaggio is paying me to retrieve. All sorts of legal crap I didn't understand over a dozen or so pages, with space for a signature at the bottom of the last one. Thankfully, Jackson hadn't gotten around to signing it.

I grabbed a quick shower and thought about how I was going to handle Jimmy Manhattan in light of recent events. I was quite open with him before, but I know a lot more than I did this morning, and there's no way in hell I'm giving the mob access to this land. As things stand, I've only got to deal with *one* crazy group of extremists. If the mob knowingly got their hands on a uranium deposit, they'd sell it to all the other crazy groups of extremists as well, which would be devastating.

I've concluded there's no easy fix here, so I gave up trying to find a solution. Instead, I rang Josh and brought him up to speed on the day's developments. His reaction mirrored my own.

"That's right, Josh. Uranium."

"Oh my God!"

"Yeah, it's pretty bad."

"I can't believe it!"

"Okay... Josh?"

"Yeah?"

"You need to calm down."

He takes a deep breath. "Got you."

There's silence on the line for a few moments. I hear him taking deep breaths. "You good?"

He lets out a heavy sigh. "Yeah, I'm good."

"Okay, so, riddle me this: who or what is Dark Rain, and how did they know to tail me before I'd even made a move against Jackson?"

"Well, the only people you've interacted with are the mob, correct?"

I see where he's going with this.

"Yeah. You're thinking someone in Pellaggio's crew is working for Dark Rain, right?"

"That's one logical scenario that springs to mind, yeah."

"I agree. Which leads us nicely on to my next problem. What do I do about Jimmy Manhattan?'

"Well, you can't give him the land."

"I know *that*. But I can't tell him why, either."

"Can you not just say that Jackson didn't have the documents with him?"

"No, because he would've expected me to keep him alive

79

long enough to find out where they were. That's partly what he's paying me for."

"Ah, good point."

"I'll think of something. The priority now is Dark Rain. I need to know where they are and what they're planning. Can you look into this Ketranovich guy that Clara mentioned?"

"I have been while we're talking."

I roll my eyes. "Of course, you have. Show-off."

"Whatever. Adrian, this guy is hardcore. He served in the Russian military and was a member of the Spetsnaz Special Forces for nearly fifteen years. He was in the thick of it back in the '80s, when Bin Laden was over there fighting and killing Russians on the CIA's payroll. He fought against the Afghans and was known for his brutal torture and relentless killing, apparently."

"Well, he sounds delightful..."

"Seriously, this guy is up there with Hitler, Stalin, and Simon Cowell. He was badly injured in a firefight and left for dead by his comrades. He survived and has been underground ever since. There's little on him after they declared him K.I.A. in the early '90s. Dark Rain must be his revenge."

"So, he's pissed at America, pissed at Russia, and is after some nuclear material? Well, this couldn't possibly end badly..."

"Exactly. Plus, if this guy is working with GlobaTech Industries, he's got some serious backing. It's conceivable that he could infiltrate the local mob."

I sigh. So far, everyone I've spoken to in Heaven's Valley is either trying to kill me or other people. You could argue I bring this shit on myself by doing what I do, but there's no denying how astonishingly screwed up this situation is, even by my standards.

"Okay, here's what we're gonna do. I have to tell Manhattan that he probably has a rat in his midst and that he can't have the land, despite Jackson being dead."

Josh scoffs. "And I'm sure both bits of news will go down a storm..."

"Oh, yeah. Like a proverbial lead balloon, I'm sure. Next, I need to track down this Dark Rain outfit and neutralize them before they can get their hands on any of the uranium."

"Have you given much thought about how you're going to stop an entire army on your own?"

"Short of knocking on their front door and asking them nicely to stop... no, I haven't. I'm open to suggestions, though."

"You never know. That might work. We rarely try the 'asking politely' route."

"There's a good reason for that..."

"Very true."

"Right, I need something to eat. Then I suppose I'll have to go and see Jimmy Manhattan."

He chuckles. "I'll keep my eye on the local news channels for any updates."

"Oh, ye of little faith. I'm sure it will be civilized, and he'll be understanding and sympathetic toward our situation."

"Really?"

I pause. "No, not really."

I hang up and strap my holster to my back before putting both of my custom Berettas in it. I pick up the deeds and hide them under the mattress. I don't want to keep them on me in case there's any security at Manhattan's club and they decide to search me. I put on my leather jacket and head out the door.

My spider sense is tingling big time. This whole thing is going to get much worse before it gets any better, and I'm going to be far behind enemy lines when it does.

I walk down the street, heading toward the Neon district. It's pleasantly warm outside, and the sky's clear of any stars. The half-moon is making a steady climb, and its greenish-white glow is getting brighter as the sun sets.

The streets are busy, although not as bad as they were during the day. There are just as many pedestrians, though —just dressed for a night out instead of a day at the office. The guys I pass are wearing expensive shirts with jeans and shoes. Women of varying ages are wearing dresses that look like they ran out of material halfway through production.

I pass by a burger joint I remember seeing earlier. I head inside and take a seat at the back, facing the door. The waitress who comes over after a few minutes is young and friendly. I order coffee and a burger with everything on it and a side of fries. She leaves with my order just as my phone rings. I clip my Bluetooth headset in place and answer.

"Yeah?"

I tend not to bother with pleasantries. There's only one person with my number, and he'll think there's something wrong with me if I'm polite to him.

"You on your way to The Pit?" asks Josh.

"I've just stopped for some food."

"Ah, okay. Well, keep your line open. Here's a little something to help pass the time."

He falls silent. A moment later, the opening guitar riff from *Highway to Hell* by AC/DC sounds in my ear.

I sit alone, wondering what the hell I'm going to say to Manhattan when I see him.

· · ·

I took my time eating, then I headed into the first bar I came across for a drink. I wasn't ducking Manhattan. It's just been a really strange day. I needed to shut off for an hour and give my head a rest.

A couple of beers later, I'm walking through the Neon district, approaching a long line of people queuing to get inside The Pit. At night, the place looks different. The sign above the door is flashing blue and white. All around me are people, lights, cars, and the constant low hum of the bass line coming from inside.

I make my way toward the front of the line, passing a selection of the half-dressed women and the over-dressed men I saw roaming the streets on the way here. A bouncer with a clipboard is standing guard at the velvet rope by the door. I reach the front and get his attention. I haven't seen him before. He's big, maybe a couple of inches shorter than me but a great deal wider—and he isn't fat. He's wearing a black T-shirt that looks three sizes too small for his chest and arms, which are bulging with muscle. He's got on a pair of black jeans, black boots and wears an earpiece.

I don't get a chance to say anything to him.

"Back of the line, asshole."

He barely looked up from his clipboard. Normally, I would take offense at such a brazen display of disrespect, which would lead to me smashing his face into the sidewalk. But on this occasion, I'll let his attitude slide. I'm not in the mood for unnecessary confrontations. I'm sure there'll be plenty of necessary ones soon enough.

I hold a hand up. "Hey, take it easy, *Conan*. I need to see Jimmy. It's urgent."

He eyes me up and down and then speaks into his radio. After a few moments, he unhooks the rope and motions me through, much to the dismay and protests from many of the people still in the line.

I look at him as I pass and smile. "Thanks, sweetheart."

I walk into the club and down into the main area, which looked so spacious this morning. Now there's easily a hundred and fifty people crammed in here. I look around quickly before I enter the throng of bodies, all laughing, dancing, and drinking. Behind the bar, at the far end, are seven people serving—three guys and four girls.

In the far corner, standing in front of the red curtain, is the big guy from this morning with the fire ax tattoo on his head. I figure that's where I need to go. I instinctively touch my lower back, checking my guns are secure, and set off through the crowd.

I glide through the masses, slowly making my way through to the other side. Two guys are standing in front of me blocking my path, seemingly trying to hit on the same girl.

I lean forward slightly. "Excuse me..."

No response. To be fair, the music—if you can call it that —is deafening, so I doubt they heard me.

I tap one of them on the shoulder to get his attention. He glances back at me, and I gesture past him—a polite indication that I need to get by. He turns toward me. The expression on his face suggests he's just scraped me off his shoe. He shoves my shoulder and turns back to his friend. They both laugh. The girl's also laughing along.

I stroke the stubble on my chin and let out a heavy sigh. It certainly appears that a large percentage of the population woke up this morning with the sole purpose of pissing me off. And they're succeeding spectacularly.

I crack my neck. I'm not in the mood for this, and I feel I've been diplomatic enough already tonight.

I tap his shoulder again. As he turns back toward me, I see him tense up, getting ready to shove me again. I wait for him to raise his hand. I quickly grab it, holding it tight. This forces him to turn and face me properly. As he does, I place my other hand flat on his chest and use my middle finger to find the little dip at the top of the ribcage, in the center just below the throat. I locate it with practiced efficiency and push my finger into him and press down hard. With the right amount of pressure, it's extremely effective. He drops to one knee almost instantly, crippled with what is a brief but excruciating pain throughout the body.

I push him back, and he goes fetal on the floor, shocked and short of breath, holding his chest. His friend goes wide-eyed as I turn to him, staring through him. I can see him thinking about making a move, but two seconds later, he decides against it and runs off through the crowd.

I turn to the girl. She seems to have overcome her initial shock and is now smiling at me. I'm probably twice her age, and at the risk of sounding judgmental, she has probably half my IQ.

She smiles and steps close to me, putting a hand on my chest. "Hey. That was really cool. D'you wanna buy me a drink?"

I gently take hold of her wrist and remove her hand, placing it back by her side. "I'm old enough to be your father..." I take a split-second to hate myself for saying that because it makes me sound older than I feel. "And forgetting for a moment you're most likely under twenty-one, I'm happily married."

She pouts. Probably not used to not getting her own way. "Fucking asshole!"

She storms off toward the exit like a spoiled child. I shake my head in disbelief and smile at the people standing nearby who overheard.

An image of my wife, Janine, drifts into my head. She would've found that hilarious. I smile to myself. God, I miss her. She's the only woman I've ever loved.

I re-focus and walk on through the sea of bodies, eventually coming through the other side and standing face-to-face with Ax Tattoo Guy. He eyes me up and down, glances over my shoulder at the hole in the crowd I just caused, and raises a quizzical eyebrow.

I shrug.

Maintaining his expressionless gaze, he steps aside and holds the curtain back, so I can walk through. Inside is a dark, narrow corridor. Ahead of me is a fire exit. On the left are two wooden doors, which I assume will lead me into Manhattan's office. I move to open them, but the big guy stops me. "Hold up."

Never mind how he looks, he even *sounds* like he's on steroids. Jesus...

I look back at him. "What?"

"Hands against the wall and spread your legs."

Shit.

This is annoying but not completely unexpected. Despite my instincts, I know there's no sense in rocking the boat any more so early in the evening.

I move over to the opposite wall. "If I see any rubber gloves, you and I won't be friends anymore."

He lets out a short, humorless chuckle. "We ain't friends anyway, asshole."

I face the wall, put my hands out in front of me, and spread my legs. He pats me down and inevitably touches the twin Berettas at my back. "Hand 'em over, asshole, nice and slow."

I reach behind me and take them out of the holster, one in each hand. I let them hang loose over my index fingers by the trigger guard and hold them out to him. He takes them from me and places them in a bucket on the floor, just inside the entrance on the left, which I didn't notice when I first walked through the curtain.

I point to them. "I want them back—they're my babies."

He doesn't respond; he simply points to the wooden doors. This time, I open them and step inside. As I thought, it's the main office of the club. In front of me is a small bar, with two sofas arranged in an L-shape before it. One's facing me as I enter, while the other is at a ninety-degree angle beside it.

The room stretches away to the left. The wall nearest me is transparent—it's one of those one-way mirrors and it makes up the wall behind the bar. You can see everything from inside here with complete privacy.

Against the far wall is a large oak desk with a computer on it and a phone. Standing behind it, looking through the mirror and surveying his little empire, is Jimmy Manhattan. Next to him, sitting in the chair, is an older man—I reckon in his late sixties—whom I've not seen before. He's balding, with what remains of his gray hair slicked back. He's got a gray goatee on his long, drawn face. His hands are resting on the desk in front of him, adorned in a variety of gold rings.

Roberto Pellaggio, I presume.

Wonderful.

11

They both look at me as I enter. Manhattan flashes me his best politician's smile. "Adrian, how nice to see you again. I hope you come here with good news?" He gestures to a chair in front of the desk. "Please, join us."

I make my way across the room. I can't see any other way of playing this besides my own. When in doubt, stick with what you know. I stare at the guy I assume is Pellaggio, who's yet to say anything. "So, are you the big boss?"

He says nothing. He just stares at me, sizing me up.

Manhattan clears his throat. "Can I offer you a drink?"

I shake my head. "I'm good, thanks."

"So, what can I do for you?"

"It's done."

He nods. "Excellent. And the deeds?"

"I don't have them. Sorry."

'Can I ask why?'

"You can ask..."

88

"Adrian, the terms of the contract were quite clear. You were to obtain the deeds to the land for us, as well as take out Mr. Jackson."

"I know, but he didn't have the deeds with him and refused to tell me where they were. He seemed more scared of what would happen if he told me than if he didn't, to be honest."

"This is... unfortunate."

I shrug. "Well, what can you do? I'll just get my money and be on my way..."

Pellaggio leans forward. "Oh, there will be no money, Mr. Hell."

His voice is like gravel, with a subtle hint of old Italy in his accent. I lean forward in my chair, matching his body language, and rest an elbow on the edge of the table. I frown, mostly for effect. "Say that again in my good ear."

Pellaggio points a fat finger at me. "I said, you won't be getting paid, *kid*. You didn't get me the fucking deeds!"

"I killed the guy you wanted me to kill. It's not my fault he didn't have some documents you wanted."

Manhattan steps in, I'm guessing to try exerting some kind of authority because his boss is in the room. "By taking the contract, you accepted responsibility for getting those papers. They were important and you failed. Therefore, you don't get paid."

I look at him, then back at Pellaggio. "There's something else. I'm being tailed by someone linked to Ted Jackson's employer. Someone was following me before I took him out."

Pellaggio and Manhattan remain silent.

"The point I'm trying to make here, fellas, is that someone knew I was in town and why, only a few hours after you gave me the contract. I haven't spoken to anyone." I let the words hang there for a moment, so they can sink in. I still get no reaction. I shake my head. "Do I need to draw you a diagram or something?"

Manhattan absently strokes his chin. "Are you suggesting we have a rat in our midst?"

"Finally, he gets it!"

Pellaggio leans back in his seat. "Huh. You got some nerve, kid—coming in here, telling us you failed to do what we're paying you to do, then accusing us of not having our house in order."

I shrug. "I'm not making any accusations. I'm simply stating the facts."

Silence descends upon us. We're at a crossroads. I've fed him the lie about Jackson not having the papers, which they seem to have bought, judging by how pissed they both are. In turn, they've explained to me why I won't be getting paid for the hit, which I honestly couldn't care less about right now. But for the sake of keeping up appearances, I'm feigning annoyance. I've also sown the seeds that they have a traitor in their ranks, which I'm hoping will distract them long enough for me to get the hell out of here without anyone noticing. The only thing I have left to worry about is what's going to happen next.

I hear the door open behind me, and I turn in my chair to see Ax Tattoo Guy walk into the room. He stands over by the sofas with his arms folded across his chest, saying nothing but staring at me with deadly intent. I take a deep breath and sigh heavily.

Ah. So, *that's* what's going to happen next...

I turn back and look at Manhattan. "There's really no need for this to escalate."

He smiles. But it's not polite. It's an obvious threat. "You *will* get those deeds, Mr. Hell, or you will disappear... become just another angel in Heaven's Valley."

Behind me, I hear the big guy walking toward me.

I stand. "Jimmy, we both know I'm no angel."

I kick my leg back, hard, flipping the chair backward and into the big guy. I spin around into a fighting stance and see him standing there smiling, holding the chair. He throws it to one side like it's nothing and stares at me. I'm going to have to do this right if I want to avoid getting hurt.

I square up to him, keeping a strategic distance. "So, what do they call you?"

He cracks his knuckles. "Pickax."

I frown, genuinely confused. "Why *Pickax*?"

He simply points to the tattoo on his forehead.

I'm actually impressed at how stupid one man can be. I start laughing. "You know that's a fire ax, right?"

He just stands in front of me, watching me laugh and getting visibly angrier by the second.

"There's a massive difference between the two things. They look nothing like each other and have two drastically different applications. The guy who gave you that tattoo ripped you off."

He reaches behind him and produces a six-inch mining ax.

I stare first at the item in his hand, then at the increasingly psychotic look on his face. I point to it. "See? *That's* a pickax..."

He growls and launches it through the air, aiming directly for my head. Luckily, thanks to years of training, I have outstanding reflexes. I avoid the projectile easily enough, but I admit it's a little too close for comfort. It whizzes past my ear, and I hear it impact into the back wall behind me.

I'm assuming I'm not lucky enough for it to have hit Manhattan or Pellaggio by mistake... I chance a split-second look behind me, just in case, but I see the pair of them staring at me with angry expressions. I turn back around and—

Uh!

Pickax runs into me, lifts me by the throat with both hands, and throws me into the wall. Time slows down as I fly through the air. I've barely had time to register what's happening, so I simply do the best I can to prepare for the inevitable impact.

Unfortunately, the wall I slam into isn't a wall—it's a one-way mirror. And I don't slam into it... I go crashing *through* it!

Time resumes its normal speed with a loud bang. The pressurized glass shatters as I go flying through the mirror and into the nightclub, showering everyone around me in shards and alcohol.

Uh!

Shit!

I land heavily on the floor behind the bar. I can't see the chaos I've undoubtedly just caused from where I am, but I can hear it because the music's stopped. The sound of screaming is second only to the sound of a hundred-plus people stampeding into each other, rushing toward the main doors.

I grit my teeth as I try to move. "Oh, you sonofabitch..."

I roll over on my front and look around, trying to shake away the grogginess. One of the young barmaids is crouching just in front of me. I can see a piece of glass about two inches long sticking out of her forearm. Blood's leaking down her hand, and she's shaking uncontrollably.

I roll on my left side, so I can see the hole I just made in the wall. Pickax hasn't followed me through, so I assume he's left the office via the doors like a normal person. If that's the case, he'll be coming out from behind the red curtain any moment.

I try to stand, but that's not happening right now. There's a noticeable pain shooting up and down my back, and I'm sure I can feel blood running down my face...

The bar staff have disappeared. I'm guessing they joined the stampede heading for the door. There's a guy helping the injured girl, which I'm glad of. I hate to see any collateral damage if it can be avoided. This isn't their fight, after all. Why should they suffer because of it?

Okay, let's try standing up again...

I manage to get to one knee but struggle to go any further. I put my hand on the bar and push myself up the rest of the way. I get to my feet and look over at the red curtain. It opens and Pickax appears.

I let out a heavy breath.

Shit.

I'm dizzy, and my head's banging so hard that it feels like Van Halen's inside my skull, playing the intro from *Hot For Teacher* on my brain. So, it might just be the concussion talking, but I'm sure this guy's grown since I last saw him...

He walks purposefully over to me with his arms outstretched, ready to grab me and inflict more damage. My survival instincts take over and give me a nice adrenaline shot. I jump over the counter and move across the mostly deserted nightclub floor, trying to put a little distance between us, so I can figure out what to do. Everything's still a bit blurry, but I'm aware enough to know that I'm in serious trouble if this guy gets hold of me.

I look around and see the odd person still lying on the floor between the door and me. The place emptied quickly

—I'm guessing they've been crushed in the panic a few moments ago. I feel bad, but I don't have time to worry about them now. It feels like I have at least two broken ribs, but it might just be severe bruising. My back's going to be a black and purple mess for a few days either way. The blood is still gushing slowly down my face, obscuring my vision, which isn't helping matters either. I wipe it clean with my jacket sleeve and blink to re-focus my eyes as much as I can.

I need to get to my guns...

I look around quickly for anything that could help me, but there's nothing. Any useful debris is over by the bar, and Pickax is in the way, walking slowly toward me. The only chance I have is using the open space to my advantage. I might've taken a beating, but judging by this guy's size, I'd still bet money I'm faster than he is. I just need to keep moving, tire him out, and look for an advantage.

The thing about *real* fights is that they're nothing like what you see on TV. There's no fancy choreography, no drawn-out back and forth battle, and the sad truth is, the good guy doesn't always win. In reality, they're quick, scrappy, and brutal, and the winner is the guy who doesn't fight fair—at least in my experience. You might not like it, but that's the dirty truth. People who fight by the rules never live to tell you about it. You just read about them in the obituaries...

Pickax charges me again, snarling like an animal with murder in his dark eyes. That's a shitload of momentum bounding toward me. Only one thing springs to mind, and I have to time it perfectly.

I let him get a bit nearer, maybe ten feet away. I take a couple of short, quick steps and slide away to the left on my knees. Timing it just right, I throw a straight right punch directly at his balls. We collide as I cut across his path. The blow connects beautifully. I can feel pelvic bone under my fist.

I don't care how big you are. *That* will always drop you.

Pickax is no different. He keels over instantly and sinks to his knees. He skids across the floor and comes to a halt about seven feet away, bent over in agony.

I try to stand up, but a wave of dizziness and nausea washes over me, and I fall forward.

Ah, damn it!

I push myself up using my arms, then bring my knees up for support. My vision is still blurry. I glance over at Pickax, who looks like he's having the same trouble as me. He's made it to one knee and is shaking his head to clear the cobwebs.

I finally stagger to my feet and make my way over to him. I need to finish this now. I'm in no condition to let this drag out any longer. I look at him professionally as I approach. He's on all fours with his back to me. There's no sense in me grabbing his neck from behind and trying to choke him. My arms won't have enough strength in them to do the job—it'll be like bear-hugging a tree.

Instead, I settle for something less delicate and more effective. I gather as much momentum as I can and jump at him, diving toward him like a spear and bringing my elbow up mid-air. I slam it down into the base of his skull with every ounce of strength I have left in me. I hear the crack as the impact shatters the top of his spinal cord, killing him instantly. He falls forward, sprawling lifelessly across the floor. I land on top of him and roll off to the side, lying on my back and breathing heavily, which stings like hell because of my ribs. I stare at the ceiling, trying to count how many different parts of my body are currently hurting.

It takes me a minute, but I slowly manage to get to my

feet and make my way back over to the red curtain. I pull it to one side and reach down, retrieving my guns from the bucket. Thankfully, they were both still there. I put one in its holster and cock the other, holding it as steady as I can in my hand, breathing in the comfort it gives me.

I walk slowly back into the office. Pellaggio's still sitting behind the desk. Manhattan moves around to the front as I walk in, putting himself between Pellaggio and me as a gesture of protection.

I walk over to them, picking up the chair I kicked on the way past. I stand it upright and sit down, grateful for the brief respite, and look at each of them in turn. I rest my gun on my lap, so they can see it. "Now... where were we?"

22:17 PDT

My entire body is screaming in pain, but I fight to keep my face expressionless for the purposes of making a point.

I look at Pellaggio. Well, I think I am, anyway—I can see three of him, so I'm playing it safe and talking to the middle one. "Let's get something straight. I couldn't give a shit who you are, nor how much of this city you own."

He seems composed, despite the fact I'm sitting in front of him looking like a car wreck with a gun in my hand. "You arrogant sonofabitch..." He stands and slams his palms down on the surface of the desk. "You've cost me millions!"

Okay... maybe he's not that composed after all.

"Shut your mouth before you give yourself a heart attack, you old prick. I'm in no mood for any of your *Godfather* shit right now, okay? In fact, medical attention and a shot of single malt are numbers one and two on my list of

96

priorities. You're *way* down the list. Now pay attention because I'm not repeating myself. You're in way over your head. You didn't properly research Jackson's involvement in all this. You have no idea what you're up against. That was your first mistake. Your second is that you're also danger-ously close to underestimating me, which will not end well for you. You want my advice? Cut your losses and move on. Find somewhere else to expand your empire."

There's a moment's silence in the room. Pellaggio stares at me, clenching his jaw muscles repeatedly in anger. Then he looks up at Manhattan. "'Jimmy... fix this."

He points a finger at me as he speaks.

I have to hand it to the guy—he isn't easily intimidated. I can understand that, I guess. A guy like him, head of a crime syndicate with half the city on his payroll and more money than half the country put together, why would he be scared of anyone? He's probably been building this empire since he was a kid. People quake at the very mention of his name. Why would *I* worry him?

Manhattan looks at me and then at my gun. He's keeping calm, but I can tell he's worried. He hasn't said a word since I came back in. "Adrian, I don't think you fully grasp the situation you're in. Mr. Pellaggio requires the deeds to that land. Life will become difficult for you if you don't do what we've paid you to do. You say Jackson is dead? That's fine. But you need to find a way to get your hands on that paperwork."

"Jimmy, let me save us all some time. You can't make me do shit. We're done here. You can keep my fee—I don't care. That corpse out there was probably the best guy you had, which means we both know there's no point sending anyone else after me. I see either of you again, I'll kill you. And it will be slow, painful, and horrific... you have my word."

Manhattan stares at me. I see in his eyes that he believes me, and if it were up to him, I suspect that would be the end of the matter. But I can also see his internal conflict because it's *not* up to him. His boss is in the room, red-faced and frowning, looking really pissed off. He told him to handle it and he did anything but.

He gestures to me condescendingly. "There's nowhere you can hide in this city where we can't find you. If you start down this road, it will be the end of you, Adrian. I can promise you that. Mr. Pellaggio doesn't forgive or forget. You should know that better than anyone. It's why you're here."

I scoff in disbelief. "So, what, you're gonna hire me to kill myself? You fucking idiot. Take a look around, Jimmy. You hired me because I'm the absolute best at what I do. There's no one you can bring in who can take me out, and we all know you've got no one on your payroll who can do it either. How's about you quit with the empty threats, accept defeat like a man, and call it a day, yeah?"

Manhattan glances at Pellaggio, who hasn't taken his eyes off me. The longer this goes on, the more obvious it becomes that I've won, and that makes him even angrier.

Pellaggio takes a deep breath. "Let me explain something to you, kid. You need to fucking appreciate exactly who I am. You talk about my payroll—my payroll includes the police. And local officials. And a lot of hired help up and down the West Coast."

I shrug. "Is that meant to impress me?"

"It should. You see, it's not just this city you can't hide in. It's this state, this time zone, this whole fucking country! You cost me millions, and I'll make you pay, you insignificant sonofabitch!"

I appear to have touched a nerve with the big boss. And

like a shark smelling blood in the water, I'm going in for the kill...

"Oh, okay. Give me a moment to finish quaking in my boots..." I pause for effect. "Now let me explain something to *you*. You keep banging on about me having nowhere to hide... What makes you think I'll be hiding? I promise you, if there ever comes a time when I want to the settle the score between us, you have my word that I'll come to your house, knock on your front door, and smile as I wipe you off the face of this earth. You can get whomever you want to come after me. I'll send them back to you in pieces. You must already know my reputation, but if you're still in any doubt —ask around. I'm sure you'll find that most people out there know that I'm not one with whom to fuck. Now from here on out, I'll stay out of your way, and you stay out of mine. Sound good to you?"

They both stare at me. There's a palpable tension in the room. Manhattan looks close to being afraid, but Pellaggio is defiant in his anger. Neither of them reply.

I nod. "I'm glad we're in agreement."

Content that's the end of the discussion, I stand and back out of the room, keeping my gun aimed at them until I reach the door. Manhattan clasps his hands on his lap, watching me. Pellaggio's just staring a hole straight through me. I can almost taste his disdain. He obviously isn't used to not being able to scare people or get his own way.

I leave the office and close the door behind me. I head back through the red curtain and make my way slowly across the empty club. Now everything's settled, I notice the place looks like a war zone. I re-holster my gun and stare at them one last time through the hole I made in the mirror. Then I turn and walk out the front door, feeling the refreshing evening breeze on my face. I head left and make my way along the street, passing people who were in the club who have congregated out front to stare at the scene. In the distance, I hear sirens.

Time I wasn't here, I think.

I cross the street and duck into the first alley I see. I break into a slow jog, anxious to put some distance between the club and myself but preferably without causing any more pain by doing something taxing, like breathing.

God, I need a drink.

12

August 22, 2013 — 14:09 PDT

Oh my God... what did I drink last night?

I open one eye and look around. I appear to be lying face-down on the floor of my motel room, beside the bed. My shoes are just in front of me by the desk.

I close my eye again and try to kick-start my brain into telling me what's happening. My head's throbbing, and it hurts to take the slightest of breaths.

I open both eyes. Images of broken glass and pickaxes rush to the forefront of my mind.

Oh, yeah. I remember now.

I take a few deep breaths, getting myself familiar with the stabbing pain in my chest so that I can learn to ignore it. Slowly, I push myself up, using the bed for support. I stand upright for a moment, finding my balance. I massage my temples and groggily look around the room. I try to stretch, but my back tells me I'm not quite ready for that yet. I let out a heavy sigh and frown. Maybe I should sit down until—

What's that noise?

I look around again, more alert this time. I hear the shower running in the bathroom. The door's closed too.

Did I leave it on last night when I got back? I don't remember much of anything after I left The Pit, and my mild concussion isn't helping. I suppose it's my own fault for getting thrown through a window.

I stagger over to the bathroom door, listening for any movement within. I reach for the handle just as the shower stop running. Someone's in there. Shit! I'm in no condition to—

The door opens, nearly dragging me to the floor because I'm still holding the handle. I stumble forward, quickly regain my balance, and look up. Clara Fox is standing in front of me, dripping wet and wearing nothing but a towel. She smiles at me.

I don't understand...

I blink hard and shake my head. The ability to think of anything intelligent to say eludes me. "Huh?"

It isn't Shakespeare, I admit.

"Morning, Sunshine!" She pushes past me and walks across the room, drying her hair with a towel and leaving wet footprints on the carpet. "Well, afternoon. Jesus, you look like shit."

"Uh... thanks? You look like you're wearing a towel..."

"I am."

"Oh, okay. Any particular reason?"

She shrugs. "I just got out the shower."

She sits down at the desk and finishes drying her hair in the mirror.

I massage my temples again in the hope it might stimulate my brain enough to form actual sentences and questions. "Yeah, what I mean is, why are you showering and walking around in a towel in my motel room?"

She looks at me in the reflection of the mirror. "You got your ass kicked last night. You know that, right?"

I wave my hand dismissively. "You should see the other guy."

"I followed you to the club. Figured you might need some back-up."

"So, where were you when Pickax was putting me through a window?"

She frowns. "Who?"

"The other guy."

"Ah, right. Strange name."

"He carried a small pickax with him. He liked to throw it at people."

"Oh, that makes more sense."

"So, wait—why did you follow me? Why would you care if I needed help?"

"Well, forgetting for a moment that I pulled a gun on you, then you elbowed me in the face and pulled a gun on *me*... yesterday was an eye-opener."

I smile weakly. "Now there's an understatement."

I recall the uranium and why I went to the club last night in the first place.

She turns to face me, crossing her legs. The towel rides up slightly, showing more of her thighs. "Why did you offer me that money?"

I finally sit down on the edge of the bed. I catch myself staring at her, so I make a conscious effort to keep eye contact.

I might as well be honest with her...

I sigh. "The truth? I kinda felt sorry for you."

She glares at me. "Do I look like I need your pity?"

"No, you look like you need to get dressed."

Those hypnotic green eyes of hers are filled with a suppressed anger. Her breathing is short and quick. Her jaw is set.

Yeah... she's pissed at me.

Damn it. "Look, I meant no offense, all right? While I'm sure you're an extremely capable and highly experienced person, I could tell yesterday that you had no idea how bad this situation with Dark Rain actually is. You looked out of your depth, and you looked mad at yourself for letting it all get away from you like this."

She doesn't say anything, but her expression softens. She looks away.

"As soon as I realized you had no idea about the uranium, I admit I felt bad for beating on you the way I did."

She looks back at me and pulls a face but stays silent.

"I don't need the money, and I didn't want you getting caught up in this any further. Easiest way to leave a bad situation is quickly and with a shitload of cash. I thought it was the right thing to do."

She lets slip a small smile. "My hero."

"Think of me more like your big brother."

She smiles again, this time openly. "Thank you."

"I think I should be thanking *you*. I'm guessing I got back here with your help last night?"

"I was keeping watch on the club. I saw you enter, and when I saw everyone come out screaming, I guessed the mob hadn't taken your news too well."

"I didn't tell them about the deeds. I just said I killed Jackson, and he didn't have them on him."

"And they bought it?"

"They seemed to. They were certainly mad enough to suggest they did."

"That was simpler than I thought."

"Yeah. The best lies are ninety percent truth."

"So, what now?"

"Not sure. I definitely need to shower and change. Are you sticking around, then?"

She stands up and looks at me. Her eyes dazzle like emeralds on her face, highlighted by the still damp blonde hair slicked to her head and resting on her shoulders. Also, her towel isn't anywhere near long enough. I'm annoyed that I have the urge to stare at her legs, and it's making me uncomfortable. I struggle to keep eye contact with her. I can tell by the look on her face that she's picking up on my distress and finding it amusing.

To her credit, she doesn't mention it. "I can't just walk away from Dark Rain. They'll find me. I don't care how much money I have. I've seen too much of their operation for them to just let me leave."

"Well, I could use your help finding them."

She pauses for a moment. "Are you as good as the stories say you are?"

I frown. "Stories?"

"Come on. You must know what I'm talking about? You're *Adrian Hell*!"

I swear to God, she just air-quoted when she said my name.

I say nothing. I know what she means. I know why there are stories about me. I've done a good job of keeping my emotions in check since arriving in Heaven's Valley. But Clara's referring to the times when I haven't—the results of which have never been pleasant for anyone involved.

I look at her, take a deep breath, and fix her with a reassuring and earnest stare. "You have my word—I'll burn the bastards to the ground. Every last one of them."

She stands quietly for a moment, looking into my eyes, presumably deciding whether or not she believes me. Then she smiles, lighting up her entire face and making her eyes sparkle. "Good. Now go have a shower. I know exactly how we can start."

14:50 PDT

I showered and changed my clothes and took some painkillers. I'm standing by the door, waiting for Clara to put her boots on. I feel slightly more human than before. A moment later, she stands and nods at me.

I smile. "You good?"

"Ready when you are."

I open the door and hold it for her as she steps out into the hall. I follow her, pausing only to shut the door behind us. We walk side by side along the corridor and out the main entrance, to the parking lot.

The sun is bright and it's hot as hell outside. I squint until my eyes adjust to the light.

I hope the painkillers kick in soon.

Clara walks over to a bright red Dodge Viper GTS with a vertical, white double stripe down the middle.

I move beside her. "I'm impressed. This is a nice set of wheels."

She pats the hood lovingly. "Sure is. It's a classic—a V10 engine pumping out four hundred and fifty brake horsepower. Zero to sixty in four seconds."

I look her up and down, admiringly. Not in a physical way. I'm just impressed. She's perfect.

She sees the look on my face and shrugs. "What can I say? We all have our toys. You have your guns, and I have Princess here."

I raise my eyebrow. "Princess?"

She laughs. "What?"

I shake my head and duck into the passenger seat. She climbs in gracefully next to me and fires up the engine, revving it and savoring the noise of a tamed beast.

I look over at her. "So, where are we going?"

She pulls out of the parking lot and turns right, stopping at a set of lights. "Well, I clearly don't know as much as I thought about Dark Rain. We need to prepare if we intend to go up against them by ourselves. I figure we can do some recon, maybe ask around and see what we can find out about their intentions. I know a good place to start."

I have to admit, I like the way she's talking as if we're a team. I've never really had a partner. Well, not out in the field anyway. Josh is my go-to guy—always has been, always will be. But Clara's operating on the same wavelength as me down here on the front line, and it feels good not going it alone for once.

I nod. "Okay, let's go."

We drive mostly in silence, and I take in some of the surroundings that whizz by outside. I've only seen a small part of Heaven's Valley so far, and wherever we're heading seems to be taking us all around the center of the city. We briefly pass through the business district, where I first saw Clara with Ted Jackson a couple of days ago. I see the large fountain where I sat waiting. We take a left turn and shortly afterward hit the freeway. We settle into a nice, steady eighty-miles-per-hour cruise.

Clara leans toward me slightly, not taking her eyes off the road. "There's a courier service with a depot on the other side of town. Dark Rain has a guy on the inside who helps them transport weapons and money around when they need it."

I raise an eyebrow. "They seem well organized…"

"They are. GlobaTech has given them a lot of money, and they've invested it well. The colonel is a smart man. They're well established in the city. They've got contacts and safe houses all over the place. It's strange to think that the people who live here have no idea their entire city is being used to organize an operation like this."

"Yeah, it's not a pleasant thought. When I spoke to Manhattan yesterday, I told him then that he was in way over his head, that he had no idea who he was dealing with. I'm starting to think I don't either."

"We just need to know exactly what their plan is and how they're carrying it out. Then we can figure out how to stop them. Simple."

I have to smile. "Your optimism is encouraging. I'll give you that."

"I just feel better now that I'm doing something positive. I felt so bad the other day when I realized what I've gotten myself mixed up in. I've done some questionable things in the past, but for the most part, I have no regrets. But this? This is off the scale. I mean, uranium? We could be talking about black market nuclear weapons. It's insane."

"I completely agree. What's worse is we don't know their endgame. That's why I've been running interference with the mob. Pellaggio's outfit pretty much owns this city. I'm surprised Dark Rain's been able to do what they have without Pellaggio finding out. But the mob isn't military, and if *they* got their hands on ready-made nuclear weapons or the raw materials to manufacture them, that wouldn't end well for anybody."

Clara navigates the traffic with ease and takes the exit on our left. "I'm thinking we scope out the courier's place, hope to get lucky and see our guy making a delivery. We can then tail him and see where he leads us."

I shrug. "Or we could just go and talk to him?"

"Seriously?" She raises an eyebrow. "You don't do subtle, do you?"

"She says, in a bright red Dodge Viper…"

She laughs. "Touché. But he won't say anything. Ketranovich has everyone wound up tight. They'd die for his cause, so there's no way you'd get anything out of him."

I look at her. "He'll talk to me."

Her jaw tightens. She bites her bottom lip, thinking. Clara knows better than to doubt me, but I think she's worrying about how this whole thing will play out.

We turn a corner, and she seems to forget her concerns as quickly as she thought of them.

"We're here." She pulls over and points to a building opposite. "That's the place."

I look across. It's a generic two-story building with a yard to its left that has six vans parked in it. The sign above the main entrance says: EXPRESS COURIER SERVICES. There's lots of activity, which is to be expected.

I turn to her. "What's this guy's name?"

"Marcus Jones."

I open my door. "Right. Come on, then."

I climb out, quickly glance both ways, and then jog across the street through a gap in the traffic.

She catches up with me as we step onto the sidewalk. "You're insane."

I ignore her. We approach the building casually and

walk in through the main entrance. Inside is a small lobby with a worn blue carpet. A couple of seats are on the left, and there's a large plant to the right that looks long overdue for some water.

Manning the front desk is a short, portly man with dark hair and a large mustache—both mottled with flecks of gray. His stomach is disproportionately large compared to the rest of his body, hanging low over his belt. I reckon it's been close to a decade since he last saw his own feet while standing.

He looks up to greet us as we walk over. "Can I help you folks?"

He has a thick, southern accent and a car salesman's smile.

I step forward and lean on the counter. "I hope so. I'm looking for Marcus. Is he around?"

"Jonesy? He's out on a job. Due back soon, though. Mind if I ask why you wanna see him? Bit irregular for folks to come in here wantin' a specific driver."

"Oh, we're old friends. We're passing through town and wanted to call in and say hey."

"Well, now ain't that somethin'?" He gestures to the chairs behind us. "You folks take a seat. Let me get you a drink while you wait. You know, Jones is a quiet sorta fella—keeps himself to himself. He'll be glad to see some old acquaintances, I'm sure."

I glance at Clara and smile. She rolls her eyes at me and walks over to the chairs.

I look back at the guy. "We're all right for drinks, thanks. We appreciate being allowed to wait, though. I promise we won't take up much of his time."

He laughs again. "No problem. You're nice folks, you know that?"

"That's kind of you to say. Thank you," says Clara behind me.

I sit down next to her, and she nudges me playfully with her elbow. "You make this look easy."

"I know..."

"It's really annoying."

I smile. "I know that too. But you love it."

She looks away, grinning to herself.

Ten minutes pass before we get lucky. The door opens and a man walks in. Clara taps my leg with her foot.

Marcus Jones.

He's average height with olive skin and a shaved head. He has a few days' growth on his face, but I wouldn't call it a beard. He's wearing a short-sleeved navy-blue shirt with a yellow logo over the breast pocket that says ECS with jeans and boots.

As he walks in, he sees the guy behind the desk smiling at him and pointing over to us. Confused, he turns and looks at me, frowning when he doesn't immediately recognize me. Then he sees Clara and his eyes go wide. I don't get chance to work out whether it's fear or surprise before he bolts for the door.

Without thinking, I rush after him. I throw the door open and step out to see him climbing into the cab of his van, parked a short distance away. His tires squeal as he flies out of the yard and turns right, nearly hitting another car.

Clara appears next to me, and we both run over to her car.

We climb in and she starts the engine. "Well, *that* went well! Did he tell you everything you wanted to know?"

We speed off in pursuit, narrowly avoiding a car coming from behind us.

I place a hand on the dash in front of me for reassurance. "Now isn't the time for sarcasm and *I-told-you-so*'s. Can you please just focus on catching this guy without killing us?"

13

I see the van up ahead, speeding down the six-lane freeway, weaving erratically in and out of the light traffic.

"Try and get next to him."

We're in a far superior car, so *getting* close to Jones isn't the problem. The problem is *staying* close to him because he keeps swerving whenever we try to move alongside him. We don't want to risk a crash, so we have to keep dropping back.

Clara's focused on the road. I'm trying to figure out how to stop him without killing him. There aren't too many options when you're both pushing eighty on the freeway.

I look at her. "Any idea where he's likely to go?"

She shakes her head, keeping her eyes on the road. "Could be anywhere. I doubt he's going to run straight to their main base of operations knowing we're following him. There's a couple other locations Dark Rain uses—a weapons drop and a safe house. It could be one of them, maybe?"

I frown. "We need to get him before he reaches somewhere we can't follow."

I open my window and lean out, reaching behind me for a Beretta.

"What the hell are you doing?" yells Clara.

"Good question!"

If I'm being honest, I have absolutely no idea what I'm doing. It's extremely difficult to hit a tire in this situation—not that I want to because it'll cause him to lose control, and at this speed, that could be fatal.

Ah, screw it. I'll just fire a few times in his general direction, see if it distracts him.

I squeeze off three rounds. I've no idea where the first two went, but the third one hits the rear door of the van, causing a high-pitched *ping*. Jones must've heard it because he suddenly swerves left, then right, fighting for control.

We drop back while he straightens up.

He takes a sharp left, narrowly missing the oncoming traffic as he cuts across the adjacent lanes and down another street. There's no way we can follow; we'll never make it across the junction without hitting something.

Clara slams her hand on the wheel. "Shit..."

I point up ahead. "It's okay. Take the next left. We'll catch up to him."

She does, and we see the van go across the end of the street. We speed up and turn right, getting behind him again in no time. Clara steps on the gas some more and gets us almost level with him on the inside, but he sees the move and edges to the left, closing us down and forcing us to drop back.

Clara lets out a growl of frustration. "We're never going to get level with him!"

I hold up my hand. "Be patient... We'll get him. Don't worry."

A heartbeat later, he tries to take another sharp turn, to the right this time. The guy's a maniac! He's going way too fast. He'll never make that...

His passenger side back wheel lifts as he skids around the corner. I see him through the windshield, fighting to control the van, but he's got no chance. The momentum carries him, and he tips over, crashing down on his side and skidding across the street. The screeching sound of metal on blacktop is deafening, but it's quickly replaced by a lower, much louder bang as he collides with a parked car on the opposite side and stops.

Clara slows down. "Jesus..."

I let out a relieved breath. "Told you we'd get him."

We pull up just before the right turn. I step out of the car, looking at the scene before me. A crowd has quickly assembled, taking photographs and pointing but making no effort to see if Jones is all right. Luckily, no one else appears to have been injured.

Clara appears next to me. "This is all my fault..."

I turn to her and frown. "How do you figure that?"

"He only ran when he saw me. If I'd let you go in alone, you might have been able to talk to him and stop him from running."

"Look, neither of us could've known he was going to bolt the moment he saw you. No one's been injured except him, and I'm okay with that. So, this is a win for us, okay?"

She forces a smile. "But we're still at square one. We didn't get anything out of him, and now Dark Rain will know we're on to them."

I put my hand on her shoulder. "Hold up a sec..."

Marcus Jones is climbing up and out of the passenger

door window. He looks relatively unhurt, apart from some cuts and bruises. He jumps down to the road and bends over, resting his hands on his knees to catch his breath. He looks around at the people staring. Then he sees our car—which, let's face it, isn't exactly hard to miss. His eyes meet mine. We hold each other's stare for a split-second, then he sets off running down the street, pushing through the crowd and disappearing.

"Oh, no, you don't, you little bastard!"

I set off after him. I sprint around the corner and barge through the crowd of slack-jawed onlookers. I see Jones just ahead of me. Unfortunately, as I realize I'm not gaining on him as quickly as I would've liked, I remember the sore back and busted ribs from last night. I grit my teeth as each rapid, deep gulp of air suddenly feels like knives in my chest. I'm usually in good physical condition, so the fact I can barely move is both frustrating and embarrassing.

I force myself to remember my old military training. Pain is a choice. I push it to the back of my mind and carry on.

That being said, I'm not an idiot. I know I can't maintain this pace for much longer. I have to catch Jones and fast.

He looks over his shoulder at me and nearly falls over a trashcan. He recovers quickly and ducks into an alley on the left, between two buildings.

"Marcus! Quit making me run, asshole!"

I enter the alleyway after him. Hopefully, I can—

Huh?

He's nowhere to be seen! It's a dead end. How did he—

Damn it! There's a fire escape just behind one of the large dumpsters against the right-hand wall. I look up and see him climbing the metal stairs up to the roof.

Shit.

I take a deep breath and move back a couple of steps. I sprint toward the ladder that Jones has ever-so-kindly pulled up, and jump. I stretch as best I can under the circumstances and... Yes! I manage to grab the bottom rung. The pain ripping through my torso is excruciating and increasingly difficult to ignore. I breathe quickly to compose myself, then start to pull myself up.

Once on the fire escape, I set off running, taking the stairs two and three at a time. I step down onto the roof of the building just in time to see Jones reach the other side and jump. Without breaking stride, I rush over and see he's made it over the next alleyway and onto the roof of the adjacent building.

I'm breathing hard and fast. "You gotta be... kidding me..."

Without thinking—because my brain would definitely tell me this is one of the dumbest things I've done—I run and jump.

Thankfully, the gap is deceptively small. I cover the distance easily enough, landing heavily on the neighboring roof. I stand, wincing in pain, and see Jones just up ahead. He's at the edge of the roof again, but this time, he's just standing there with his back to me. It takes me a moment, but I realize we're on the edge of the block. There's nowhere left to go.

He turns to face me, glancing over his shoulder at the ledge, which is now behind him. We're easily five or six stories up, so the drop would most likely be fatal. Let's just hope it doesn't come to that... at least not before I get some answers.

I slow down as I approach him, catching my breath. I draw my gun and take aim one-handed. "Finally! Have you finished being a dick now? You and I need to have a chat."

He shakes his head. "I ain't got nothin' to say to you, man."

"You don't know that. You don't even know who I am or what I want. Don't write off your ability to be helpful before we even start talking."

Jones shrugs. "Okay, so who the hell are you?"

"I'm a concerned citizen who wants to know what Dark Rain is planning."

I see the flash of concern on his face, but he seems set on pleading ignorance. "I ain't ever heard of no Dark Rain. You got the wrong guy."

"Bullshit. I saw your reaction when you laid eyes on Clara. Why did you run?"

He glances over his shoulder again. "Fuck you! I ain't talkin', and you can't make me! They're gonna hunt you down and slay you in the street for this!"

I fire once, above his head. "Enough. If you're gonna talk, stick to what I want to know, not what I couldn't give two shits about."

I step closer to him. Again, he looks over his shoulder at the street below. This time, he inches himself backward a tiny bit, so he's standing right on the edge.

He wouldn't jump, surely?

"Uh-uh. Don't even think about it, Marcus."

I'm maybe ten feet away from him. I see the defiant look in his eyes. His jaw is set, his breathing fast.

Shit. He's going to jump, isn't he?

Screw it.

I take a chance and shoot him in his kneecap. He falls forward, screaming in pain and clutching his leg, which is pumping out blood on the ground around him.

The kneecap is one of the most painful places to get shot. I didn't do it to make him suffer, though. I needed him to fall forward. If I'd shot him in the arm or shoulder, the impact would've sent him backward and over the edge. At least putting one in his knee meant he'd keel over and drop straight to the ground.

I walk over and crouch beside him. I place the barrel of my Beretta to his head. I go to speak, but there's a loud bang behind me. I spin around, aiming my gun, preparing for anything. I see Clara walking toward us. The door that leads to the roof must've hit the wall as she opened it.

I lower my weapon. "Hey. How did you find us?"

She gestures to the street with her thumb. "I was following you in the car. I saw you on the roof. When you reached the end of the block, I figured the chase was over so I came up through the building."

She walks over to Jones, looks down at him quickly, then turns to look at me. "Can you interrogate *anyone* without shooting them?"

I shrug. "Not usually..."

"Maybe I should handle this?"

"Be my guest."

I take a step back as Clara crouches next to him. "Marcus, I need your help."

He looks up at her. His teeth are clenched in agony. "Screw you, bitch! You're a traitor, and you're gonna die!"

Seemingly unfazed, she places her hand on his throat. "Marcus, did you know about the uranium?"

"Do you have any idea what they're gonna do to you if they find you? Or to me if I talk to you? Kiss my ass, *traitor*!"

Clara squeezes his throat. His eyes widen as he gasps for air, but he can't breathe. After a few moments, she loosens her grip again. "Do you have any idea what *I'm* gonna do to you if you *don't* talk? I can make the agony you're in right now last for days. Weeks, if necessary."

He starts to cry... the poor bastard.

"Please—they'll kill me!"

"Marcus, you're dead anyway. You're going to bleed out on this rooftop in a lot of pain. But if you help me, tell me something we can use against them..." She pauses. I see a look on her face that reminds me of a nurse comforting a patient. "You can rest knowing you've done the right thing. I can ease your suffering."

I have to admit, she's good. This is probably more effective and quicker than me shooting him and beating on him until he talks. I'm not going to admit that to her, though.

"Please, Marcus. Did you know about the uranium?"

"Y-yeah, I did."

"What's the big picture?"

"Once it had been mined, it was going to be my job to transport it to their lab."

"And then what?"

"I'm not sure."

"Marcus, come on..." She squeezes slightly on his throat again.

"Please! I swear, I don't know. I heard talk that they're holding a scientist somewhere until the uranium's ready. They're going to make him process it into weapons-grade material."

Clara looks up at me. My jaw muscles tense. I'm guessing we share the same concerns.

I step toward them. "Marcus, where are they keeping this scientist?"

"I s-swear I don't know. I just heard a couple of people talking."

Clara stands and motions to me to follow her. We walk a few paces away from Jones, just out of earshot. She rubs the base of her neck and sighs. "I believe him."

That's good enough for me.

I nod. "Okay."

"Ketranovich doesn't tell any one person everything. He tells people only what they need to know to carry out their individual assignments. That way, if he's betrayed, he'll know who did it based on what information has been leaked."

"That's smart. So, now what?"

She looks over at Jones, then back at me. She lowers her gaze, and her body visibly tenses. That tells me she believes we've got all the information we're going to get from Jones. And we obviously can't leave him here...

I smile empathetically. "Do you want to do it?"

She shakes her head.

I nod. "That's okay. Wait here."

I walk over to Jones and take aim. Without another word, I look him in the eye and put a bullet in his head. The shot rings out, and neither of us moves until silence falls once more.

I take a deep breath, choosing to ignore the stabbing pain in my chest.

At least we've got more to go on now, which is good. We know Dark Rain is hiding a scientist somewhere until the uranium is mined. It's interesting to hear that Dark Rain intended to process the material themselves. I wonder if GlobaTech knew... It's kind of funny that both parties were intending to betray each other. It would've been interesting if the material were mined, and they both tried to convert it at the same time...

I'm assuming, given what's at stake, no one's going to let the fact that *I* have the deeds stop them from mining the uranium. With Jackson dead, I reckon that will delay things from GlobaTech's point of view for a while.

So, the next step is to find this scientist. If we can get to them before the mining starts, Dark Rain will be forced to delay things too, based on their inability to do anything with the material once they have it. The last thing Ketranovich will want is to be sitting on tons of uranium that's useless on the black market.

We need to act fast, but for the first time this week, things are looking up.

Clara walks over to me. "What now? We need to get out of here before the cops arrive..."

I nod. "Agreed. Fancy a drink?"

14

We're sitting across from each other in a booth, sipping our drinks. The bar isn't too busy or loud. Music is playing low in the background. There's a contemporary feel to the place. The interior is a mixture of brown leather and dark wood, as is the furniture. The people here seem more refined than the patrons in the places I usually drink. Everyone is in business dress or smart casual attire, talking in small groups like civilized people.

I'm cradling two fingers of Johnnie Walker. Clara's holding a bottle of Bud between her hands on the table, staring silently into space.

She looks up at me. "So, what's the plan?"

I shrug casually. "The way I see it, we need to start by tracking down this scientist. Any ideas where Dark Rain could be holding him?"

"There are a few places they might use. It'll be within

the city limits. They wouldn't want to risk transporting the uranium too far. Especially over state lines."

"Good point. I'll get my guy to look into it. You can give him the locations you know of, and he'll work his magic from there. He might be able to narrow down the search and track them by process of elimination."

"Sounds good."

She seems distracted. She probably has a lot on her mind, which I can understand. "Hey... you all right?"

She smiles wearily. "Yeah, I'm fine. I'm just thinking about what Marcus said to me on the roof, about being a traitor. It's like I told you, Adrian—you can't walk away from these people."

"Hey, you're gonna be fine. You have my word. We're going to stop them, okay?"

She smiles but says nothing. We fall silent again for a few minutes, but it doesn't feel awkward.

She takes a sip of her drink. "Can I ask you something?"

I nod. "Shoot..."

"Before, in your motel room, I was wearing a towel..."

"Yeah, you were."

"And we had a long conversation..."

"I know. I was there, remember?"

"You didn't check me out *once*."

I raise an eyebrow and burst out laughing, prompting a disapproving look. "I'm sorry... but you're such a woman!"

"What gave it away?" She points to her breasts and pulls a face. "These?"

I make a conscious effort not to look. "Let me ask *you* something. If I *had* checked you out, would it have gotten me anywhere?"

She seems to be genuinely considering her answer. After a moment, she smiles apologetically. "Probably not."

I hold my hands up. "There you go! So, if we both knew I wouldn't have stood a chance anyway, why does it bother you that I didn't try?"

She shrugs. "A girl likes to be noticed, y'know? It makes her feel... special." She pulls another face, playful, and smiles. She's messing with me.

I massage my temples in frustration. "Shoot me now..."

We laugh together. She finishes her drink and points to my glass. "Want another?"

I take a final gulp to finish it and nod. "Please. Same again."

She slides out of her seat and walks over to the bar. I notice a group of men at a table across from us stop and check her out. I smile to myself and stare absently at the table.

Why didn't I check her out? I mean, it's not like she's unattractive. She's one of the most gorgeous women I've seen in a long, long time. I just... I don't think about stuff like that. I focus on my job and that's it. After losing...

I rest my head in my hands and sigh.

I'm angry at myself now because I'm worried I offended her in some way. I wonder if I've actually hurt her feelings. Women are complicated creatures sometimes. She being playful, but there's likely an underlying reason that prompted her to ask.

Or am I over-thinking it?

I let out another heavy sigh.

"What's on your mind, champ?"

Clara appears next to me, places my drink in front of me, and then slides back into her seat opposite.

I shake my head. "Nothing. Just thinking about what you said before, about not checking you out. I—"

She waves her hand and smiles. "I was just kidding around. Forget about it."

"No, it's fine. I need to give you a real reason for my own peace of mind, okay?"

She shrugs, still smiling. "Go ahead."

I take a deep breath and a gulp of Johnnie Walker. "Six years ago, I was working a contract over in Philadelphia. A guy hired me to take out a local drug dealer called Darnell Harper, who sold some cocaine to his son. The boy died of an overdose, and the coroner's report said the coke had been cut with some kind of cleaning fluid, which made it toxic. The guy was beside himself but knew he couldn't do anything on his own. He reported it to the police, but they did nothing, so he hired me to kill the guy that sold it."

She listens intently, occasionally sipping her drink.

"I looked into the guy. He was just a small-time dealer. He had a modest operation in the local area, but he wasn't in the big leagues. I tailed him for a couple of days, learning his routines and his hangouts. Then, on the third day, I waited until he was alone, and I put a bullet between his eyes with a sniper rifle from a rooftop two streets away."

She nods approvingly. "Nice!"

"Thanks. Unfortunately, it turned out Harper was the son of Wilson Trent, the drug kingpin who runs most of Pennsylvania. I didn't find that out initially because no one on the street knew about it. Apparently, Harper used his mother's maiden name, so he wouldn't be associated with his old man. He wanted to make his own way, not on Trent's coattails."

Clara leans forward. Her smile's faded. "So, what happened?"

"Trent put the word out that his son had been hit. It didn't take long for him to track down my client, and it took even less time to convince *him* to give me up. Within a few days, I had five guys kicking down my front door, intent on killing me. An example needed making to send a message, to remind everyone that you didn't mess with Wilson Trent."

I pause to finish my drink as I'm inundated with memories and images. Visions from that day that will haunt me forever... and of the darkness I tried to crawl out of in the years that followed.

She reaches over, placing her hand on my arm. "You all right? You don't have to explain anything to me, y'know? I'm serious—I was just kidding around before."

I nod. "I know. Thank you. But it's okay. I want to tell you."

Clara smiles and leans back against the seat as she takes another sip of her beer.

I take a deep breath. "I wasn't home when they came for me. But they kicked down the door and stormed in to find that my wife and daughter were. Maria was just seven years old..." I let the sentence trail off. I picture my baby girl smiling at me. "When I got home, I found them both hogtied on the kitchen floor with bullets in their heads and chests. Trent's men had turned the house upside-down and trashed it almost beyond repair. At the time, I had no idea what had happened. I just panicked, packed a bag, grabbed my guns, and left. I rang the police a couple of hours later and said I was a concerned neighbor who had heard gunshots. I've not been back home since."

"Jesus, Adrian. I'm so sorry..."

Her eyes are filling up with tears.

"That's why I wouldn't have dreamed of making a move on you—as beautiful as you are. As far as I'm concerned, I'm still married."

Clara nods and smiles, casually wiping away the single

tear rolling down her cheek. "That's admirable of you. So, how come you've never gone after Trent since?"

"I hadn't been in the freelance business long when it all happened, and back then, I was out of my league going up against a man like Trent. I just ran, keeping clear of the East Coast, even to this day. Nowadays, yeah—I'm more than capable of going after him, but... I'm not ready to face my past yet, nor my guilt for running away in the first place. I was in a bad place for a long time. If it wasn't for my friend, Josh, getting me through those dark times, I probably would've eaten a bullet years ago."

"Well, you shouldn't feel guilty, Adrian. Anyone in your position would've done the same."

I smile. "Thank you for saying so, but that doesn't make living with it any easier."

"No, I imagine it doesn't... I'm sorry." She pauses. "So, your life since then has basically involved traveling around the country and killing people for money?"

I chuckle. "You make it sound so glamorous. But yeah, that's pretty much it. I learned the hard way not to take jobs in my hometown. So, now I don't live anywhere—makes things much easier. Over the years, I've earned my reputation and made plenty of money doing something I'm good at. Things could be a lot worse."

"It must be lonely though, all that traveling on your own?"

I shrug. "I'm used to it. I've always got Josh to talk to, and I've learned to embrace my anonymity."

"You're hardly anonymous, though, are you? Every criminal in North America who's worth a damn has heard of you."

I smile. In truth, my reputation isn't limited to North

America, and it isn't limited to criminals. Let's just say I've been around...

"That may be, but I still can't be found unless I want to be. I'd call that pretty anonymous."

I take another sip of my drink and glance around the bar. Outside, through the front window, I see a black Humvee pull up. It mounts the curb at a decent speed, sliding to a halt with a loud screech. The doors fly open and four people step out.

What the...

Are they holding guns?

I see them form a line in front of the bar.

Yes, those are *definitely* guns... assault rifles, in fact.

They take aim...

Oh, shit!

"Everybody get down!"

I grab Clara's hand and drag her out of the booth as the bullets start flying. The air fills with the rapid, thumping roar of automatic gunfire and the bitter stench of gunpowder.

I flip one of the tables, pulling us both down behind it.

Clara looks at me. "What's happening?"

"We're getting shot at..."

I look around and see people running and screaming in blind panic. The furniture and decor are getting shredded by the onslaught from outside. The glass behind the bar shatters, exploding everywhere. Nearby, I hear the dull squelch as bullets impact someone's body, piercing their flesh with an unholy fury. A lucky few seem to have found cover, but nothing's going to protect anyone for long against *this*.

I risk a quick peek over the table to get a glimpse of who's attacking us. I can see the four figures through the smoke and haze. There's a woman who, judging by her figure and outfit, I'm assuming is Natalia Salikov—the super-scary assassin Clara mentioned yesterday. The other three are guys I've not seen before. But if Natalia's here, that means Dark Rain has found me.

Or found Clara.

I look over at her as she looks at me, clearly coming to the same conclusions.

"You packing?" she asks.

I reach behind me and produce my two babies. "Always."

I hand her one, then reach into my pocket and pass her a spare mag. She nods at me gratefully, checks how full it is, and loads the gun. She works the slide, chambers a round, then flicks the safety off.

I motion for her to stay where we are, behind cover. She nods. I take another quick look at the front. Happy they're all momentarily pre-occupied with causing as much damage as possible, I run to my left and fire three rounds blindly in their general direction. I slide across the floor on my knees and stop behind another batch of tables, taking cover again. I look over at Clara, who's doing her best to return fire.

I tense my jaw muscles as I think. We've got no chance of winning a shootout against these people—we're too heavily outgunned. I glance around for some inspiration and see a door at the far side of the bar. That must lead into the back area and, hopefully, out of the building...

Clara breaks cover and runs to my side, letting off four rounds that cause one of the gunmen to momentarily duck away. She can certainly handle herself. I'll give her that. I have to admit I'm glad to have her on my side.

I look at her as she crouches beside me. "We can't stay

here. There's a door behind us. We're gonna have to make a run for it."

She nods, then squeezes off a few more rounds just as the table splinters just above her head. I look over to see which of the gunmen has locked on to us. They're standing in a line, with Natalia second from the left. The guy on the far right is emptying another mag in our direction.

I duck back down to avoid another burst, then spring up and unload three more rounds at the guy on the right. The first one misses, but the second and third hit the spot. One hits him in the chest, making him stagger back and spray bullets in a wide arc toward the ceiling. The other catches him on the jaw, and the bottom half of his head explodes in a pink and white mist, sending bone and blood flying off in all directions.

The guy standing next to him shouts something as he watches his comrade's body drop lifelessly to the sidewalk. In a blind rage, he steps forward into the bar and opens fire, fanning his bullets wildly from side to side.

Clara reloads, and I note the concern creeping across her face. We're both down to our last few bullets.

"C'mon, we're leaving!"

I stay low and fire blind as I run over to the side of the bar. She does the same and follows me. I point at the door just behind it and count down from three on my hand...

Three...

Two...

One...

We both stand and run, barge through the door, then slam it shut behind us. It won't be long before the gunmen follow. Probably just a few seconds.

There's a fire exit ahead of us on the left. The entrance to the cellar is before that on the right, halfway down the corridor. Clara points to it. "There's gotta be a way in and out through there. It's where they unload the barrels from the delivery trucks out back."

It's sound logic, and I think she's right.

I nod. "Okay, you take the cellar. I'll go out back. If we can split them up, we stand more chance of surviving this thing. Meet back at my motel room, okay?"

"Okay. Be careful, Adrian."

I smile. "You too."

I turn around and take aim at the door we just came through, providing cover. She opens up the cellar doors and descends into the darkness below. Once she's inside, I shut them behind her just as our attackers burst into the narrow corridor. I fire at them, aiming awkwardly behind me as I run for the fire exit up ahead, forcing them to duck back inside the main bar area. It buys me a few more valuable seconds at least. I push through the fire exit shoulder-first and come out in a small parking lot at the back.

"Freeze!"

I skid to a halt and look around. There are three police cars, each with two officers standing behind their open doors. They're all aiming their guns at me.

You've got to be kidding me...

15

I hold my arms out to the side instinctively, so I don't appear threatening—despite the fact I'm holding a gun in my hand.

Time slows down, and every second that ticks by feels like an hour.

"Drop your weapon now!"

I frown, feeling my jaw muscles tense as I try to subdue the frustration. "Guys, you've caught me at a *really* bad time here..."

Before anyone can reply, bullets explode into the door behind me, interrupting the standoff. Without thinking, I duck and dive away to my left, taking cover in a small alcove. I look over and see the police ducking for cover and resting their guns in between their open doors and the body of their cruisers. They're aiming at the fire exit.

"Stay where you are!" shouts one of the officers.

I look over at them. "Oh, don't worry about me, officer. If

133

I were you, I'd be more concerned about what's coming through that door!"

There's another burst of gunfire. The fire exit swings open, falling from its frame and crashing noisily to the ground. Two of the gunmen step out, holding their assault rifles in front of them, and stand ceremoniously in front of the police. They're using AK-47s, which makes sense, given Dark Rain's run by a former Russian soldier.

A moment later, Natalia steps out and walks over to them, standing in between her comrades. She's got two Heckler and Koch MP7 submachine guns, one in each hand. I think they're officially classed as personal defense weapons nowadays. They're used out in Afghanistan, and they're some serious pieces of hardware.

Natalia's dressed in a similar outfit to what Clara was wearing when I first saw her—all black and tight. But Natalia's looks slightly different. It's more of a cat suit, and there's visible padding over vital organs and limbs. I figure she'll survive a stray bullet, which doesn't bode well.

They must know I'm here, but I'm assuming the six armed police officers are a more pressing concern for them right now.

I watch the scene unfold, keeping quiet behind the wall of the alcove.

Natalia steps forward. She's got bright red hair and dark eye make-up. She glances over at me and smiles. She has the brightest blue eyes I've ever seen. The excessive eyeliner accentuates them even more, so they look like searchlights. I stare back at her. There's a void in her eyes where normal human emotion should be.

For a split-second, dark moments from my past come flooding into my mind. I remember staring at my own reflection in the mirror and seeing that exact same look staring back, tempting me to stick the barrel of my Beretta in my mouth and pull the trigger...

This woman has some serious, unaddressed anger management issues, and that could become a problem.

Natalia looks back at the police officers, who haven't said anything since Dark Rain emerged through the fire exit. They're exchanging hesitant and frightened glances. With no warning, Natalia and the gunmen level their guns at the small squadron of cops.

They wouldn't...

She screams something loud in Russian that I don't understand. Then all three of them open fire, emptying their mags at the police.

My eyes go wide. "No!"

The loud clunking noise of bullets hitting metal fills the air, causing the officers to scatter. The don't even bother returning fire. The three police cruisers are about thirty feet away from the Dark Rain assault team, and it doesn't take long for the middle one to explode.

The noise is deafening and leaves me with a ringing in my ears as the heat from the blast forces me to duck completely into the alcove. After a moment, I look back round at the scene. An eerie silence descends, broken only by the crackle of flames from the destroyed car. The gunmen seem unfazed, despite their close proximity to the blast. The force from the explosion shifted the other police cars out to the sides a good twenty feet, removing any chance of cover the cops might have had left.

Through the smoke and fire, I can't see where the officers have disappeared to. The firing stops, and Natalia turns her attention toward me. As I see the maniacal grin on her face, I realize I've been standing here watching like an idiot this whole time instead of putting some distance between me and the hit squad sent to kill me. One gunman turns and runs away to the right, presumably going after Clara...

I hope she's managed to get a decent head start.

As the remaining gunman aims his weapon at me, I snap back into the moment, re-focus on the situation, and take aim. My arm moves like a reflex. I unload three bullets, which all hit him dead-center, square in the chest. He falls to the ground as my gun clicks down on an empty chamber.

I look at Natalia, who momentarily regards her fallen comrade with complete indifference. Then she looks at me and raises her MP7s.

"Oh, shit!"

I turn and run around the corner of the building, narrowly avoiding a burst of gunfire that chips away at the brick just behind me. I head down an alleyway that runs alongside the bar, which leads me back to the main street. As I emerge onto the sidewalk, I'm genuinely shocked to see how much it resembles a warzone. There's broken glass everywhere. The Humvee is still parked outside the bar at a hurried angle with the doors all open. The building looks derelict, having been almost completely destroyed in the gunfight.

The street is littered with bodies—some dead, some alive but injured. There's constant screaming nearby and a cacophony of sirens approaching in the distance. A crowd of onlookers has congregated across the street, all talking excitedly into their phones or taking pictures and videos of the scene for the internet.

I can't head that way. Natalia won't think twice about firing at them to get to me...

I look behind me and see her rounding the corner, heading for the street. I run quickly over to the Humvee, carefully pick up a shard of glass from the ground nearby, then use it to slash both front tires. I sprint away to the right, down the street.

As I pass the alleyway again, Natalia is just stepping out onto the sidewalk. She shoots from the hip, arcing a spray of bullets upward in my general direction. I raise my arm, shielding my head—which I know is futile but instinctive, nevertheless.

The sirens are getting louder. I need to get off the main street…

I see another alleyway off to my left. I head down it, not bothering to look if Natalia is in pursuit. I quickly reach into my pocket and put my Bluetooth earpiece in, dialing Josh as I navigate the alleyways.

He answers. "Josh?"

I wince in pain from the effort of speaking and running at the same time. I'm still hurting from chasing down Marcus Jones, and now that I'm breathing heavily yet again, my bruised ribs are actively complaining.

"Adrian, are you all right? You sound… flustered."

I can barely manage to say more than a few words at a time as I gasp for air. "Long story… gunfight… Dark Rain… Google Maps… my motel…"

"On it."

It's like we have our own language sometimes. He fully understood my request and knows it's not the time to ask questions. We've known each other for so long, we're like brothers. We understand each other well, and it's times like these when that really comes in handy.

I chance a look behind me but can't see Natalia. As Josh

works his magic, I briefly think of Clara. I hope she got away all right.

"Okay, Adrian, listen up. Take the next left up ahead. On the right is an alleyway that cuts through the block and brings you out two streets over from your motel but approaching from the back. That's the best I've got."

"Thanks, man."

I hang up and pick up the pace, running as fast as my body allows me as I follow Josh's directions. I step out of the alleyway and slow to a casual walk, taking deep breaths in through my mouth and out through my nose to slow my heart rate down as quickly as possible. Two police cars speed past me with their sirens blaring. I remain calm, knowing they won't be looking for someone so relaxed and so far away from the scene. As long as I don't draw attention to myself, they won't show any interest in me.

I wait until they're out of sight and jog over to the back of my motel. I walk around to the front and scan the area to make sure I've not been followed. Satisfied I'm in the clear, I head inside, walk past the front desk, through the double doors, and down the hallway toward my room.

As I approach, I see the door's open slightly. I take a quiet breath to steady myself and draw my gun. I know it's not loaded, but no one else does. Usually, the sight of a gun is enough to throw someone off their game.

I can't imagine Clara leaving the door open, which means Dark Rain must've found out where I'm staying. These guys are worryingly adept at going after people...

I push the door open gently and walk in, dropping to one knee and raising my gun.

Ah, shit.

The room has been completely trashed. All the furniture is upturned and scattered across the floor.

But two things in particular catch my attention. The first thing is that my mattress isn't on the bed frame anymore. It's been thrown unceremoniously into the corner by the window. This means that whoever did this now has the deeds to the uranium mine…

The second, arguably the more concerning thing is that Clara's lying face-down on the floor in a pool of steadily expanding blood.

Jesus Christ!

I holster my gun, fighting to stay calm. "Clara?"

No response.

Shit.

I kneel next to her body carefully, so as not to step in any blood. I feel for a pulse. It's there, but it's weak.

"Clara, can you hear me?"

Still nothing.

Double shit.

I quickly assess her, calling on some long-buried first aid knowledge. I conclude there are no broken bones. The blood's coming from underneath her, and I can't see any exit wounds on her back, so I know the bullet's still inside.

I grab her right shoulder and roll her over gently on her back. I examine her body again. There's a bullet wound in her left shoulder, just below her collarbone and to the left of her breast. It's not fatal, but she's lost a lot of blood. She's been lying face-down, and gravity's done its job annoyingly well. She needs urgent medical attention, but under the circumstances, a general hospital probably isn't the best idea.

Triple shit.

I look over at the bed, quickly thinking about the land deeds. If Dark Rain is responsible for this, then I've drastically underestimated them. They've managed to track me down and nearly kill me before I've barely had chance to learn their name.

I look back down at Clara.

Maybe they're not after me at all... or maybe not exclusively. This attack could easily have been an attempt to kill Clara, not me. They might not consider me a threat—just an obstacle to overcome in order to get the deeds to the land...

The Beretta I lent to her is lying on the floor a few feet away. I pick it up and holster it at my back, next to its brother. I look around the place, my mind going into survival mode. The room was rented under a fake name, and I paid cash, so no one can link me to the scene. I quickly move around, wiping down surfaces and checking the bathroom for any trace of forensic evidence. I then grab my shoulder bag and jacket, which thankfully hadn't been taken. With one last glance at Clara, I leave the room.

18:43 PDT

I walk at a brisk pace and put a few minutes between me and the motel before I call an ambulance from a payphone. I feel guilty because I'm putting Clara in a bad spot. The doctors are going to question her, and she could find herself in a lot of trouble. On the other hand, she needs medical attention, and she'll be much safer in a hospital than with me.

I'll ask Josh to track her progress once she's admitted. I'm sure he'll be able to hack his way into the hospital databases without too much trouble.

I need to stay clear of any kind of authority for the time being. After the attack at the bar, and with the police being caught in the crossfire, I'm probably close to the top of everyone's priority list at the moment.

The first thing I need to do is find a new place to stay. I'll keep to the back streets and alleyways where I can and make my way into the city center. I'll need to be careful and make sure no one picks up my trail—not the police and definitely not any Dark Rain operatives.

After another ten minutes, I come across a small park behind a row of convenience stores. It's been a long day, and I need time to get my head straight. I don't envisage any major recovery time coming my way, so maybe five minutes sitting down in a quiet park will have to do.

I walk through the wrought iron gates and down a path lined on either side by small flowerbeds. The path snakes through the middle of the park and brings me to an open area with a large water fountain surrounded by wooden benches. The sky's turning orange as the sun slowly begins its descent. It's quiet and peaceful here. I take a good look around to make sure I'm alone before sitting down and allowing myself some time to relax.

I lean back on the bench, stretching my legs and carefully lifting my arms up, feeling my sore ribs crack in protest.

Oh my God, it feels so good to not move!

In fact, in the last twenty-four hours, this is probably the longest I've gone without someone trying to kill me.

I take out my cell and dial Josh's number. He answers as I'm letting out a heavy and painful breath.

"You okay? Did you make it back to your motel?"

"Yeah, thanks for that before. But I got back to find Clara unconscious and bleeding on the floor."

"Shit! What the hell is going on there, Adrian?"

"We tracked down a guy called Marcus Jones. He's a

courier in the city that Dark Rain employs to move stuff around for them. After some initial resistance, he told us they've kidnapped a scientist to process the mined uranium to make it weapons-grade."

"Which I'm assuming our friends at GlobaTech are blissfully unaware of?"

"I think that's a fair assumption, yeah. So, afterward, me and Clara grabbed a drink and started planning our next move. Then a Humvee pulled up outside. Four people got out and proceeded to completely annihilate the place. We fought our way out and split up. I know I killed two of them, and I've not seen the one that peeled off to chase Clara. The only one who survived for sure is a woman named Natalia Salikov. Some big-time Russian mercenary who has Clara spooked. I got away, and that's when I called you. Then I got back and found Clara."

"Oh my God, man! Seriously, what the hell have you stumbled into?"

"I'm trying to figure that out. But it gets worse. Whoever broke into my room and shot her also took the deeds to the uranium mine."

"Shit!"

"That's what I said."

"Okay, this is bad... You gotta be careful, Adrian. I'm serious. Dark Rain is two steps ahead of you, and you're alone in a town where everyone seems to wanna shoot at you as soon as they see you."

"I'll cross those bridges when I get to them. I need a few things. First, can you find out which hospital Clara's been taken to and what condition she's in?"

"I'm on it."

"Also, I need to find out where they could be holding this scientist... Can you look into any well-known or respected scientists that haven't been seen lately? See what comes up. If we can find out *who* they've taken and *when*, I might be able to work with Clara and get an idea of *where* they're holding them."

"Yeah, I'm on that too. Gimme a sec..." The line goes silent for a few moments. "Ah, bollocks."

"What's wrong?"

"I just searched all hospital databases within a twenty-mile radius."

"That was fast."

"It's not exactly hard to do, Adrian."

"All right, show-off. So, what's with the British cussing?"

"No one's been admitted today fitting Clara's description. No Jane Does, no gunshot wounds... nothing."

"I definitely called the ambulance. There's no way they didn't get to her."

Now I'm worried. After everything that's happened, for Clara to disappear after being shot and left for dead is the last thing I need to deal with.

Could Dark Rain have gotten to her before the ambulance arrived? I checked the area before I left, and there was no one around. But if they found my room and took the deeds, it's feasible they were hiding somewhere nearby.

"Shit!"

"Adrian, you all right?"

"Yeah, I'm fine. Goddammit! I shouldn't have left her."

"You did the right thing. Don't blame yourself."

"Listen, I've got to find her. Can you focus on finding this missing scientist?"

"Will do. What are you thinking of doing?"

"I was going to find somewhere else to stay, but now I'm going to head back to my old motel and see if I can find anything that might give me more of an idea what happened to her."

"Okay. Well, watch your back, man."

I hang up and look around, more paranoid now that I'm being watched. I take another minute to relax and focus, then make my way out of the park and back toward the motel.

16

After searching the room and the surrounding area carefully and discreetly, I found no clue as to what happened. Clara was gone, and the old guy working the front desk confirmed an ambulance arrived. So, where the hell is she?

I decided it was becoming less productive to keep focusing on what had happened, so I made my way back toward the city center and started thinking about what's going to happen next. I lost track of time and must've been wandering around aimlessly for a good couple of hours before I finally made it to the center.

Most of the stores have closed, and streetlights have flickered into life now that the sun has crept down behind the horizon. The bars and restaurants have filled up, and the sidewalks are bustling with people out for the evening.

Up ahead, I can see a street vendor on the corner, selling

hot dogs and burgers out of his cart. I walk over to him, realizing I can't quite remember when I last ate. He's an older man, probably mid-sixties. He has dark skin with gray hair and dark eyes. He's whistling a tune to himself and looks happy and carefree. I get the impression he's been standing on this street corner with that same cart for most of his life.

I stop just in front of him. "Hey, can I get a cheeseburger, please?"

The guy's eyes widen slightly. He looks me up and down, then chuckles. "Oh, man, you look like shit! You all right?"

I must admit, I'm not in the mood for small talk, but I'll be courteous. I smile with little humor. "Rough day. I'll be better when I've eaten."

He nods. "Man, I heard that! I'm gonna give you the works, son. You can thank me later."

He produces a burger from inside the cart and places it between two buns. He then lays a slice of cheese on it, another burger, some relish, ketchup, mustard, and another slice of cheese. Finally, he tops it off with a sprinkling of grated onion. He wraps it in a napkin and hands it to me.

I take it from him and look at it admiringly. "That's gotta be the best-looking burger I've ever seen."

His smile is laced with confidence, like he's secure in the knowledge that it's obviously the best-looking burger I've ever seen. "You're welcome."

"How much do I owe you?"

"For you... gimme five bucks. The extras are on me. It looks like you need 'em."

"You're a kind and generous man. Thank you."

I pay him the five dollars and walk on down the street. I take a bite of the burger and I feel my eyes go wide. It's the nicest cheeseburger I've ever tasted... and I'm not just saying that because I'm so hungry!

I step to one side and lean against the front window of a closed store to finish eating. I don't want to walk and not appreciate the food. Back in the day, when I was on a mission, I could easily go a couple days without the opportunity for food. You soon learn to eat all you can when you can—and be damn grateful for it. You never know when or where your next meal will be...

I finish up and toss the napkin in a trashcan near the curb, then walk on down the street. There's a crossing up ahead. I glide past a small group of women and stand by it, waiting for the green light.

A black, stretched limousine appears and stops on the crossing in front of me, much to the dismay of the other drivers, who are now sounding their horns and gesturing angrily.

The window buzzes down, and Jimmy Manhattan leans out. "Get in."

I let out a deep breath in frustration.

At least he waited until I'd finished my cheeseburger. Nothing pisses me off more than someone interrupting me while I'm eating.

I stare at him. "That's a little forward, don't you think?"

The driver's door opens, and I look over to see my old friend, Stan, getting out. He stands up straight and pulls his jacket apart, showing me the gun holstered at his side.

I look back at Jimmy. He's smiling. "I said, get in."

He opens the door and gestures to the seat in front of him. I wait a moment, take a quick look around, and then climb inside.

The interior is nice—smooth leather with a dark walnut trim all around. The windows are tinted, offering total privacy.

I sit in the seat opposite Manhattan. I don't like the fact

I've got my back to the driver, but I figure if anything's going to happen to me, it'll be Manhattan who attempts it.

The car pulls away and gathers speed. He produces the gun from inside his jacket and aims it at me. "I think we have some things to discuss, don't you?"

I say nothing. I just stare at him, smiling.

He raises an eyebrow. "Under the circumstances, I don't see how you have much to be happy about."

I'm smiling partly to wind him up because that's just what I do before a fight... and yes, I'm working on the assumption that there'll be a fight, during which I intend to break Manhattan's neck.

But the main reason I'm smiling is because for the first time in three days, I have an advantage. I know something that no one else does. Before I got in the car, I saw a black, leather-clad figure on a blue and white motorcycle parked across the street. I couldn't tell for sure that they were looking at me because of the helmet, but after today, I'd recognize Natalia Salikov anywhere.

I tend to remember the people who try to kill me.

I also heard her bike start up as we drove off. I subtly glance over Manhattan's shoulder out the rear window and see a single headlight behind us. I know she's not exactly on my side, but it's going to be interesting when she catches up with us.

Still, let's keep that a surprise for now.

My smile fades. "Jimmy, I told you to leave this alone. In fact, I remember explicitly saying I'd kill you if I ever saw you again."

He says nothing, but he reaches into the other side of his jacket and produces some papers, which I recognize instantly as the deeds to the land from my motel room. He waves them in front of me. "Let's start with you explaining why you lied to me."

I stare at them for a moment, not saying anything. I can't find any words. I'm too busy processing the fact it was clearly Pellaggio's men who raided my room and shot Clara. I need a minute to let my anger subside. If I weren't in a moving vehicle, Manhattan would already be dead. As it is, right now isn't the time nor the place to rip his throat out.

I take a deep breath in an effort to remain calm. "Like I told you and your boss last night, you're in way over your head here. The best thing you can do is walk away. Whatever money you believe you've lost as a result of all this, you can easily recoup elsewhere."

He says nothing.

"Now let me ask *you* a question. Was it you personally who broke into my room?"

Manhattan smiles. "You're wondering if I pulled the trigger and shot your little girlfriend? How touching."

It's more of a statement than a question.

"You're on thin fucking ice, Jimmy. I suggest you tread carefully."

"We don't intimidate easily, Mr. Hell, as I'm sure you can understand. Besides, you're hardly in a position to be making threats, are you?"

I look behind him again. The single headlight is still there and gaining slowly.

"How do you figure that?"

"I have the deeds to the land for Mr. Pellaggio, which I managed to get without having to pay you a cent. Your girlfriend's been shot and is currently lying in a hospital bed somewhere. After seeing what was left of that bar earlier, I can only assume you've managed to piss off a few other people along the way..." He pauses, seemingly for effect. "Stop me if I've missed anything."

"Actually, yeah. You've missed one very important fact."

"Which is?"

"Those other people I've pissed off? Right now, they're more pissed at you than me."

His eyes narrow slightly with a mixture of concern and doubt.

"And I'm the only one who can tell you why. Do you wanna know?"

He gestures theatrically with his gun hand. "Enlighten me."

I figure now is as good a time as any to introduce him to the rest of the players on the field.

"You ever heard of Dark Rain?"

He shakes his head. "No. Should I have?"

I shrug. "I guess not. They're a militia outfit based somewhere in Heaven's Valley. As far as I can tell, they have designs on committing an act of terrorism on U.S. soil. Ted Jackson's company is funding them—some kind of off-the-books deal. Originally, he was going to sell that land to you, on the side, to make some money for himself. But then GlobaTech Industries ordered him to broker a deal and sell the land to Dark Rain. That's why he screwed you over."

Manhattan considers what I've said for a moment, then shakes his head again. "I don't care about any *militia outfit*. Roberto Pellaggio runs this entire city and owns half of it. They're of no concern to us."

"Yet again, you underestimate the game you're playing, Jimmy."

Before Manhattan can speak, Stan's voice sounds out over the intercom and announces we've arrived at our destination. The limo slows to a stop. I hear Stan get out, and a moment later, the door opens for us.

Manhattan points his gun at me. "Get out, nice and slow."

I step out and stand up, stretching slowly to my full height, being careful not to show that my ribs are sore. As I do, Stan hits me flush on the side of the head with a big straight left. It takes me by surprise. Given the beating I've taken over the last twenty-four hours, it's enough to drop me to one knee. Stan reaches behind me and takes my guns away. Then he picks up my shoulder bag and drags me to my feet by the scruff of my neck.

I look around but don't recognize where I am. I figure we're close to the city limits. There are no buildings anywhere—just desert and the vague silhouette of the mountains in the distance. In front of us are the beginnings of a construction site. There's a digger parked over to the left, and straight ahead are a couple of those portable cabins that people use as offices. Far back on the right is a large billboard with floodlights along the top edge, illuminating it in the night, despite it not yet having a poster displayed.

I look back the way we came but see no signs of the motorcycle that's been following us. I'm certain it was Natalia, and I must admit it's concerning that she's disappeared.

Manhattan gets out after me, holds his hands out, and gestures to the location. "Here we are. This is what you've been so desperate to keep from us."

He waves the deeds at me and walks on ahead. Stan still has his hand wrapped around my neck. He pushes me forward, following Manhattan as we head over to one of the cabins.

My headache's back with reinforcements thanks to that punch, but I'm still able to think clearly enough to figure out where we are.

I'm walking on a goddamn uranium mine.

22:35 PDT

We enter the cabin, and they sit me down in front of the desk at the far end, opposite the door. Manhattan sits on the edge facing me as Stan ties my hands behind me. For good measure, he hits me across the face again.

This is nowhere near as much fun when you're the one sitting in the chair...

The cabin's practically empty, save for the desk and a notice board on the left-hand wall. There's a small window in the wall opposite with vertical blinds pulled together.

Stan steps to one side, letting Manhattan look at me. He's sitting on the edge with his hands clasped on his lap. He's holding the gun loosely still—not aiming it at me, just making sure I know it's there. The deeds are next to him on the desk.

I stare at him. "I'm almost offended that you've only brought Donkey Kong over here with you for backup. Especially given I've already handed his ass to him once this week."

I turn to Stan and smile.

He unleashes another big right hand that catches me square on my cheek.

Oh, man, that hurts...

My head's spinning, and my brain's shouting at me to

stop getting hit, but I ignore it and laugh at him. "Come on, asshole. This isn't a tickling competition. Give me a shot that doesn't feel like it came from a girl scout."

He winds up his right hand again. I'm my own worst enemy sometimes. If he lands this, it's going to take my goddamn head off! I grimace slightly, preparing for the impact.

Manhattan holds up a hand. "Enough. We want him alive long enough to get what we need. Then he's all yours."

Stan smiles at me. I throw him a dismissive look with my eyebrows to show my complete lack of concern before turning back to Manhattan. "So, what now? You gonna threaten me some more?"

He shakes his head. "Not at all."

He reaches behind him and opens the top drawer of the desk. He pulls out what looks like a medical kit. It's a small, green box with a zipper running all the way around. He places it next to him on the desk and opens it, so I can see. Inside is an array of stainless-steel surgical equipment—all of which looks sharp.

His lips curl slightly, more of a smirk than a smile. Full of bad intentions. "I'm going to ask you nicely to explain to me everything that's happened since we first spoke a couple of days ago. You're going to leave nothing out, and you're going to take particular care when telling me why you kept the deeds for yourself."

I look at the surgical blades on the table. I can't see any way that the next five minutes won't end up sucking massively. I mean, there's no way Jimmy Manhattan is a qualified surgeon, which means he won't have the dexterity to handle those blades with care and precision. It's going to be ugly, and it's going to hurt. A lot.

But it's okay—I can take it. I reckon I've been through worse in my time. Which speaks volumes about the kind of life I've had, I guess.

I crack my neck. "Jimmy, with all the love and respect in the world... you're a dick. You have absolutely no idea how much trouble you're in. And that's in addition to how pissed off *I* am at you. If you go down this road, you will cross people who can turn your entire organization to ashes in minutes."

With a speed not becoming someone his age, Manhattan reaches over, grabs one of the steel blades, stands, and lashes it out toward me. The blade stops about a quarter inch below my left eye. The tip touches my skin. Not enough pressure to draw blood but enough that I know it's there.

I don't flinch. I stay calm and still, despite my shock.

Manhattan leans in close to me. "I could turn you into a memory with a flick of my wrist. So, keep your advice and idle threats to yourself."

I look down at the blade, then back at Manhattan. His old eyes are cold and his gaze steady. I've pushed him as far as he's willing to let me. But there's no way I'm telling the mafia that we're sitting on top of the only natural uranium deposit in North America. I need to think of something to stall him.

"As I've said, Dark Rain has a working relationship with GlobaTech Industries. Ted Jackson was in town selling this land to them because of that relationship. I fully appreciate *your* view on things, but I'm the only one who does. Dark Rain doesn't care about you or Pellaggio. They just want their land back. They feel they have just as valid a claim on it as you do."

Without a word, Manhattan presses the blade harder, piercing the skin.

Ah!

Shit!

I feel a warm trickle of blood run down my cheek as the cold steel slices through my skin. My flesh splits apart like a ripe melon, opening up a cut on my face running from my eye down to my jaw.

I let out a guttural growl through gritted teeth. The pain is white-hot, and the cool air stings my exposed flesh.

"Answer my goddamn question! What is it about this land that everyone's so interested in? What are they planning?"

He places the blade against me once again, but this time, it's against my throat. He isn't quite piercing my skin, but he's as close as he can be without drawing more blood. Instinctively, I tilt my head back and take shallow breaths, trying to reduce the pressure of the blade against my trachea.

I can't tell him the real reason, but I can't think of a good enough lie.

I close my eyes. I don't honestly know if I'm trying to think clearer or just accepting my fate.

Seconds tick by in agonizing silence. I'm—

Wait... what's that?

It sounds like tires on the gravel outside. Lots of them. Manhattan straightens up and moves over to the window, peering through the blinds. I turn and look. There seems to be quite a few headlights out there...

He looks back at me. "Who the fuck are these guys? Friends of yours?"

I smile. "I don't have many friends, Jimmy. But let me guess... Black Humvees?"

He nods. "Four of them."

I laugh out loud, prompting both Manhattan and Stan to look at each other in confusion.

Showtime.

17

I look at Stan, who has both of my Berettas in his hands, preparing for a fight. I'm not going to tell him that they're empty, nor that the spare mags are in my bag...

"Hey, douchebag, use your own guns."

He ignores me, seemingly too bothered by how concerned his boss is getting.

"Jimmy, meet Dark Rain. You remember what these guys did to the bar when they came after me the first time, right?"

His initial concern is giving way to something more potent.

Fear.

"Imagine what they're going to do to you. All the crime families in the world can't protect you now. But I can."

His jaw muscles clench. I see the panic in his eyes. "How?"

"Untie me and give me my guns. You guys don't even

register on their radar. All they're concerned about is this land. And killing me, seeing as I made Clara betray them."

I hear car doors opening and the crunching of boot on gravel, followed by the unmistakable sound of automatic weapons being cocked.

I turn to Stan. "Untie me now, or we're all going to die here."

Stan looks at Manhattan, who nods. He bends down and removes my restraints. I stand, rubbing each of my wrists in turn to get some feeling back in them.

I hold out my hand. "Now give me my guns."

He hesitates, but after one look from Manhattan, he hands them over. I holster one of them and hold the second in my right hand. Without any warning, I smash the butt of it into Stan's nose. He stumbles backward, holding his face, and falls to the floor. I quickly turn and aim at Manhattan. "Put your gun down... on the floor... right now."

Reluctantly, he does.

"Kick it over to me."

Again, he does, albeit with an impatient and heavy sigh. "Now what?"

"Now? You keep quiet and let me handle this. They're after me, not you."

I step back, all the way across the cabin to where my shoulder bag is. Keeping one eye on Manhattan, I crouch, open it, and retrieve a couple of spare magazines. I load my Beretta with one and pocket the other.

Manhattan frowns. "Why are you helping me after what I've just done to you?"

I laugh. "An outstanding question. Look, I'm no master strategist. I simply do what I can to survive. I'm a fighter, and right now my fight isn't with you—despite the fact you're trying to pick one with me. Be grateful and leave me the hell alone. You're the only person I've ever warned twice. Take heed, as there won't be a third time. Understand?"

He sighs. "I—"

"Adrian Hell!"

The voice came from outside. It was loud and had a thick Russian accent. It reminds me of the guy from that Flash Gordon movie in the '80s—with the beard and the wings. Man, I loved that film...

It definitely isn't Natalia, so I can only assume it's Dark Rain's illustrious leader, Colonel Ketranovich.

I look out the window. The Humvees are parked with their doors open. Standing in front of them are twelve armed soldiers, all dressed in black. They're in a line, holding assault rifles loosely at their sides.

In front of *them* are three more people. On the far right is Natalia Salikov. The one in the middle must be Ketranovich. I've never seen the guy on the left before, but he looks strangely familiar. I'm guessing he's important. Otherwise, he'd be standing with the rest of the grunts.

Natalia and the other guy also have assault rifles aimed directly at the cabin. Ketranovich isn't armed, but then, why would he be?

I let out a heavy sigh. It's been a really shitty week so far...

"Adrian Hell, come out of there unarmed, and I promise you we will not shoot."

Yeah, right.

Still, I don't really have a choice. There's no cover in here. If they open fire, the cabin will be decimated within seconds, along with everyone inside it.

I turn to Manhattan. "You wanna get out of here?"

He shrugs nonchalantly. "There's no reason I won't anyway. You just said yourself that their issue isn't with me."

"You're right, it's not. But they didn't have an issue with anyone in that bar earlier, and that didn't stop them opening fire regardless, just to get to me."

He thinks about it for a moment. "What do you want?"

"The deeds to this land. It's the only reason they're here, and it's my only bargaining chip."

He shakes his head. "You can kiss my ass, Adrian. You're not having them."

In response, I raise my gun and put a bullet right between Stan's eyes. His head snaps back and smashes against the wall, leaving an explosion of deep crimson all around him. The gunshot sounded extra loud inside the cabin, and the muzzle flash was so bright, even I see flashes every time I blink.

I hear agitated voices and the sound of weapons being checked from outside. I have to act fast. I point my gun at Manhattan. "I have a million reasons to shoot you and very few not to. Give me the fucking deeds."

Slowly, he picks them up off the desk and holds them out to me. I reach over and take them, placing them in my back pocket. I quickly jab the butt of the pistol into Manhattan's nose. I hear it break from the impact. He goes sprawling to the floor, clutching his face. He looks up at me, his eyes wide with a mixture of shock and fear.

I take aim at his head. "We ain't done, Jimmy. I've got big plans for you. But for now, if you wanna get out of here, you're gonna have to trust me."

I take aim just to the right of his head and put a bullet through the floor. He catches his breath as his eyes roll in silent relief. I kneel beside him. "Be seeing you soon."

I slam the butt of my gun down hard on his left temple, knocking him out cold. I slide it back into my holster and wipe the blood from my face as best I can with my sleeve. I walk over and pick up my bag, putting it over both shoulders.

I move over to the door, ready to step outside. I touch the cut on my face again, wincing slightly. That's going to scar like a bitch...

I must admit, I prefer not to have much more than a vague outline of a plan. Any significant amount of detail, and you feel compelled to stick to it as best you can, which means you risk losing sight of the bigger picture. Not seeing everything clearly in front of you can be a deadly mistake.

Luckily, I have no fucking clue what I'm about to do or what will happen as a result.

When in doubt, improvise.

I take a breath. "I'm coming out! I'm unarmed."

I open the door and step out to face the firing squad.

23:17 PDT

The moon is shining bright in the clear night sky, bathing the area in a pale, white glow. My boots crunch on the gravel as I walk toward Ketranovich and his gathering of armed followers. I'm holding my arms out to the sides like a cross with my palms open. It's a passive gesture and gives the impression I'm not a threat.

I might as well try the diplomatic approach first. Granted, diplomacy isn't exactly my strong suit, but at least it will engage them in conversation and buy me some more time.

"Get your men to lower their weapons. We can sort this without any more violence or bloodshed."

Ketranovich laughs. "You have some balls, Adrian Hell. I give you that."

"I didn't realize you could see them from over there..."

He laughs again and motions for his troops to lower their guns, which they all do immediately. Apart from Natalia. She keeps hers trained on me the whole time. Our paths have crossed before, though, so you could argue she knows better than the rest of them.

And I don't blame her. If this goes south, I'll have both pistols drawn and the first bullets fired in less than two seconds. You can be damn sure I'll take out Ketranovich and Natalia before I get cut in half by machine gunfire. I'd count that as a victory. If you cut off the head, most organizations like Dark Rain will simply crumble.

Roman Ketranovich is an impressive man. I can't deny that. He's tall with short graying hair and dark eyes. He's wearing a green vest and camouflage pants. Tattoos cover his huge arms; his muscles are toned by years of combat and killing. He has a scar down his cheek.

I wonder if I'm going to look like that now, thanks to that prick, Manhattan?

He turns and speaks to Natalia in Russian. I have no idea what he's saying, but she finally lowers her weapon. Satisfied, he turns back to me. "I have heard a great deal about you, Adrian Hell. It is an honor to meet such an accomplished soldier."

Normally, this is the point where I'd start winding him up, goading a reaction out of him and capitalizing on his overly emotional state of mind. But given the circumstances, even I recognize that's a pretty stupid idea.

I shrug. "Thanks. Can't say I've ever heard of you..."

He smiles. "That's okay, Adrian Hell. Soon, the whole world will have heard of me."

"Yeah, about that. Listen, I'm not sure I can allow you guys to carry on with your crazy plan for world domination or whatever. Sorry."

He laughs loudly, prompting his followers to do the same. Everyone except Natalia, who's staring a hole right through me.

I frown. "I'm sensing you're not taking me seriously..."

"We have partnership with your military. Our *crazy* plan will happen regardless of what you do."

I shake my head. "I killed your liaison with them, and he never finalized the deal to sell you this land. I have the paperwork in a safe place, so your plan is dead in the water."

Ketranovich's smile fades. "Yes, that's... unfortunate, but no matter. We will begin mining here in a couple of days regardless."

Natalia takes a step forward, raises her gun, and shouts at me in Russian. She's spitting her words out, and I see the venom in her soulless eyes. I don't know what she's saying, but I'm probably safe in assuming she's not declaring her unrequited love for me...

I take a small step back and lift my arms a bit higher to emphasize I'm still unarmed. "Hey, I don't speak Communist, sorry."

Ketranovich turns to the other guy standing with him and gestures at Natalia with an impatient nod. The guy lets go of his rifle, allowing it to hang loose by its strap, and walks over to her. He's a little shorter than Ketranovich but similar in build. He has buzz-cut blond hair and blue eyes. He shouts something at Natalia, and she turns to him—the anger still etched across her face. He places his hands on her shoulders and begins talking to her—again, in Russian. His tone is soothing, almost hypnotic.

I notice the soldiers behind them are looking at each

other and shifting nervously back and forth, muttering among themselves. I get the impression Natalia's the resident freak show, but everyone's too afraid to say it out loud. Ketranovich is also looking on but with far less concern than the rest.

The blond guy is calming her down, but it's interesting to see how she went from zero to psycho in the blink of an eye. This woman has some serious issues, and she's definitely not the type of person I'd trust with an automatic weapon. But hey—that's just me.

Ketranovich looks over at me. "Forgive me. Little Natalia sometimes gets wound too tight. Her brother relaxes her."

Her brother? That makes sense. He looks familiar because he bears a striking resemblance to Natalia. They might even be twins.

I shrug. "Hey, I'm passing no judgment. I kill people for a living."

He laughs again. "You are funny man, Adrian Hell. I like you. Would you consider joining our cause, maybe? We could use a soldier like you."

"Thanks for the offer, Roman, my old friend, but I'm not a terrorist. I'm not going to let you profit from this land, and I'm not going to let you manufacture nuclear weapons. I *will* stop you."

"I'm afraid you are—how you say?—pissing in the wind, my friend. No one can stop what is already in motion. It's a shame you won't be around to see my plan come to fruition. It will be a whole new world."

He points at me. Everyone raises their rifles, cocks them, and takes aim.

Oh, shit.

I breathe out heavily and close my eyes, content that whatever small plan I might've had didn't work. I mentally prepare for a shower of bullets to rain into me. I suppose the blessing is that I won't really feel anything after the first couple of rounds anyway...

Seconds pass that feel like hours.

I'm still alive?

I open one eye and look around.

Well, they're all still there...

Hang on, what's that noise?

I see Ketranovich looking up. I follow his gaze.

In the sky, a line of lights appears in the distance, heading toward us. The noise I can hear is the unmistakable sound of helicopters.

So, who have we here?

The soldiers look at each other, unsure how to react. Natalia and her brother stand close to Ketranovich, who hasn't moved or said anything. He's just staring at the night sky.

It only takes a few moments for the three black helicopters to reach us and hover overhead, forming a triangle above our little showdown. The noise is deafening. Everyone, including me, has to shield their eyes against the dust that the rotor blades are kicking up.

Inside the helicopters are soldiers, all dressed in black with a red trim, aiming their guns at Dark Rain. There's also a mounted minigun on one side, with a single soldier manning it, covering the whole area.

The chopper nearest to me drops lower. A rope ladder falls down, stopping a few feet off the ground next to me. I have no idea who they are, but going with them can't possibly end worse than if I stayed here with a bunch of Russian psychopaths...

I step on the ladder and hook my left arm through the rungs. I look at Ketranovich. "Hey, Colonel—you know what they say about people who piss in the wind: they always get their own back!" I flip him the finger. "Be seeing you soon, you Commie bastard!"

I smile as the helicopter climbs once again. We fly off, followed closely by the other two in a loose formation. I carefully make my way up the ladder, doing my best not to look down. I'm not a massive fan of heights.

One of the soldiers reaches down, extending a hand to help me up into the back of the chopper. I take it gladly and climb aboard as we race across the sky.

I look around at the expressionless faces all staring at me. I smile at them. "My parents always told me not to get in cars with strangers." I get no reaction. "No?" I let out a low whistle. "Tough crowd."

Well, these guys seem like a friendly bunch. I wonder who my new friends are?

18

The silence in the chopper is borderline awkward. I'm sitting in a seat flanked by two men with guns. I look around, trying to find out as much as I can about who these guys are, but I've got nothing. Their uniforms are devoid of markings, so I've no idea who they work for. I'm guessing they're friendly. Or at least not trying to kill me.

But my spider sense is still tingling.

Outside, the other choppers peel away, flying off in different directions. We carry on straight for what feels like another ten minutes before I feel us begin our descent.

I see landing lights below us and realize we're setting down on the roof of a building. It's dark and there's minimal lighting, so I'm not sure what the building is, nor even where I am.

Everyone files out. I jump down, flanked again by two armed men. There are five guys in total—one leading us across the roof, one on either side of me, and two behind.

Keeping low, we hurry over to a fire escape, head inside, and walk down three flights of metal stairs.

We stop at a door on the fourth floor of wherever we are, judging by the large sign on the wall next to it. The guy in front opens the door and holds it for the rest of us to go through.

We come out into a waiting area of some kind. The familiar, sickly smell of disinfectant that you only ever find in a hospital stings my nostrils. It's eerily quiet, and our footfalls echo on the permanently waxed tiled floor. Nobody is offering any conversation. We're just standing in a conspicuous huddle.

The front desk is on the right, with a corridor leading away from it on either side. Two nurses are busying themselves behind the waist-high counter. They look up curiously for a moment but say nothing and soon resume their duties.

On the left, facing the desk is an array of chairs with two more corridors disappearing out of sight, mirroring the others.

The guy in front looks at me. "Wait here."

He disappears down the nearest corridor, leaving me surrounded by the other four. After a few minutes, the guy re-appears with another man I've not seen before. He's wearing a nice navy-blue suit, with his white shirt untucked and no tie. He has thick, dark hair parted to the side and is clean-shaven. I figure him for early forties. He heads straight for me, smiling.

He extends his hand. "Adrian, I'm glad you could make it."

I wouldn't normally, but under the circumstances, I shake it firmly. "Not as glad as I am. If it weren't for your boys, I'd have been cut to shreds back there. I owe you my life."

"Don't mention it. I'm actually hoping you can do me a favor in return?"

"You have me at a disadvantage. Who are you, exactly?"

"Forgive me. My name's Robert Clark. For the last..." He pauses to check his watch. "...twenty-seven hours or so, I've been acting Head of Finance and Development for Globa-Tech Industries."

I fail miserably to hide the look of surprise on my face.

GlobaTech? I didn't expect that.

Why are they helping me?

I quickly assess my options. There are five men with guns surrounding me, and I'm in a hospital, probably on numerous security feeds. There are nurses nearby who are witnesses. I have my guns at my back, but there's zero chance of success if I draw them.

They must be friendly because they've made no attempt to disarm me.

So, violence probably isn't the answer. What a strange concept! I guess I have to settle for talking. At least for the time being.

"GlobaTech? As in, the same GlobaTech who's funding Dark Rain and selling land to them, so they can mine uranium and make nuclear weapons?"

Clark smiles, slightly embarrassed. "That's us, yeah."

"You'll have to forgive my hostility. It's just I've spent the last few days getting my ass kicked all over this city by pretty much everyone I've come into contact with. I came here on business, and I ended up being either shot at or tortured almost hourly..."

"Yes, I'm well aware what your *business* is, Adrian. I guess I should thank you for killing Ted Jackson. Aside from the fact he was nothing but a greedy, selfish sonofabitch, his job pays much better than my old one did."

I shrug. "You're welcome, I guess? Hey, wait—how do you know what happened to Jackson?"

The nurses are looking at us but suddenly find something to do elsewhere.

Clark smiles apologetically. "Listen, Adrian. You've had a rough couple of days and obviously have a lot of questions. I completely respect everything you've done so far, and you absolutely deserve some answers. But before we get to that, I want to show you something."

"Well, you certainly seem nicer than Ted was, and I appreciate everything *you've* done for me, but that's a little forward, don't you think? Maybe a drink first?"

Clark smiles again. "I see you're a fan of using humor as a defense mechanism. It's nice to know that the money we spent compiling a psychological profile of you was a sound investment."

"You spent money on what?"

"I like to know everything I can about the people I do business with. I'm sure you can appreciate that, what with your history of paranoia and borderline obsessive/compulsive behavior..."

"Okay, stop talking like you know me. It's freaking me out, and it's liable to get you shot."

He smiles a company smile and holds his hands up, as if conveying his apology and explaining he meant no harm. He turns and walks back the way he came. When I don't follow, he looks over his shoulder at me. "Come on. It's fine. You can trust me. If I wanted you dead, you already would be."

While trusting him is a little optimistic on his part, he

does have a point about me not being dead... I guess it can't hurt to see what he's selling.

I follow him down the corridor to the end and turn right. Ahead of us is a set of secure double doors with a keypad on the wall for access. Clark produces a card from his pocket, swipes it down the side of the machine, then enters a code. The doors click and hiss open automatically, and I follow him through.

This corridor isn't as brightly lit as the others and is quieter. It's a dead-end, with three doors on either side. We walk to the second one along on the left and stop level with it. He knocks once as a courtesy, then opens it without entering, holding it as an invitation for me to go through.

I stand in the doorway and look around the room. There are no windows, but an air conditioning unit hums in the background, keeping it nice and cool. There's a TV mounted on the wall to my right and a couch facing me, opposite the door. On my immediate left are two chairs, presumably for visitors, and against the left wall is the bed.

I raise an eyebrow, which is the only reaction I have the energy for. Lying there, hooked up to monitors and IV drips, is Clara Fox.

She looks at me and smiles. "Hey."

I'm confused.

Clark places his hand on my shoulder. "I'll give you two a minute."

He closes the door, leaving me alone with Clara. Neither of us speaks until the sound of his footsteps has faded away.

She looks good, considering. She seems a bit out of it, but she looks well.

She waves weakly. "You all right?"

I move over to the bed and sit down in one of the chairs. "Never mind me. What the hell happened to you?"

She takes a deep breath and closes her eyes momentarily. She looks at me and smiles again. She seems happy to see me. I've not seen anyone happy to see me in a long time. It's nice.

I hesitate, then grab her hand and squeeze it gently. I'm glad she's okay. She squeezes back in appreciation.

"After I left through the cellar in the bar, I climbed out of the loading dock around the other side just as the shooting started. I took a quick peek around the corner and saw Natalia unloading at the police. That's when they split up, and one of them came after me. I turned and ran, but the guy was too quick and soon caught me. Long story short, I shot him a couple of times, and he died."

I have to smile. Clara has a similar approach to conflict as I do. It's refreshing.

"I avoided the YouTube vultures on the main street out front and made my way to your motel. I got there and found two guys in suits I'd never seen before searching your room. I was exhausted and completely unprepared, so they got the drop on me. One of them shot me. I must've blacked out, but the last thing I remember seeing was one of them lifting your mattress. I'm sorry, Adrian, but whoever they were, they took the deeds."

I squeeze her hand gently again, offering reassurance. "It's okay. I got them back."

I reach behind me, pull the papers out of my pocket, and wave them at her, smiling.

She breathes out a heavy sigh of relief, wincing slightly. "How did you manage that?"

"It was Pellaggio's men who raided my room. I had another run-in with Jimmy Manhattan." I point to the cut running down my cheek. "We had a disagreement."

"Ouch. Is he dead?"

"He's not. I left him unconscious on the floor of a portable cabin on the construction site above our favorite uranium mine."

"Oh, fair enough."

"So, come on—what happened after the motel? I asked Josh to search for you, but you weren't registered as being admitted to any hospital nearby."

"Yeah, I came to in the ambulance. There were two nurses patching me up, a guy dressed in black with a gun, and Bob."

"Bob?"

"Yeah, the GlobaTech guy."

"You mean Robert Clark."

"He said to call him Bob."

"Uh-huh..."

She struggles and sits up slightly in bed, giggling to herself. "Adrian, do I detect a hint of jealousy in your voice?"

I scoff, mostly to hide the embarrassment. "Me? Jealous? No, of course not!"

She looks at me with a raised eyebrow but says nothing.

"I'm just highly skeptical of the new, overly friendly Ted Jackson replacement who works for the people funding the terrorist organization who've been trying to kill us both all day."

Clara rolls her eyes and pulls a silly face. "Well, when you put it like *that*..."

I shake my head in comical disbelief. "Anyway, you were saying?"

"Yeah, so I woke up surrounded by these guys, and Bob... *Robert* said he was going to make sure I received the best medical care available. I've been resting up here ever since."

"Have you spoken to this guy since you woke up?"

"Not really. He came in to see how I was about an hour

ago, but that's been it." She shifts in her bed again, trying to get comfortable. "How did you get here anyway?"

"After we got to the uranium mine, Dark Rain showed up in force. Ketranovich and Natalia were there. I met her brother too. He needed to calm her down after she went all psycho."

"Yeah, that'd be Gene. They're twins."

"I thought they might be. Ketranovich said her brother's the only one she'll listen to when she goes a bit crazy. That's a family in need of some serious therapy."

"You don't know the half of it."

"I bet. So, the colonel and I had words, which didn't go well."

"Let me guess. He offered you a job, and you openly antagonized him?"

"I'm hurt you would even think such a thing..."

She raises an eyebrow and stares at me again.

"Okay, yes. I might have poked a little fun at him."

She laughs. "There we go!"

"Anyway, just as I was about to get gunned down by fifteen armed soldiers, three blacked-out helicopters show up out of nowhere and give me a lift out of trouble. Dark Rain didn't try and stop them either—they just stood there as stunned as I was."

She shakes her head. "You're one lucky bastard. Do you know that?"

I smile. "I'd hardly call myself lucky, given how my visit to this city has gone so far."

We share a moment of laughter, and the conversation dies down. We sit in silence for a few minutes. I'm genuinely glad she's all right. Despite what Josh said earlier about me doing the right thing, I know I would've struggled to forgive myself if anything had happened to her because of me.

The door opens, interrupting the silence. Robert Clark walks in. "You guys all caught up?"

I glance at Clara and smile before looking at him. "Yeah, we're good. Thanks for taking care of her. Now I want some answers, Bob."

He nods. "Fair enough." He pulls up a chair next to me and sits down. "Ask away."

"Okay, how the hell did you get involved in all this?"

Clark shrugs. "I knew Jackson was neck-deep in the Dark Rain deal. I've been keeping tabs on him as part of an investigation I'm conducting into suspected corruption within our organization. I knew he had protection..."

He pauses to gesture and smile at Clara.

"And it wasn't long before you came on the scene. You're an easy man to find out about if you know where to ask. Given we have a lot of contacts in the private security business—some more reputable than others, I confess—I found out who you were and put two and two together. A bit of digging revealed you were hired to kill Jackson by Roberto Pellaggio. I kept you both under surveillance after your visit to the Four Seasons. Oh, and I've left Jackson's body in his room—figured it's best GlobaTech doesn't get involved in whatever business you've got here."

He smiles and gets to his feet. He moves over to the window, puts his hands in his pockets, and stares out for a moment. Then he turns to look at us.

"We saw what happened back at the bar. I had a team move in to pick up Clara, thinking I'd left you both out in play long enough. Unfortunately, we were a little late getting to her."

I frown. "So, you knew what was going on before we did, but you left us to fend for ourselves anyway?"

"I needed to see how far this went and who was running

things for Dark Rain. Thanks to you... both of you, now we do."

"I don't like being played, Clark."

"I know you don't. You like to know exactly what's going on before you involve yourself, just like I do. I just happen to have more money and resources, so I'm better at it. There are no ill feelings between us, Adrian. At least not as far as GlobaTech is concerned. We're on the same side."

"Are we now?"

"I think so, yes. Tell me, after you killed Jackson and took the deeds for the mine, why didn't you take them straight to Pellaggio? I'm assuming he wanted them because of his property deal."

"How do you know about—"

Clark holds a hand up and smiles. "Money and resources, remember?"

I shrug, sighing heavily with defeat. "I couldn't allow the mafia to have access to that land, knowing what it was. It would be just as dangerous as if I'd allowed Dark Rain to keep it."

Clark nods, like he's interviewing me and assessing my answers. He turns to Clara. "And you—why did you turn your back on Dark Rain after the years you'd spent fighting for them?"

She looks at me, then at Clark. "Same reason Adrian kept the deeds. I had no idea their endgame involved selling uranium, and I wanted no part of it. It's just difficult walking away from someone like Ketranovich."

Clark nods. "You're right. It's difficult. In fact, I have the exact same problem."

I frown. "You do?"

"Yes. Like I said, I'm running an internal investigation at GlobaTech. We've uncovered evidence that a small group of people were working toward their own agenda from within the organization. It was this group who were using their own department's budgets to fund Dark Rain. Jackson was a part of that, acting as a go-between for Ketranovich and this group. I've discovered it was their plan all along to extract the uranium and shift liability over to Dark Rain, under the pretense that they were working *with* them. Once the material had been processed to make it weapons-grade, their intention was to either turn their backs on Ketranovich and sell the material for additional funding, or to frame him should things go wrong. Either way, they believed they had things covered. However, since you killed Jackson, Dark Rain's lost their link to GlobaTech. The board of directors has ordered an immediate halt to all activities currently ongoing involving these departments, pending further inquiries. All assets relating to the Dark Rain project have been frozen."

"You expect us to believe that you've pulled your funding from Dark Rain and screwed them the way Jackson screwed Pellaggio? And that's supposed to immediately absolve you of any accountability and make you the good guys?"

"Adrian, I think we both know that there are no good guys and bad guys in this world. Things are too gray. But yes, whatever ties my company had with Dark Rain are now severed. We're actively looking to clean up the mess Jackson made, but as I'm sure you can imagine, Colonel Ketranovich isn't happy about his deal with us being terminated."

"So, what happens now?" asks Clara.

"We need to stop Dark Rain. They're heavily armed and well prepared. They have roughly three thousand men tucked away at their compound, ready to fight for them, according to the last status report from Jackson. We can expect some retaliation, and we're working on a strategy to neutralize them as we speak. For now, your part in this is officially over."

I stand up. "What, just like that? After everything we've been through?"

"Just like that, Adrian. You can't take on an army by yourself. You need to get your affairs in order and get out of town. You're almost done here."

"Almost?"

"There's just one tiny thing I need you to do for me first."

"I can't believe after all this, you're asking *me* for a favor. What is it?"

"I need you to give me the deeds to the land. I will personally sign them over, on behalf of GlobaTech Industries, to the U.S. government, who will make sure the land gets mined clean and the uranium disposed of safely."

"That's a big ask under the circumstances. I appreciate you saving my life, but that doesn't mean I trust you."

He nods curtly. "Fair enough. Perhaps this will put your mind at ease a little..."

He pulls out his cell phone, dials a number, and puts it on speaker as it's ringing. He places it on the edge of Clara's bed, so it's in the middle of the three of us.

"Yes?"

He smiles at us both. "Sir, it's Robert Clark, GlobaTech Industries. I'm sorry to disturb you at this hour, but I have you on speaker with Adrian Hell and Clara Fox. We spoke of the situation in Heaven's Valley yesterday..."

"Ah, Bob, good to hear from you." The voice has a distinctive Texan drawl. "Adrian... Clara... this is Ryan Schultz, and I'm the Secretary of Defense for the United States."

19

Holy shit!

I mean, it's obvious this whole situation is bad, but it's hard to believe I've managed to get myself wrapped up in something that's on the White House's radar.

I stare at the phone. Schultz clears his throat. "Adrian, I'll make no secret that I dislike what the rumors say you do for a living, son. But I cannot deny you're a resourceful sonofabitch. Your actions so far in Heaven's Valley have been impressive and of significant value, and you've done your country a great service."

How do I address him?

"Well, ah, Mr. Secretary... I didn't do it for my country. Everything I've done, I've done for no other reason than to stay alive. But I appreciate you calling and thanking me—that means a lot. I just did what anyone else would have, I guess."

"Well, whatever your motivation, your contributions

have proved invaluable to our efforts. But if you ain't doin' it for your country, you need to help us now as a service to your fellow man. I need you to hand what paperwork you have relating to the uranium mine over to Bob Clark. Globa-Tech are one of our biggest independent contractors, and we trust them implicitly in this matter."

"With respect, sir, how can you trust an organization that funded an underground militia and attempted to supply them with nuclear material?"

"That was a deal brokered by a clandestine group of individuals operating independently within a larger company. Those people have ceased all activities on the project, and management of the resources has been given to Bob Clark. Bob here is one of us. Do you understand?"

"I do."

"Good man. I read your file, Adrian. You were a helluva soldier. You're wasting your life as a hired gun. And if we could actually prove you'd done half the shit I've heard rumor of, I'd personally make sure they gave you the chair, and I'd throw the damn switch myself!"

"Well, while I appreciate the sentiment, sir, I'm happy as I am. What I do is my own business. This country trained me to be the best, and that's exactly what I am."

"That may be, but you're still a goddamn killer. I don't condone it. But this once, I'm willing to overlook it."

"That's kind of you."

"Now it should go without saying that the details of what's happening down there are classified at the highest level. I would hate to think there's any risk of information getting out about such things."

"You have my word, Mr. Schultz. The moment I'm outta this city, the whole thing will be completely forgotten."

"We appreciate your cooperation, son."

Clark picks up the phone and takes it off speaker. He has a quick, one-sided conversation, agrees a lot, and then hangs up. He looks over at me. "So, shall we?"

I look at Clara, who nods. I let out a heavy sigh and hand him the paperwork. "Screw me over and I'll hunt you down."

He takes the deeds and smiles. "I expect nothing less. But you have nothing to worry about. We're on the same side and want the same thing. Now, if you'll excuse me, I need to get these over to our legal department. Thank you again, Adrian."

"Don't mention it."

He turns and leaves the room, closing the door gently behind him. I start pacing the room, running everything through my head.

Am I right to trust GlobaTech after everything they've done? Maybe not... but my gut's telling me I'm right to trust Robert Clark, regardless of whether the secretary of defense vouched for him.

But now what? I can't just leave, can I? I know I've got no chance taking on Ketranovich and Dark Rain on my own. But I still feel responsible—and consequently obligated—to finish what I've inadvertently started. There's no doubt Dark Rain are out to kill me. And Pellaggio is definitely going to want my head on a spike after everything that's happened. I'm not convinced it's as simple as just picking up my bag and taking the first Greyhound out of here. Ketranovich might be as good as dead if GlobaTech and their private army are after them, but Pellaggio won't let me walk away. He'll keep coming until I decide to stop him.

I look over at Clara, who's lying comfortably now. I see her fighting to stay awake. What about her? Dark Rain is after her too. I'm assuming she still has the money I took from Jackson.

I just have to convince her to use it and get out of town. I don't want her to go through anything else. She's suffered enough already. If she lies low until GlobaTech finish dealing with Dark Rain, she can start a new life somewhere else.

I know that sounds a little hypocritical. We're both in exactly the same situation. I'm contemplating how I can fix things by staying when anyone in their right mind would tell me to cut and run. Yet here *I* am thinking of how to get Clara to leave because it would be stupid to stick around...

Maybe it's male pride. I'm sure she'll understand. But I also know she'll think like me. She'll want to see this through to the end.

"So, what's the plan, Adrian? I can see you thinking."

I figure I'll go down the chivalrous route first.

"Once you heal up, you should get out of town. Use that money I gave you and start a new life. Between me and GlobaTech, I promise we'll stop Dark Rain."

Clara laughs. "You macho asshole! I'm not going anywhere, and you knew that before you even opened your mouth to feed me that bullshit line."

I smile and hold my hands up. "You got me."

"So, seriously, what's the plan? Me and you—we're in this until the end, no matter what, right?"

See? I knew we were on the same wavelength. I admit I find the sentiment touching. I think I'm getting soft in my old age...

"Well, forgetting that we're top of Dark Rain's hit list for the moment, we still need to find this scientist. Once Ketranovich realizes GlobaTech have turned their backs on him, taking away any chance he had of accessing the uranium mine, that scientist is as good as dead."

"Agreed. But where do we start?"

"You said you knew a few places Dark Rain could use to house them, right?"

"Yeah, but I don't know for sure if they're in use."

"It's okay. Right now, that's all we've got to go on, so it's worth a shot."

I pick up a pen and some paper from Clara's bedside table and take down the address details as she reels them off. Then I take out my cell and call Josh, putting him on speakerphone.

He answers after three rings. "Hey, Boss. Still alive, then?"

I quickly shake my head. How can he still sound *that* happy with everything that's going on?

"Just about. Listen, Josh. You're on speaker and Clara's here. We're in her hospital room."

"You found her? How's she doing? Sorry—Clara, hey. Are you all right?"

She laughs. "I'm fine. I just got shot a little bit."

Josh chuckles. "I can see why you like her, Boss."

"Thanks, asshole." I actively try to avoid Clara's gaze. "Have you had any luck finding our missing scientist yet?"

He sighs. "I got nothing, man. No one of any significance has been reported missing in the last six months."

Clara sits up a little in bed and leans closer to the phone. "Try searching back eighteen months. Dark Rain will have been planning this for a long time, so it's feasible this scientist has been in play a lot longer."

I never thought of that.

"Huh, good idea. Also, Josh, Clara's given me a few locations of safe houses that Dark Rain use. Can you look into them, see if there's any recent activity, et cetera?"

"Yeah, of course."

I give him the address details and ask him to call me if he finds anything. I hang up and the room falls silent again.

I like to know how something is going to end before I start it. I like to play out every possible outcome first, so I can prepare for anything going wrong. I hate surprises. Josh —along with everyone else, apparently—thinks I have OCD, but I just like being thorough and covering my ass.

This whole thing has been a disaster from the moment I entered Heaven's Valley. I need an exit strategy. I need to stop Dark Rain from doing whatever the hell it is they intend to do. I know it's not going to involve uranium anymore, which is a small comfort, but if they have the numbers, the weapons, and the token megalomaniacal leader with a grudge against the western world, nothing good is going to come of whatever they decide to do instead.

I also have the mob to contend with. Whichever way I look at it, Jimmy Manhattan has a point—I *did* go back on my contract by not fulfilling every stipulation of it. And I told them to shove it up their ass when they questioned me about it. That's something I've never done before, and in doing so, I've broken the only golden rule in the world of contract killing. Nobody wants to hire someone who might not do what you pay them to. I know these are extenuating circumstances, but nobody else will ever know that. I can't outrun Pellaggio's far-reaching empire, nor any bad press they might put out about me.

I look over at Clara. She's fallen asleep. I smile to myself and look at the clock on the wall. It's the middle of the night, and it's been a long couple of days with little rest. I sit back in the chair and put my feet up on the table in front of me. I rest my head back and stare up at the ceiling to stop my mind racing at a hundred miles an hour in every direction at once.

I close my eyes and take a deep breath, letting it out slowly.

At least the pain in my ribs is easing...

08:45 PDT

I startle myself awake, snorting a little. I'm still sitting with my feet up on the table. Outside, the sun is shining brightly through the blinds. I look around, a little dazed. I must've nodded off.

Where—

Oh, yeah. I'm in Clara's room in GlobaTech's hospital. I remember now.

I look over at her bed. It's empty!

What?

I stand and check the time. I've been asleep over eight hours, Jesus!

I massage my temples and think for a moment. All right, one thing at a time, Adrian...

I don't know if it's because I got some sleep and I'm thinking a little clearer now, or I've had an epiphany, but in my head is a concise plan of how I can solve my current problems.

Excellent.

Right, now where's Clara?

I pick my phone up off the table and check it. There's a missed call from Josh a couple of hours ago. I call him back.

"Josh, it's me."

"You sound half-asleep. You all right?"

"Yeah, I dropped off in Clara's room. I just woke up and saw your missed call. Clara's gone from her room as well."

"Uh-oh…"

"What do you mean, *uh-oh*?"

There's silence on the other end of the phone.

"Josh?"

"Well, I rang you and she answered. She said you were sleeping. I told her I'd had some luck and got a hit on both the missing scientist and one of the locations you gave me."

"That's good news, isn't it?"

"I told her what I had, and… I think she may have gone off on her own to rescue them…"

"What?"

"That's why I tried calling you back, but there was no answer."

"What exactly did she say?"

"She said she'd go and check out the address. I said she should probably wait for you. She said she felt fine and wanted to go on her own. Said she felt responsible."

"Ah, shit! What's the address?"

"It's a few miles from the hospital you're in, so you're gonna need a car. Listen, Adrian. I'm sorry—I had no idea she was basically a female version of you!"

"It's okay. I just need to find her. I'll call you back."

I leave Clara's room and run down the corridor to the waiting room where I met Robert Clark a few hours ago. A couple of soldiers are pacing around, still dressed in their nondescript black and red fatigues.

I walk over to one of them. "I need a car."

He looks at me, a little surprised. "What for?"

I quickly explain why, strategically omitting any details about the scientist that Dark Rain has kidnapped. The soldier looks over at his partner, who shrugs back at him. He then reaches into his pocket and pulls out a set of keys. "It's the black Jeep out front. Don't scratch it."

I take the keys and get in the nearby elevator. I ride to the first floor and run outside. The 4×4 is right outside the entrance. I climb in, start it up, and pull out of the semicircular driveway. The tires screech as I hit the gas and navigate the light traffic on the street.

I call Josh again and put him on loudspeaker. "Right, I'm on the road now. Give me directions."

"Okay, keep straight for another two miles, then turn right at the intersection."

"Will Clara be there by now?"

"Easily, yeah."

"Shit."

"Adrian, I'm sure she can take care of herself. You worry too much."

"They sent a hit squad to shoot up an entire building just because she was in it. And now she's heading to one of their safe houses trying to save a scientist who just became disposable. Plus, as far as I know, she's unarmed."

"All valid points. You wanna know about our missing scientist?"

"You've found out who it is?"

"Well, the search results were surprisingly narrow. Once I filtered by location, I was left with literally one name: Jonathan Webster. He's a nuclear physicist who worked out of Columbia University in New York. He apparently went to a conference about fifteen months ago and never came back. He sent a note to his colleagues a couple weeks later saying he was resigning from his position at the university. No explanation, and he hasn't been seen since."

"Sounds like our guy. We sure he's at this particular safe house?"

"Satellite imagery from the last three weeks shows regular movement at this address. Out of all the locations

Clara gave us, there was only one other that showed any activity, but I ruled it out because it's miles away on the other side of town, close to the state lines. It makes no sense to keep him there. Plus, this other place is reasonably close to the mine."

"How the hell do you find this stuff out?"

"Trade secrets. If I told you, I'd have to kill you."

I can hear him smiling smugly down the line.

"Josh, even if you *could* kill me, you'd have to take a ticket and get in line."

"Yeah, you do seem quite popular at the moment, eh?"

"Looks that way. Good job I'm not heading to a building that's likely to be filled with people who have guns and orders to shoot me on sight. Oh, wait!"

Josh laughs. "Even when faced with such adversity, it amazes me how you always find time to practice your sarcasm."

"I'm glad someone's impressed. I'm turning right now. Where do I go from here?"

"Okay, carry on and take your fourth left, then your first right. It's the second house on the right-hand side."

"Got it. Thanks, Josh."

"Just add it to the list of things you owe me. Be safe."

I hang up and navigate my way to the house. It's in the middle of a quiet, suburban neighborhood. They're all large, detached houses with expensive cars on the driveways and well-manicured front lawns. It's hard to believe that somewhere so quiet and peaceful could house soldiers fighting in an extremist militia. What goes on behind closed doors... even in neighborhoods like this one.

I take the last right turn and hear several loud cracks that take me by surprise. I swerve right and slam the brakes on, sliding to a halt across the width of the street as the windshield spider-webs.

"What the fuck?"

I duck behind the wheel. I hear the rapid, deep *clunks* as more bullets pepper the Jeep's bodywork. I reach behind me, drawing one of my babies and checking to make sure the magazine's full. Thankfully, it is, but I have no spares with me.

I take a few deep breaths to compose myself, immediately cursing at the sharp pain each one causes. I completely forgot to pick up any painkillers while I was in the hospital... I'm aching all over, but it's getting easier, and I can certainly live with it.

I take one final, deep breath and let it out in a heavy sigh, steeling myself for what comes next.

I chamber a round and reach for the passenger door, ready to leap out.

I'm getting too old for all these gunfights...

20

I push open the passenger door and clamber out, ducking behind the front wheel arch. I take a quick peek over the hood at the house, which is to my right. I see two guys, both dressed in black. One is in the doorway, and the other is kneeling on the front lawn. I'm assuming there are more inside, but I don't have eyes on them.

No sign of Clara, either. Christ, I hope she's okay.

I duck back behind the wheel, crouching on my haunches with my elbows on my knees. I rest my forehead on the barrel of my Beretta.

How the hell did they know I was coming? They opened fire the moment I turned into the street. I could've been anybody, so they must've known it was me...

Hang on...

I look forward, back the way I came. I scan all the houses and the vehicles. No sign of movement. Then I look up and check the rooftops.

Ah-ha!

Directly ahead of me, I catch a glimpse of a shadowy figure crouching low next to a chimney stack. He's partially obscured from *my* view by the shape of the roof, but *he'd* have had a clear view of me as I approached, just before turning right.

They've got a scout, the sneaky bastards!

Well, the good news is I found him... The bad news is I'm now aware that I'm surrounded with minimal cover.

Shit.

I've got to take out that scout first. He's got the high-ground advantage, which means he can see me better than I can see him. He can also potentially relay my movements to people in the house, meaning I'll lose any element of surprise I might have with my approach.

I sit down on the road and lean back against the wheel, adjusting myself so I'm comfortable. I take a deep breath and aim my gun at the rooftop, holding it in my right hand and clasping my left around it tight to steady it. I close my left eye to help line up my shot.

There's hardly any breeze, so wind speed isn't a factor. I'm aiming up at an angle of around thirty-five degrees, and the target is approximately three hundred feet away, now almost completely hidden by the chimney stack at the arch of the roof...

I'll need two shots, on target, in quick succession. The first will be to draw him out, and it needs to be as close as I can get to his position without being able to hit him. I need to put it to the left of where he's hiding—he's unlikely to be expecting any heat, so his instinct will be to move away to the right. The second bullet needs to follow immediately, aimed where he's *going* to be, so it hits him as he breaks cover.

Good job I'm a helluva shot.

I aim as close to the top of the roof as I can and practice the slight movement between shots—up and right—to catch his head as it pops around the corner to return fire. One... two. Bang... bang. Nice and quick.

Okay, here we go.

I take a deep breath. Then another and hold it. I squeeze the trigger. I see roof tiles and brick go flying from the impact. A fraction of a second later, I re-adjust and squeeze the trigger again. At the exact moment the scout leans out of cover to shoot, his head snaps back, disappearing out of sight and leaving a small puff of red mist lingering in the air.

I breathe out a sigh of relief.

Easy!

I get back up into a crouch and re-focus my attention to the two guys at the house. The guy out front is keeping low behind a large bush. The guy in the doorway has taken cover just inside the hallway.

Where the hell is Clara? She must know I'm here. What else would these assholes be shooting at?

Bullets intermittently strike the Jeep and the ground around me as I try to figure out how I'm going to get inside the house. I don't have enough ammo to trade pot shots with these pricks and hope I get lucky. Plus, I'm running out of time. They know I'm here, so whoever else is inside is likely preparing to either move the scientist or kill him.

I pull my other gun from my back holster and check the mag to make sure it's full. I quickly run through every possible outcome I can think of. If I go left or right, if I stay put and trade bullets, if I move the Jeep, if I don't move the Jeep—everything. I disregard anything that will get me shot and work with the options that won't. I see everything like a game of chess, looking three, four, five moves ahead, reading people and calculating the outcomes...

It only takes me a few seconds to realize the quickest and most effective way inside the house.

Fuck it.

With a gun in each hand, I quickly stand and walk around the hood toward the house, aiming my left at the guy in the front garden and my right at the guy in the front door. I line up my shots in my peripheral vision, seeing both targets as best I can and pick my moment.

I fire both guns simultaneously and put a round in each of the targets as they break cover. The guy crouching in the bushes out front falls backward as the bullet hits him in his chest, sending him sprawling across the lawn. The guy at the door catches it in his stomach, which punches him back against the wall. He slides down and sits lifelessly in a crumpled heap in the doorway.

I quickly run over to the guy out front and search him. There's no ID, but I find a knife in a pouch strapped to his leg.

I'll take that. Might come in handy.

I put my guns away and take his assault rifle. It's Dark Rain's weapon of choice: the AK-47. I check the mag and see it's half empty, but he has two spares on him. I pocket them and head over to the front door.

There's no point searching this guy in the doorway. He won't have any ID, and I've got enough ammo to finish up here. I step past him and enter the house, keeping low and pausing in the hallway to look around.

In front of me on the right is the staircase. I'll deal with upstairs in a moment. To the left is a long hallway, leading straight through to the kitchen. Along the left wall are two doors. I move slowly and carefully toward the first, holding the rifle ready. I listen at the door but hear nothing from within. I try the handle and open it, pausing for a moment before swinging it open cautiously and stepping inside. The room stretches away to the left, but it's empty. There's not even any furniture. It's just floorboards and peeling paint.

I head back out to the hallway and try the next room along. As before, I listen outside the door for a moment. This time, though, I hear movement within. I give it another minute, breathing as softly as I can and listening intently...

I reckon there's only one person in there, and if they're moving around, they're not going to be a prisoner.

The movement stops, and I hear a noise that's eerily reminiscent of a gun cocking...

I don't even think about it. I step back and kick the door open, pushing my foot through, close to the frame, just above the handle. It nearly comes off its hinges as it flies open, banging loudly against the wall. I step inside and drop to a crouch. I quickly assess the layout.

There's a dining table with four chairs in the center of the room, with an old-fashioned fireplace built into the far wall. Besides the threadbare carpet, the room is otherwise empty...

Apart from the guy standing in the far corner with his gun aimed at me.

I don't give him the chance to react. I instinctively spin and take aim, unloading a quick three-round burst to his chest. He drops to the floor and I breathe easy once again.

I back out of the room and quickly stick my head inside the kitchen. It's empty, which I half-expected. I turn and head back toward the front door, stopping at the bottom of the staircase. I take a quick look up. From what I can see, it's clear.

The hardest part is always going upstairs. If someone's

up there already, they have the angles and the cover. If you're the one on the stairs, you have nothing. You can't view every angle, you don't know where every door is, and you're firing up as you're climbing stairs, so your accuracy will go to shit.

I crouch next to the stairs and weigh my options. I *have* to go up, so I'll need to keep my back to the wall and aim high, making sure—

BANG!

What the...

BANG!

They were gunshots...

And the dull thud I heard after the second one was definitely a body hitting the floor above me.

Oh, shit! Clara!

Ignoring all training I've had for these situations, I quickly stand and rush up the stairs. I'm holding the rifle loose in front of me, ready to fire from the hip if need be. I move from room to room, kicking in each door and quickly sweeping inside before moving to the next.

Finally, I reach the main bedroom at the front of the house. The door's open, and a thick pool of blood is creeping into view over the thin, beige carpet.

With my gun raised, I run in.

Clara's standing where the bed would've been, behind the door. The gun in her hand is still smoking slightly from the bullet she's just fired. I look at the dead guy on the ground, lying spread-eagled with a bullet hole between his eyes.

I rush over to her. "Jesus! Clara, are you all right?"

She's staring vacantly into space. I drop my gun and put my hands on her face, making her look at me. I examine her eyes and can see the onset of shock behind them.

"Clara, are you okay? Answer me. Are you hurt?"

She finally focuses on me but looks blank and disoriented. There's a bloodstain on her top from where her bullet wound has re-opened. "I was too late... I'm so sorry."

She turns her head, and I follow her gaze to the opposite wall.

Sweet Jesus, Mary, and Joseph...

The sick, twisted bastards have stripped Jonathan Webster naked and nailed him to the wall by his hands and feet, like a starfish. His body is a mess, covered in deep cuts and a mixture of fresh and dried blood. There's a pool of blood on the floor beneath his body too. The bullet hole in his forehead is recent.

She must have killed that guy on the floor seconds after *he* killed Webster.

I look back at Clara and feel overwhelming sympathy for her.

But it only takes a few seconds to start feeling the darkness and the anger building inside me. I'm completely blind with rage, and I clench my jaw muscles and my fists as I struggle to contain it.

Yet again, these pieces of shit were two moves ahead of me. Ketranovich hasn't just disposed of the scientist—he's tortured and sacrificed him, needlessly, knowing we'd find him. Webster's body is a message meant for Clara and me to find.

Well, message received.

He isn't going to like my response.

I look at Clara. "Come on. We need to get out of here."

I take her by the hand and lead her out of the room, down the stairs, and outside to the street. We get in the Jeep and I drive off. I need to get her back to the hospital, so she can get her gunshot wound looked at.

As I turn left, I glance to the right and see her Dodge Viper parked further up the street. I slam the brakes on and reverse quickly, stopping level with her car. She looks at me inquisitively.

I nod toward the windshield. "The bullet holes in *this* are even more conspicuous than your Viper. We should switch."

Within minutes we're back on the road in the Viper, heading to the hospital.

Clara's sitting in silence, staring at the dashboard. She hasn't said a word since we left the house. I don't think she's even blinked. She's in shock, and I have no words of comfort to offer her. Things aren't going to be okay. Things won't get better soon. We're officially at war, and it's going to keep getting worse until I kill Ketranovich.

The best thing I can do is stay productive. If I dwell on what's happening with Dark Rain, I'm going to end up in a disturbing place that may well result in a lot of dead bodies —and that's not the best way to play this. But until I figure that out, I need a distraction, so I'm going to focus on getting Pellaggio off my back.

I'll leave Clara at the hospital. It's the safest place for her right now. My bag's still in her room, and I need it to help me deal with Pellaggio.

I pull into the hospital driveway. The roar of the engine in the Viper sounds even louder than usual outside the quiet building.

I look over at her. "Come on. You need to go and get yourself patched up again."

She shakes her head absently. "It's all right. It's just a flesh wound."

"Yes, but it's a flesh wound that's bleeding all over your top. Now come on."

She doesn't bother arguing again. We get out of the car, and I put my arm around her waist, offering support. We walk into the hospital and take the elevator up to the fourth floor. There's no sign of any GlobaTech personnel as the doors ding open. They must've cleared out after I left earlier. They obviously weren't *that* bothered about their Jeep...

Good job, really.

As we approach the front desk, a nurse rushes round and takes over supporting Clara, shouting for a doctor. One quickly appears, along with another nurse. I follow them all back to the room. I watch them lay Clara gently back in her bed, then cut away her top and set to work on stopping the bleeding. I quickly retrieve my bag from next to the chair I slept in and move back over to the door.

I gently tap one of the nurses on her shoulder. "Is she gonna be all right?"

She doesn't look around. "She'll be fine. The stitching burst, but it wasn't a serious wound. We managed to remove the bullet from the shoulder during surgery, and there was only minimal damage to the muscle tissue. She was lucky, but she'll recover completely. She just needs to rest."

"Thanks for taking care of her. Will you tell her I wish her well? I have to go."

She glances back at me, nods, and smiles. "I will."

I quietly walk away and head back outside. I slide in behind the wheel of the Viper and call Josh.

He answers almost immediately. "Adrian, are you all right? What happened?"

"I'm fine. I found Clara. I was too late to save the scientist. The sick bastards tortured him. They were leaving me a message. I've just brought Clara back to the hospital."

"Christ... how's she doing?"

"She's been better. She's resting up now, though."

"What's your next move?"

"Well, Ketranovich and Dark Rain are a huge pain in my ass, but I can't do much about them on my own. So, instead, I'm going to work on getting Pellaggio out of my hair."

"Be smart, though, Boss. They're still big enough that messing with them could have consequences."

"I know. I'm going to frame Manhattan for the Jackson murder and use his arrest as a distraction to get out of the city."

Josh laughs. "Wow... that's arguably the smartest thing you've said or done in a long time! All without my help... you're finally learning!"

I smile to myself. "Kiss my ass, Josh."

I hang up, start up the engine, and set off down the street toward the center of the city.

21

Any assassin worth a damn knows how to cover their tracks. If you do it right, most of the time it's like you were never there. But when you can't deny someone *was* present when a hit took place, the trick is simple: make it look like someone else was there instead of you.

I pull up outside the Four Seasons, walk in, and head straight for the elevator. I press the button for the sixteenth floor and make the short ride up to Ted Jackson's suite. The elevator dings open, then I step out and walk casually toward the Summer suite. I take out the key card I took the other day and open the door. Thankfully, the *Do Not Disturb* sign is still on the handle, and no one's been in to clean. The room's exactly as I left it. Jackson's still tied to the chair— and still dead. The bloodstains are now just dark, sticky patches on the carpet.

I walk over to the table in front of Jackson's body and set my bag down beside it, taking care not to disturb the scene unnecessarily. I take out a pair of surgical gloves and put them on. Then I take out a tub of cocoa powder, a teaspoon, some tape, and a small basting brush.

Stay with me—I'm not pausing for a hot chocolate or anything, I promise.

Finally, I take out the envelope Manhattan gave to me the other day with Jackson's photo inside. I place it on the table and dip the brush into the cocoa powder, covering the bristles with a thin film. I gently brush over the surface of the envelope, specifically where Manhattan is likely to have held it.

Fingerprints are made up of tiny ridges on your skin, and in between those ridges are sweat glands. When you put your fingertip on something, it leaves a residue on the surface in the shape of your fingerprint. The cocoa powder on my brush is going to stick to that residue, highlighting the fingerprint. It's how forensic investigators dust a crime scene. I use cocoa powder because it's fine and easier to brush lightly, but CSI teams will use a special dust that does the same thing.

I find a full print near the top of the envelope, so I carefully lay a strip of tape over the top of it, pressing it down firmly. I then carefully peel it off the envelope, bringing Manhattan's print with it. Holding it between my thumb and index finger, I walk across the room to the gun on the floor that belonged to Clara. I press the tape down on the butt and rub my finger over it firmly, transferring the print onto it.

Voila! Jimmy Manhattan now killed Ted Jackson!

I know there are more holes in that theory than your average sponge, but it's enough to justify arresting him, which is all I'm aiming for. The gun fires the same bullets as my Beretta, so there's the initial link. A detailed forensic test will prove the bullets that killed Jackson weren't fired from this gun, but those things take time, and they'll have Manhattan in custody while they do all that stuff. Plus, any competent detective will take one look at the room, see there's a frightening lack of workable forensic evidence, and determine it's too clean a crime scene, meaning it could be a professional hit.

Which is true.

The result is that Manhattan is out of my hair for the immediate future, which buys me plenty of time to settle up with Dark Rain and get the hell out of Dodge.

I pack up my things and do a quick sweep of the place, retracing my steps and making sure I've not contaminated the scene. I leave the room and take the elevator back down to reception. I walk over to the front desk and attract the attention of the young woman with dark hair who checked me in a couple of days ago.

"Excuse me, Miss?"

She looks at me and smiles. "Hello, Mr. Aday. How can I help you today? Are you enjoying your stay with us?"

"Oh, yes, the place is lovely. Listen, I'm growing concerned about my associate, Mr. Jackson. He hasn't been to either of our meetings, and there's no answer when I knock on his door. Can you please send someone up to check on him?"

"Of course, sir. I shall arrange a courtesy call right away."

She walks over to a phone, dials a number, and quickly starts explaining what she needs. I smile to myself and walk out of the hotel. I climb into the Viper and drive off.

I'll give it three hours...

14:14 PDT

. . .

I was close—it took two and a half hours.

After leaving the hotel, I drove to Manhattan's nightclub in the Neon district. I parked a reasonable distance away but where I could still see the main entrance. I figured after he regained consciousness in the portable cabin the night before, he would make his way back to where he could protect himself. I bet he's gathered as many local goons as he can, and he's sitting in his office with the broken mirror, on the phone to Roberto Pellaggio, asking advice and planning their revenge against me.

Talk about ungrateful! I mean, if you overlook the fact I broke his nose, killed his bodyguard, and left him unconscious, I did *technically* save his life.

It would've taken ten minutes from me approaching the front desk at the Four Seasons to someone opening the door to Jackson's suite to check on him. He was a rich and important guest, after all.

I imagine the guy whom I recently found out was on my payroll would've volunteered for the job. He would've raised the alarm straight away, and the hotel manager would have called the police.

They would've wanted the whole thing handled discreetly. A hotel like that has to think of its reputation. They would've insisted the police deal with it quickly and quietly, so a forensics team would've been there within the hour. They would've needed a good half-hour to conduct their examination of the crime scene. The first thing they'd go to is the body. Next would be the weapon.

The trick is to make it all look natural. Too much detail in the phony evidence, and it's too obvious it's a set up. Too little, and they have nothing to go on. In the case of Ted

Jackson, it will immediately seem strange that someone would use a gun to kill someone, not wear gloves, and leave the weapon at the scene of the crime. But the fact they'll find a fingerprint means they'll have to bring the owner of it in for questioning, even if they don't have enough evidence to convict. The room is completely clean apart from the gun, so it'll look suspicious, and they'll assume it was a professional hit. They'll look into Jackson, and it'll take a few minutes to find the link to Pellaggio. Factor in Manhattan's fingerprint, and it all makes perfect sense. A mob hit.

So, I'm parked half a block away from The Pit in Clara's Dodge Viper. I've been waiting two hours and thirty-five minutes, but I finally hear sirens.

After a few moments, two police squad cars and a van pull up outside the entrance to the club, all at different angles, so they're facing the building. There are seven officers in total, all armed and moving toward the door with practiced efficiency.

A four-man team lines up with their backs to the wall, poised to enter through the main doors. Three officers remain stationed behind their open car doors, weapons trained at the entrance.

The officer at the back of the line runs to the front and works the door. Once open, he holds it so that the other three can file in. He falls in behind them, disappearing into the gloom of the nightclub.

Less than five minutes pass before the officers emerge back onto the street. Two officers appear first, walking backward, guns trained on Jimmy Manhattan and three men in suits—all handcuffed and looking pissed off. They're arguing and shouting.

Still, it's better to be pissed off than pissed on, as the saying goes.

The two officers bringing up the rear come out and load Manhattan and his band of merry men into the back of the van. Everyone then climbs into their cars, and they speed off, sirens wailing.

I call Josh. He picks up after a couple of rings. "Hey, Boss. How's everything going?"

"It went exactly as planned at the Four Seasons. They might not make much stick long-term, but for the foreseeable future, Jimmy Manhattan is no longer a problem. I just watched the cops arrest him."

"Very nice. Well, to add to your good news, I've got some of my own."

"Oh, yeah?"

"I've just been speaking to Robert Clark from GlobaTech."

"And that's good news?"

"They contacted me and said they'd spoken to you and Clara about a plan of action for Dark Rain. They wanted to know if they could rely on me for logistical support."

I'll admit I'm not happy at how easily people seem to trust Clark. I'm the first to admit I'm a sociopathic, paranoid cynic who hates most things and most people, but that doesn't mean I'm wrong for being skeptical of the company that has, up until recently, been funding the organization that has spent all week trying to kill me. I'll take more convincing than most.

"And what did you say?"

"I asked what they were planning and what my involvement would entail. At the end of the day, I work with you, Adrian."

I smile to myself. "Thanks. So, what *is* their plan, exactly? I know they're handing the land over to the U.S. government, so at least *that's* no longer an issue. But Dark

Rain has the numbers and plenty of funding. I can't take on an entire army on my own."

"You don't have to take them on at all. Their plan is to mount a two-pronged attack on the ground and in the air. GlobaTech has its own private military, don't forget. They regularly work out of Afghanistan and Korea, subcontracting for the U.S. government. With their resources, it'll be like a hot knife through butter."

"Sounds good to me. Where do you fit in?"

"Given our background knowledge, along with your contributions so far, they've asked if I'll help coordinate their attack. They're giving me temporary access to their satellite network."

"Which means..."

"Which means I'll be giving myself *permanent* access to their satellite network."

I laugh. "Nice. I'm sure that'll come in handy somewhere down the line. I'll just be happy when we can walk away from this. I don't even care that I didn't get paid for taking out Jackson. This has been a nightmare from start to finish. I can't wait to leave Heaven's Valley once and for all."

"How come you haven't already?"

"I'm just waiting to get an update on Clara's condition. Once I know she's okay and safe, I'll leave town."

"Sounds good. Let me know how she's doing, yeah?"

"Will do."

I hang up and sit for a few moments, thinking about everything.

Is that it? Am I done? Dark Rain is about to get wiped off the face of the earth by GlobaTech Industries. Jimmy Manhattan is now in police custody under suspicion for the murder of Ted Jackson, which will keep Pellaggio's mafia off my back long enough for me to disappear. And the uranium mine is now the property of the U.S. government —which, granted, may or may not be a good thing. Aside from Clara being in the hospital and me not finding Jonathan Webster in time, I reckon this has ended about as well as it could've, under the circumstances. As much as I want to see things through to the end, realistically, I think I've done all I can.

My phone rings, interrupting my train of thought. I look at the screen. It's a withheld number.

Strange.

I answer it. "Yeah?"

"Adrian Hell? This is Roberto Pellaggio. I think me and you need to talk, kid."

Oh, for fuck's sake...

"What can I do for you, shit stain?"

"I'm assuming that Jimmy's recent issue with the police is down to you?"

"I don't know what you're talking about..."

"Sure, you don't, kid. As things stand, I figure you owe me. Big."

"Really? See, the way I figure it, I owe you fuck all. So, how about you piss off and forget you ever hired me?"

"That mouth of yours is gonna get you into trouble one day."

"So people keep telling me. I thought I told you to leave this well alone?"

"I want my goddamn land back!"

"Oh, well, seeing as you asked so nicely..."

"Don't fuck with me, kid. I don't care who you are. I'll see to it they find pieces of your body in all fifty states!"

I fail to suppress a chuckle at his last threat, which I can tell does nothing to improve his already sour mood. "Listen, I don't have the deeds anymore. I gave them away. Sorry."

There's a brief silence. "You can't possibly be that stupid, kid."

Despite having nothing to hurry to, I'm still not in the mood to argue with this guy. I understand he's the head of a large and powerful mafia family. And yes, I fully appreciate there are many, many ways in which he can come after me. But after the week I've had, I simply don't care. I figure it's irrelevant how much I tell him now. I mean, what's he going to do? Threaten the U.S. government?

"You're right. I'm not that stupid. In fact, I'm probably one of the smartest people you'll ever meet. But that doesn't change the fact that I no longer have the deeds."

"So, get them back. They're mine."

"Actually, that land is now the property of the United States government. I spoke to the actual secretary of defense, who persuaded me to hand the deeds over to a private military contractor called GlobaTech. Ted Jackson worked for them in case you've forgotten. They're handling the legalities of it all, but the bottom line is this: let it go. You've lost."

I hear his frustrated breathing on the line. "Bullshit."

"I'm afraid not. Sorry. See, it turns out that underneath that little plot of land lies the only natural uranium deposit in North America. Crazy, I know. But I couldn't let you keep it once I found out, and since then, lots of things have happened that culminated in the secretary of defense ordering me to hand the deeds over."

"You've cost me millions of dollars..."

There's an icy calm in his voice. I suspect that means he's so angry, he doesn't quite know how to express it.

"Well, if you'd known about the uranium and started selling *that* as well, you could argue I've probably cost you *billions*. If it's any consolation, you *did* manage to get away without paying me for the Ted Jackson hit. Although, I did kinda screw you over and frame Jimmy for that, didn't I? Huh... how about we call it even?"

"You're a fucking dead man. You hear me, kid? Dead!"

"I think not, Bobby, old buddy. See, you're now a member of an exclusive club for people whom I've warned more than once. There are two members. One of them has just been arrested for a murder we all know he had nothing to do with. His nose is broken, his pride is hurt, and he's fully aware that if I see him again, I'll put a bullet in his head. The other is you. So, listen up and listen well. If you ever see me again, you run as fast as you can in the opposite direction. If I catch you, the last thing you will ever see will be my gun pointing at your face. I'm not threatening you. I'm simply stating an irrefutable fact. Take the hit on this one, walk away, and fight another day."

"You talk a lot, kid. And you seem to forget exactly who the fuck I am. You've caused me a lot of trouble, and there are countless bodies buried in the desert that can vouch for the fact I don't take too kindly to people fucking with my business. You're one man, and soon, you'll be a dead one."

He hangs up before I have the chance to say anything else. I look at the phone for a moment and sigh. To be fair, I've probably said enough. He's likely calling everyone he knows right now, rallying his troops and showing them *my* picture. I suspect things are about to get really interesting...

So much for getting out of Heaven's Valley!

I sit in silence for a moment, thinking things over. Then it comes to me. I call Josh again, who answers promptly. "Hey, quick question. You got a number for Robert Clark?"

"Yeah, I'll text it you now. Why? What's up?"

"I need a favor from our new best friend."

Josh sighs heavily on the other end of the phone. "What have you done, Adrian?"

"Josh, I'm sure I don't know what you're talking about…"

Silence.

I roll my eyes. "Okay, fine. Pellaggio just called me and demanded I give him the deeds. I told him about the uranium mine and how the secretary of defense ordered me to give them to GlobaTech. He advised me I won't be alive for much longer."

"To which you replied…"

"I *may* have suggested I'll shoot him in the head if I ever see him again."

"So, not only did you basically commit treason by divulging classified military information, but you succeeded in pissing off one of the biggest mob bosses on the West Coast?"

"He was already pissed at me."

"Yes, but *now* he's gonna be pulling together his vast array of resources and dedicating his every waking moment to killing you."

"Well, there is that, I suppose."

"You did it on purpose, didn't you?"

I pause. "Maybe…"

"I swear, sometimes I think you're suicidal."

"Oh, it'll be fine. Stop being such an old woman about it. We've dealt with worse."

"What are you going to do?"

"Can you get me his address?"

"Pellaggio's? Why? Do you intend to knock on his door and say hi?"

"Something like that."

"Can I have all your guns and money when you die?"

"Knock yourself out, but I'm being buried with my Berettas."

"I can live with that. When this goes wrong and you're buried in the desert, where you'll be heading, you'll need all the help you can get."

22

14:36 PDT

I'm on my way back to the hospital to check on Clara one last time. I've spoken with Josh about what I have planned for Pellaggio before I leave. He's skeptical, to say the least, but he texted me Robert Clark's number a few moments ago, as well as Pellaggio's address and directions.

I figure I'll pop over on my way out of here and see if we can't sort this out like gentlemen.

This car is one of the best I've ever driven. The powerful roar of the engine sounds like someone tried to tame nature itself—and struggled. For a true sports car like the Viper, you have to drive it straight, drive it fast, and have a helluva soundtrack in the background.

I'm messing with the radio to find something suitable. There are a couple of local radio stations playing up-to-date chart music, which is no good at all. After another moment or two of fine-tuning, I stumble across a station with an older-sounding guy talking, introducing three tracks to be played back-to-back, all classic rock.

That'll do nicely.

I crank up the volume as the opening riff to *Since You've Been Gone* by Rainbow starts. This song is what I like to call hundred-mile-an-hour music. I put my foot to the floor and blast down the street—windows down, music loud. For the first time in what feels like a lifetime, I feel relaxed and free, away from all the burdens and bullets that this city has thrown at me. It's just the music, the open road, and me.

I pull into the hospital parking lot and turn the volume down to a reasonable, boring level. There aren't many cars parked nearby, considering it's a hospital. I don't want to get out of the car, but as the saying goes, there's no rest for the wicked...

I climb out and head over to the main entrance. I walk inside and take the elevator up to the fourth floor. The doors ding open, and I step out into the waiting area. One of the nurses behind the desk looks up and smiles. I recognize her from when GlobaTech brought me here early this morning. I smile back as I walk past the desk and down the corridor toward Clara's room. The doors with the keypad are standing open, which is helpful, as I don't have a keycard.

It's not very secure, though.

I walk through and knock on the door to Clara's room. There's no answer, so I open the door slowly and look inside, in case she's sleeping or getting changed.

The bed's empty.

Seriously, I wish she'd stop doing that! The woman can't stay still for more than a couple of minutes, let alone be trusted to seek medical attention when she needs it.

I walk back out to the waiting area and signal to the

nurse who smiled at me. "Excuse me, can you tell me where Clara Fox is? She was in room five, down the corridor."

She checks the computer in front of her for a moment. "She discharged herself a couple of hours after she came in. We cleaned the wound and stitched it back up, then she insisted on leaving almost immediately."

I take a deep breath, sighing heavily. "Okay, thanks for your help."

I take the elevator back down to the first floor.

Where the hell is she now? Why would she have checked herself out? There's nothing left for her to do. GlobaTech will handle Dark Rain, and Pellaggio was never her problem to start with. Where could she be?

I step outside, take my phone out, and dial Clark's number.

"It's Adrian," I say as he answers. "You got a minute?"

"I don't know where she is either, if that's what you're calling to ask."

"How do *you* know Clara's not in the hospital?"

"I came by a couple of hours ago, hoping to run into you, funnily enough. I went to check on her while I was there, and the nurse said she'd checked herself out."

"Well, with a bit of luck, she's left town with Jackson's money, like I told her to."

"Ah, I did wonder where his briefcase was. Technically, you should return that to me, y'know."

"Sorry. I gave it to Clara not long after taking out Jackson. She was worried about trying to leave Dark Rain, so I told her to take the money and run. I think she's resourceful enough to disappear for a while."

"How noble of you. Well, I'll consider it an investment for the future."

"How diplomatic of *you*. What did you want me for, anyway?"

"I wanted to thank you again for giving up the deeds to the uranium mine earlier today. Thanks to you, GlobaTech have strengthened their delicate relationship with the U.S. military. Moving forward, we'll be working closely with them on a number of projects both domestic and overseas."

"Glad I could help."

"Did you want me for something?"

"Yeah, I was going to ask you for a favor. But since I just helped you secure lots of business and money, it's probably more like a commission payment."

Clark laughs. "Go on. What do you need?"

I spend a couple of minutes running through a comprehensive list of things I want, as well as details of what I intend to do with them. Under the circumstances, I figure he deserves full disclosure.

He's silent for a few moments. "Well, you're officially certifiable. You do realize that, right? I mean, I wouldn't send an entire unit to do that."

"So, can you help me?"

"Yeah, I can get you what you need. I'll text you an address where you can pick it up. I can have it ready for you in a few hours."

"I appreciate that. Thank you."

"Adrian, are you serious about this?"

"Completely."

"And you think you can pull it off?"

"No doubt at all."

"When all this has blown over, if you ever want a job, you call me, okay? I could use someone as clinically insane as you."

"I've got a job, but thanks for the offer."

I hang up and walk over to the parking lot. It still isn't busy, although there's a few more cars here now compared to when I arrived five minutes ago.

I see Clara's Dodge Viper up ahead. It's maybe twenty-five feet away...

There's a brilliant, burning flash in front of me.

What the...

The air fills with a deafening roar, and—

14:47 PDT

I open my eyes. I hear a loud ringing sound coming from somewhere. I seem to be lying on the floor, looking up at a large, dark gray cloud of smoke billowing into the sky. There's a voice in my head telling me not to move, so at least I know I'm alive and my brain's working.

My entire body feels hot, like I'm on fire...

What the hell just happened?

I cautiously try to move my arms, one at a time.

They hurt, but they're attached and functioning.

I check the rest of my body instinctively to make sure I'm in one piece... I can't feel any protruding bones, but my chest is wet. I feel around and realize I'm bleeding from my mouth, and it's dripping down my front. I use my tongue to search the inside of mouth.

Ah! Shit!

A blinding white pain surges through my face.

I stop moving my tongue.

Man, this sucks.

I try to move my legs, one at a time.

Yup, they work.

Okay, I'm going to try to stand…

I put my arms out behind me and bring my knees up to my chest. I take a few deep, painful breaths, then try to push myself upright.

Oh, no—this isn't going to work!

I fall slowly and pitifully over on my side. My equilibrium seems to be all over the place. I look around, but my vision's blurry, and I can't focus on anything nearby.

Great—another concussion…

I'll settle for sitting up for now. I resume the position of arms behind me and knees to my chest. I start looking around, taking slow, deep breaths to calm myself. My bruised ribs and back are hurting again with renewed vigor. I feel sick too.

Definitely a concussion.

What's that? Two so far this week?

For fuck's sake!

I look ahead of me, staring to give my eyes chance to focus. There's a blazing wreck in the parking lot. The remains of the bodywork are red with patches of white…

Jesus! The Viper exploded? How?

In the distance, I hear lots of commotion—sirens wailing, people screaming and running in all directions…

Hang on.

That's all happening around me!

I guess I'm quite fortunate because I've been blown up in a hospital parking lot. At least I don't have far to travel.

I feel hands on my shoulders.

Shit, who's that?

Immediately, I try to fight them off, but when I look down, I realize I'm not thrashing my arms and twisting my body violently to escape their grasp, like I was trying to do. In reality, I'm hardly moving.

How embarrassing.

I give up. I let the hands guide me backward, so I'm lying on the ground again. A face looms into view above me. I recognize it as the nurse from the fourth floor who smiled at me. She's saying something, but I can't really hear her.

This is all getting a bit much. I have no idea how the car exploded, or why. I can't really move, besides sitting upright, which isn't going to get me anywhere... I might as well get some rest. This nurse looks friendly, so I doubt she'll try to kill me. I just need a bit of peace and quiet ...

??:??

I open my eyes again and see long, bright lights rushing past above me.

How long have I been out?

I try to lift my head and look around. There's a person on either side of me, walking quickly and looking ahead.

Oh, man. My head feels like it's been split in half.

The person on my left looks down, clearly having noticed me moving. They say something to me that I can't hear, but they don't look frightened, angry, or concerned.

Whatever they're saying can't be too bad, then, right?

I'll just close my eyes for a—

21:27 PDT

I open my eyes slowly. A heavy mist slowly lifts, revealing my surroundings. I'm lying in bed, in what looks like a hospital room. There's a clock mounted high on the wall opposite.

Christ, I've been out well over five hours.

I blink a few times, urging my brain to start functioning properly again.

I definitely feel a lot better than I did the last time I was awake.

I look around the room. There's a window on my right, overlooking some trees and the parking lot—I can see lots of flashing lights reflecting from below. Attached to the far wall, below the clock, is a TV. Next to that, on the left, is a man dressed in black with a balaclava on, standing to attention and holding an automatic submachine gun. There's the door on my left, which is closed, and there's a metal stand next to my bed with an IV drip hanging on it. I follow the tubing and realize it's feeding into a nozzle that's sticking in the back of my left hand. On the table next to my bed is a—

Hang on.

Window. TV. Man with gun. Door. IV drip.

That's not right.

I look over at the man in black. I can only see his eyes, which are brown. He relaxes his stance as he sees me looking at him, holding his gun loose—not primed for action. He waves at me.

What the hell's in this IV?

I slowly wave back with my right hand.

I'm not convinced that this isn't some kind of hallucination...

He walks over to the door and opens it. He sticks his head out to the left and whistles, then holds the door open. After a few moments, Robert Clark enters the room.

He moves over to the side of the bed, smiling. "Hey there, sleeping beauty."

I sigh and roll my eyes. That's something Josh would've said.

"Ugh. Come closer, so I can hit you."

"How are you holdin' up?"

"Been better. Let me ask you something. Is that guy over there with the gun real?"

Clark looks over his shoulder at the guy standing guard by the door, then back at me. He nods. "He's as real as it gets."

"That's all right, then. Thought I was going strange for a minute."

"Adrian, what the hell happened?"

"I don't know. I got off the phone with you, walked over to Clara's car, and it exploded. My guess would be that Pellaggio's got a head start on trying to make me dead."

"That was a serious explosion, Adrian. You're lucky you're alive. I've got a couple of guys working on the car now. Or what's left of it at least. We've managed to keep the local authorities away for now. It's a shame—that was a sweet ride."

"It really was. Man, Clara's gonna kill me."

"Not if someone else beats her to it. We think the bomb was C4, intended for remote detonation from somewhere nearby. It was underneath the car, near the driver's door. From what we can determine after our preliminary investigation, whoever did this configured the device to detonate via a cell phone transmission. My personal guess is that for some reason, our conversation triggered the explosion early. Your phone must've used the same frequency as the device programmed to detonate it."

"Well, they *do* say cell phones will kill you..."

"Look, if this *was* Pellaggio, you need to proceed with caution. He clearly has the means to get to you whenever he wants. And he definitely seems intent on killing you. Maybe you should—"

"Let me stop you right there."

I reach over and take the IV out of my hand, causing a thin trickle of blood to run down on to the bed sheets. I throw the covers back and swing my legs over the side. I put my feet flat on the floor and tentatively put my weight on them. They seem to be working fine, so I commit fully and push myself off the bed. I stand up straight and turn to face Clark.

"In the last two days, I've been shot at, mildly tortured, shot at *again,* and now blown up. I've been thrown through a mirrored wall, and I've had to see innocent people die horribly because of me."

I walk slowly toward him. He looks a little uncomfortable, which is fine by me. He needs to know who he's talking to. He needs to know what's going to happen now.

"Do you know why they call me Adrian Hell, Robert?"

"Ah, no. No, I don't."

He looks even more uncomfortable now I'm standing almost nose to nose with him.

"I live with a daily struggle to keep all my anger, hatred, and horrible thoughts behind a locked door in my head. Occasionally, if people push me hard enough, they run the risk of that door opening. If it does, what they find behind it is their problem to deal with. And God help them. Dark Rain is your problem now. And frankly, you're welcome to them. But Pellaggio has just blown my door off its hinges. Literally, as well as figuratively. So now..."

I pause as I clench my jaw muscles, fighting to keep the burning rage inside me in check. I feel a lust for violence coursing through my veins, touching every part of my body and filling it with a dark energy that's bursting at the seams, desperate to be unleashed.

"Now Roberto Pellaggio will know what it's like to feel the wrath of my Inner Satan. I'm going to rip his entire world apart. I made him a promise not so long ago, and I aim to come good on that. I appreciate you helping me out, but if you want some free advice, *Bob*—stay the fuck out of my way."

23

Clark and his bodyguard quickly left my room. I got dressed and discharged myself from the hospital. The nurses strongly objected, but they weren't going to stop me. I finally took some painkillers to help with my ribs and my back, then made my way outside.

I'm standing in the doorway, looking at the goddamn circus out front. It's been over five hours since the car exploded. There's still a fire truck on site, although the fire itself was put out hours ago. The police are here too, along with a forensics team and a bomb disposal unit. They've cordoned off the area, but some members of the public are moving around in front of the police tape, trying to see what's happening. Away to the right, spilling onto the street, a crowd of journalists and local media are trying to describe the scene to the curious masses.

I want to avoid any kind of attention. I head to my right and work my way around the back of the hospital, onto the next street over that runs parallel to the building. I use side streets and alleyways where I can, keeping my exposure to prying eyes down to a minimum.

My hearing is almost completely back to normal, and my tongue has stopped bleeding, although it still hurts to talk. Luckily, the time for talking has long since passed.

Wars aren't won with words.

I have no idea at this stage whether Pellaggio's aware I've survived the blast. Ideally, he'll think I'm dead. That way, he'll forget about me and absolutely won't expect me to show up on his doorstep, which gives me a huge advantage.

However, I think we all know I'm not that lucky.

Working on the assumption he knows I'm still alive, I figure I should try to keep a low profile until I'm ready to make my move.

As we agreed, before I was blown up, Clark has arranged a little care package for me. He's texted me the address. The drop point is a storage locker at the main bus terminal. He's given me the combination to the lock and confirmed it's accessible twenty-four hours a day.

I know what I need to do. I'll admit, I usually like to take more time to plan an operation—especially one like I've got planned for Pellaggio—but I can't afford to wait any longer. I'm done trying to do the right thing and play the diplomat between everyone. The door's open, and the devil inside is hungry for blood.

I find the bus terminal easily enough and quickly locate the locker. The combination works. Inside is a black sports bag. I remove it, putting my shoulder bag inside in its place. I walk over to an empty bench and quickly open it to check everything I need is in there.

Holy shit! Clark delivered and then some...

Everything's here. It's all high-end equipment—perfect for what I'm about to do.

I zip the bag back up and walk out of the bus terminal, carrying it by my side as I keep to the alleys and the side streets, like before. I instinctively touch the Berettas at my back. I'm glad I didn't leave them in the car, and I'm fortunate the nurses kept them with my belongings. I suspect that particular hospital benefits from some extra funding, courtesy of GlobaTech. They all seem perfectly comfortable with the comings and goings of guns and bullet wounds.

My phone starts vibrating in my pocket. I take it out and see Josh's name on the screen. I'm not in the mood for talking, but I should probably answer it.

"Yeah?"

"Whoa, you all right, big fella?"

"Aside from being blown up by a car bomb, I'm peachy."

"What?"

"Yeah, Clara's Dodge Viper got blown to shit in the hospital parking lot as I approached it. I think Pellaggio's started his campaign to kill me. Dunno if he knows he failed or not."

"Jesus! You all right?"

"I've got a helluva headache, and my ribs and back have taken another pounding, but I'm fine. I was blown clear by the blast. Any closer and I'd have been evaporated."

"This has gotta be one of the shittiest weeks ever! Listen, have you spoken to Clara yet?"

"No, I haven't seen or heard from her. I went back to the hospital to check on her, but she'd discharged herself... again."

"Right. Well, that's why I was calling you—she just called me."

"She did? Is she all right? Where is she?"

"She's fine. She was asking after you, actually. Said she felt bad leaving the hospital without telling you but couldn't allow Dark Rain to get away with what they did to Webster. She felt responsible and wanted to do something."

"What did you say to her?"

"Well, she asked what the plan was and how she could help, so I told her about my involvement with GlobaTech and what their operation entails. She said she'd do some recon and give me intel from the ground, to help me coordinate the attack."

"Sounds like a good plan. She needs to watch her back, though. Dark Rain is gunning for her just as much as they are for me."

"I'm sure she'll be fine. Anything she can give me will be invaluable. So, what are you doing now?"

"I have a gift from GlobaTech, thanks to our friend, Bob. I'm going to pay Don Pellaggio a visit."

"Is this gift, by any chance, in the shape of a black bag full of evil things?"

"It is."

"And have you used the words 'Inner' and 'Satan' in the same sentence recently?"

"I have."

"Oh, bloody hell! I'll be under my desk until you're finished!"

I smile. "That's probably wise."

I hang up and continue navigating the back streets. After a good half-hour, I find myself walking down a poorly lit street just outside the center of the city. It's clearly a rich area of the city because the houses are well spaced and all look like mansions. About halfway down, on the right, is a particularly enormous house set within gated grounds. There are high walls all around, but a security hut is visible on the right of the large, wrought iron gates. Beyond that is a circular driveway with a huge water feature in the middle. The house itself has three floors, with a large, stone pillar on either side of the front door. There's light coming from a few windows, but other than that, the place is in darkness.

Roberto Pellaggio's estate.

I smile to myself.

Showtime, asshole.

22:34 PDT

I crouch behind some bushes at the front of the house opposite. It's dark and the lights aren't on, so I doubt anyone will see me. I open the bag, take out a pair of black coveralls, and quickly put them on over my clothes. I then carefully unpack all the equipment and weapons, kitting myself out, preparing for war.

I look across the street. My first problem is getting into the estate. I can easily get over the walls, but I have no visibility of what's on the other side. I don't know if there are guys patrolling the perimeter, if there are any attack dogs, what the positions are of security cameras... Basically, I'm completely blind and therefore justified in assuming any attempt to get inside at this stage would result in a swift and painful death.

Luckily for me, I have Josh.

I clip my Bluetooth earpiece in place and call the man who's been my eyes and ears around the world for half my life.

He answers. I take a breath. "You ready?"

He sighs. "I am, but for the record, I'd like to say again

that I'm completely against this. I think it's the dumbest thing you've ever done—and that's saying something because I've known you a long time, and I've seen you do some really dumb shit. I just want that made official, so my conscience is clear in case you die."

"Josh, given I'm relying solely on you for navigation here, if I die, it'll be your fault. And if that happens, be prepared for me to come back and haunt you."

"Fine. Are you in position?"

"Yeah, I'm across the street, hidden in some bushes. I'm invisible and ready to go."

"Okay, let's do this."

Josh mentioned earlier that GlobaTech gave him access to their satellite feeds and thermal imaging technology. He's going to work with Clark to help coordinate the attack on Dark Rain, which he said is going to happen at some point tomorrow. I figured, seeing as he's got that access, he might as well use it.

He's explained to me that once the satellite is in position over Pellaggio's estate, he'll have a real-time view of where all the guards and dogs are, both inside and out, as well as where the security cameras are and which way they're look-ing. He'll be able to view all the heat signatures on the grounds and direct me safely inside.

He's already taken a look at the place, which is how I knew exactly what to ask Clark for.

"Right, Adrian, I'm picking up your signature across the street, facing the west wall of the estate. That's good because that's where the main security desk is."

I frown. "Why's that a good thing?"

"Because if the main security hub is there, there'll be no need to have any other security patrols on that side of the building, which means once you're past it and inside, you shouldn't run into anyone else."

"Great. So, how do I get past it?"

"The guard's hut and main gate is about forty feet to the left of where you are now. If you look about thirty feet to your right, you'll see a group of trees. Work your way level with them and wait for my signal."

"Got it."

I negotiate my way through the bushes and under-growth, doing my best not to tread on any flowerbeds these people have scattered around their garden. There's a skill to making no noise while walking through things that crack and rustle. Thankfully, it's something I learned a long time ago.

It takes me less than a minute to get where I need to be. "Right, I'm here. The trees are directly in front of me."

"Good. There's been no movement, which means no one's heard you moving over there."

"Or they *have* heard me and they're pretending, while secretly planning to gun me down the moment I'm over the wall."

"Adrian, do you really think *now* is the time for your particular brand of pessimism?"

"I prefer to think of it as realism, but let's not split hairs. So, now what?"

"Once you're over the wall, dive to your right. You should then be covered completely by trees and darkness. It's a black spot in their security coverage, but that just means there will likely be at least one sentry checking the area now and then, so we need to keep an eye out for him."

"Got it. Just say when."

I check my equipment for the fourth and probably not

final time. In addition to my black overalls, I'm wearing a Kevlar vest and tactical night vision goggles on my head. I adjust the chinstrap again, ensuring it's tight and the goggles are firmly in place. I've moved my Berettas so that I now have one holstered on each leg. Both have their suppressors fitted. At my back, in their place, is a belt kit for a rappelling hook —good for two hundred feet. More than enough for what I need it for. Fed over both shoulders are two MP5 submachine guns—both silenced and set to fire three-round bursts. I also have the knife with me that I took from the guy at the safe house where I found Webster. Figured it might come in handy. Finally, in the pockets sewn into the legs of my coveralls, I have some grenades—two frags and two smoke.

I hear Josh clear his throat down the line, interrupting my last-minute checks. "Right, one guard is approaching the security gate now. Possibly switching shifts. Hold steady." There's a moment of silence on the line. "Okay, he's walking away again now. On my mark, stay low and move fast to the wall. Flatten against it until I give you the all-clear to scale."

I nod to myself. "Roger that."

More tense silence.

"Okay, Adrian... move!"

Staying low, I sprint across the road and stop when I reach the wall. I press my back against it and catch my breath. The painkillers are doing their job—breathing isn't causing me any discomfort in my torso, which is a pleasant change. I should've taken some days ago...

I lower my voice to a whisper. "I'm in position."

"Okay, up and over the wall on my count—remember to land and roll right. Three... Two... One... Now!"

I scale the wall, heave myself up, and lie flat along the top for a moment, catching my breath. I then swing my legs over and drop down into a crouch on the other side. As I land, I roll to my right and come to a stop behind the trees, exactly as Josh had instructed.

I lower my goggles into place and activate the night vision mode. Everything flickers in front of me and turns a pale green. I quickly scan the area. I see the southwest corner of the house in front of me. To my left, in the distance, is the security hut. To my right is a long lawn with two sets of garden furniture positioned along it. No sign of any movement.

I look up at the house. There are a couple of lights on in windows on the top floor, which flare up and obscure my view through the green glow of the goggles.

"Josh, I'm in."

"Okay, this next bit is the tricky part."

"The tricky part? I've not seen the *easy* part yet. So far, all of this has been tricky, Josh."

"True. But this next part in particular will suck more than the rest."

"I can barely contain my excitement..."

"From here, you need to head left. You should see a wine cellar entrance. You got it?"

I look over and see the alcove, maybe a third of the way along the side of the house. In the middle of the alcove is the entrance—two doors open out at an angle leading under the house and to the cellar. Decent-sized gaps on either side are completely covered in darkness.

"Yeah, I see it."

"You should have enough cover at the side of that, but to get there, you're going to have to run across open ground. You'll be completely exposed for close to fifteen seconds."

"Oh, wonderful..."

"I'm tracking the patrols now. I see a total of six guys working the perimeter in teams of two, with a lone guy based in the security station. You're clear to your left, as you're out of sight from the station, but to your right, you've got two guys patrolling. It's gonna be tight, but you should make it. Once there, you'll be in total darkness again, so they shouldn't see you."

I lift my goggles up and look at the world as it is. Josh is right—there's no way anyone will see me, and I doubt Pellaggio's goons are equipped with the same tech I am. I pull my goggles back on and turn the world green once again.

"Okay, when I say—run like hell, yeah?"

"I'll do my best."

Just up ahead, I catch a glimpse of one of the guards. He's walking toward me down the left-hand side, carrying an assault rifle, which he's holding loose, letting it hang in front of him from the shoulder strap. I figure that means the other guy is walking away from me, down the right side. Plus, as I suspected, he's not wearing any night vision goggles, so I'll keep my advantage as long as I don't get too close to anyone.

Seeing what I have to do, the enormity of the risk begins to sink in. As soon as the guy nearest to me turns his back, Josh is going to tell me to run. By the time I reach my cover, the guard will be out of earshot, but the guy patrolling the right-hand side will be coming toward me, and I'll be horribly close to his line of sight. Even in the dark, if he's facing my direction and I'm running, he'll see enough by what light is coming from the house that he'll be suspicious, prompting him to move in for a closer look. That means there's a high chance of someone discovering me, and if *that* happens, it's game over.

Shit.

"Be ready..." says Josh.

I stand slowly, preparing to run.

"Okay, go now!"

I set off like a sprinter out of the starting blocks. I have to cover almost three hundred feet in less than fifteen seconds. As I run, my weapons bounce around, adding extra resistance. I feel myself slowing down.

Five seconds.

"Adrian, the guy on the left should be out of earshot by now, but the guy coming toward you on the right will have line of sight any second. You gotta push the pace..."

I grit my teeth and press on. I'm usually pretty fast, but I'm not an Olympic sprinter by any means. Plus, despite normally being in good shape, the pounding my body's taken recently is making quick, heavy breathing a very painful experience. Subconsciously, I know I'm not running as fast as I'm capable of.

Ten seconds.

"Adrian, he's almost in position. You need to get to cover *now!*"

I approach the cellar doors at full speed. I drop and do a baseball slide into the corner. I stop by slamming into the wall, and I struggle to suppress a grunt of pain caused by the impact. I look out across the lawn and see the other guy almost level with my position. I'm gasping for breath. My lungs are burning—each intake is sending a white-hot stab of pain pulsing into my ribs. I lift up my goggles, and the guy disappears in the darkness.

"Don't move, Adrian. You're not clear yet."

I do everything I can to slow my breathing down as the seconds tick by. There's nothing out of the ordinary just yet. But the big test will come when the first guy comes back toward me down the left flank.

"Okay, the first guy is heading your way now. Don't move. Don't breathe. Don't do anything."

My breathing is finally returning to normal. The guy on the left is approaching the cellar doors. I curl up into a ball in the small alcove, tucking myself away in the shadows. I can't see my hand in front of my face, which means he shouldn't be able to see anything if he looks my way. I slip my goggles back on and see the guy walking right in front of me. He can't be more than ten feet away...

I hold my breath, causing fresh waves of pain to course through my chest like a fire spreading through a forest. My eyes water, blurring my vision through the goggles.

Come on... move, you piece of shit...

The guy's almost past me, but I can't hold it in any longer.

I grimace at the burning sensation as I let out a breath.

Fuck!

I immediately clasp my hand over my mouth, but it's no good. The guy stops, listening intently. Then he takes a couple of paces backward and stares into the small abyss where I'm crouching against the wall. He doesn't know it, but he's looking right at me.

Josh sighs down the line. "Oh, bollocks..."

24

The guy's standing directly in front of me, squinting into the same darkness I'm desperately trying to hide in. I'm convinced he can hear my heart beating inside my chest. He takes another step closer, his hand tightening around the barrel and stock of the machine gun he's holding.

I know Josh is watching via satellite. I'm silently begging him to give me some clue as to what my next move should be, but he's staying quiet. Probably worried his voice would be heard in the silence.

I run through my options but soon arrive at the annoying conclusion that there's really only one way out of this... If this guy doesn't move away, he's going to have to die.

I move my hand slowly away from my mouth and down to my leg. With infinite care, I reach for the knife which I've strapped to the front of my thigh. I slowly grip the handle. I can't risk drawing it right away in case the blade makes a noise, but I want to get ready to use it if I need to.

Come on... move, goddammit!

I'm willing him to walk away, but he remains where he is, trying to focus and see into the dark shadows ahead of him. He takes another pace toward me, pointing his gun out in front of him.

Each second that passes feels like an hour. I need to decide and fast. I can't afford to blow this, not after coming so far. But if this guy finds me, it'll be hard to deal with it without alerting everyone else. And if I lose the element of surprise, I'm as good as dead. Unless I run for it...

Let's be honest—that's never going to happen. I would rather die.

Ah, fuck it.

In one swift and silently brutal movement, I draw the knife and lunge toward the guy, pushing up with my legs and thrusting the blade forward. It carves into him effortlessly, catching him in the fleshy part of his throat just below his jaw and above his Adam's apple. I aim it perfectly and sever his vocal cords, preventing him from making any noise as he dies. He falls forward lifelessly. I catch him and guide his body gently to the ground.

That's one issue resolved, but now I'm left with a whole new one. The other guy's going to notice his friend's missing in the next thirty seconds.

"Josh, where's the second guard?"

"Yeah, I can't help but notice that the heat signature near you is disappearing..."

"I had no choice. Where's the other one?"

"He's still walking away from you on the far side. He'll be turning around any second. Just be careful the other patrol at the far side of the house doesn't see him drop."

"I'll wait for him to head back toward me. Don't worry."

I remain where I am, making sure the same darkness

hiding me is completely cloaking the dead guard. The next twenty seconds feel like a lifetime, but eventually, Josh comes back on the line.

"Right, the second guy's approaching you now. You should see him coming from the left any second. You can't let him get too close. Otherwise, he'll notice his partner's missing."

"I'm on it."

I move forward slightly, crouching on the edge of the alcove, just inside the shadows. After a couple of seconds, I have a clear view of the other guy, walking casually but alert across the lawn. I grab the knife by the blade and line it up, ready to unleash it at my target. I'm a good aim, but I'm trying to hit either his throat or the top of his chest with a knife from about eighty feet away. It's not going to be easy, but I don't want to use my guns. Even though they're fitted with suppressors, there's still a risk of noise or commotion. Plus, I'm going to need every bullet I have for what comes later.

I take a few deep breaths to slow my heart rate down, ignoring the pain.

"Adrian, whatever you're going to do, you have to do it now."

I clench my jaw. "I've got this..."

Just another couple of paces toward me... and...

I whip the knife across the lawn, following through with my arm so that it gains maximum velocity as it travels with deadly intent toward the remaining sentry. It takes a little over a second to hit him.

Bullseye!

It hits him at the bottom of the throat, penetrating his skin with ease and completely burying itself inside. He instinctively clutches at the knife, his face contorted in shock and pain. But it's too late for him—he's dead before he hits the ground.

I breathe out a sigh of relief.

Josh startles me by shouting down the line. "Fuck me! Good shot, man!"

"Thanks. How long do I have?"

"It'll be a few minutes before he's noticed, I would think. I've not seen any previous interaction between the two patrols."

"Good." I stand and quickly check the rest of my equipment's still in place. "Right, give me a minute."

I edge forward out of the shadows of my alcove and glance both ways. I can't see any movement, but I leave it a few moments just to be sure, then I sprint over to the dead body.

I crouch low next to him and retrieve my knife. I wipe the blood off the blade on the grass and sheath it.

"Josh, how's it looking?"

"Still clear for now. I wouldn't hang around, though."

"Don't intend to."

The dead guy's lying on his right side, partially facing the ground. Still crouching, I grab hold of his right arm and sling it over my shoulder. I put my hands around his waist and gradually get a grip underneath him. Taking some quick, deep breaths, I steel myself. In one last monumental effort that hurts every inch of my body, I stand and heave him over my shoulder in something akin to a fireman's carry. I take a quick look around again and set off back to the alcove. I try to run, but under the weight, it's more of a slow jog.

"Hurry up, Adrian—the patrol on the far side is coming up fast and will see you if they look your way."

"Going as... fast... as I can..."

It takes me twice as long to cover the same distance going back, but I manage to retreat into the shadows undetected. I drop the body next to his partner and push them back against the wall, making sure they're fully hidden.

I take a moment to catch my breath. I step out onto the lawn and look back at the alcove, checking the bodies aren't visible. They're not.

"Right, now get me on the goddamn roof."

Josh chuckles. "This is going to be the fun part."

"I doubt that..."

"To your left, as you approach the end of the south wall, there's another small alcove between a window and the corner of the house. As you face the alcove, there's a drainage pipe on the right-hand side that leads almost all the way to the roof."

"Okay, the key words I picked up there were *window* and *almost*. Care to elaborate?"

It's these kinds of situations where Josh and I really come alive. Don't get me wrong. I love my job as much as someone *can* love killing people for a living. But this—the thrill of the assault, the adrenaline, the danger, the close quarters battle—it's what I miss from the old days on the unit most of all.

Before the dark times.

Josh is no different. He was a good soldier, and I would entrust him with my life, but he's always been better acting as the eyes, ears, and brains for everyone else. He's a strategist, and he excels at logistics and planning. He always wanted to be the one directing everyone else to victory from behind a desk of hi-tech toys. I'll never forget the way he phrased our relationship to me once. He said: "Adrian, you've always wanted to be *the man*. I've always wanted to be the one *the man* relies on."

No truer words have ever been spoken.

He laughs, sounding like he's enjoying this way too much. "Sure. By *window*, I mean a massive bay window that I'm hoping will have the curtains closed. Otherwise, you'll be on full view to whoever's in that room. And by *almost*, I mean that the drainpipe stops about six feet below the main roof, where the top floor of the house sticks out and the roof angles for drainage. You're going to have to balance on that, jump, then climb up the rest of the way."

"Excellent. Glad I asked."

"The good news is, once you're on the main roof, there's a decent-sized skylight above a large room. *And* it looks like tonight's your lucky night because there's some kind of meeting going on in there. I count at least fourteen heat signatures gathered together, with five... no, *six* more dotted around just outside that main room."

"That'll be a Pellaggio crisis meeting. I suspect the word's out I survived the car bomb."

"You just gotta get to that roof unseen. You ready?"

"Always."

"Okay, stay low and as close as you can to the wall. Be careful as you approach the bay window. I reckon you've got two minutes to get in that end alcove and up the drainpipe, at least above eye level, before the other patrol realizes they're two men down."

"Copy that."

Staying low, I set off and head for the end of the south wall. My goggles are back in place, and I see no movement ahead of me. I cover the distance quickly, and I soon reach the bay window. It juts out like a big square a good three feet from the house. I can see the next alcove on the other side of it. The two sides and the front of the window are all glass, from ceiling down to about waist height. The curtains are open, giving whoever's standing there a full view of the south lawn.

Shit.

"Josh, are you picking up any heat signatures nearby?"

"I've got one near the window, yeah. Hold position. It's hard to tell which way he's facing. If his back's to the window, you'll be all right, but until he moves, I can't tell."

"All right, standing by."

I crouch low, close to the wall. I'll be fine as long as no one walks into the bay and looks out the right-side window. If they do, at this range, they'll see me even in the darkness.

Almost a full minute passes in silence.

Josh sighs with relief. "He's got his back to you. Stay low and move fast, I don't know how long you've got here."

"Done."

I move silently, sidestepping in a crouch with my back to the window. I duck low enough to stay out of view, but again, if anyone walks right up to the window and looks out, they'll see me instantly.

I hold my breath as I move.

"You're clear, Boss."

I breathe out as I settle into the alcove undetected.

I test the drainpipe with my hands. It's solid and well attached, so it should take my weight. I grab hold of it with both hands and place my right foot on the side. I push with my legs and pull with my arms, heaving myself slowly up toward the roof.

It's not as easy as it should be, but I manage to shuffle up gradually, like a monkey climbing a tree. I reach the top without incident.

Oh.

I see what Josh meant about the last few feet...

The roof is made of old slate tiles and is on a reasonably

steep slant with a gutter around the edge. Standing on it with any degree of balance is going to be difficult. The main roof of the house is roughly six feet above that. I pull myself up and slowly stand, as if I have one foot on a step, with my arms out to the sides for balance. I find my footing and look up. The ledge of the main roof is technically about head height for me, but because I'm on the slant, it looks impossibly high...

I don't know why because heights aren't my favorite, but I have a sudden urge to look down...

Holy crap!

Man, I wish I hadn't done that! Basically, if I fall, I'm almost certainly dead.

Brilliant.

I take a few deep breaths to calm myself and think about how best to attempt this.

I don't like it at all. That's a big jump to make from a standing start on a downward slope. Given the damage I've done to my chest and ribs over the last few days, especially in the last half-hour, it's going to be difficult pulling myself up there...

"Adrian, what's wrong?"

I shake my head. "I don't think I can make the jump to the main roof from where I'm standing. The angle I'm balancing on is too steep."

"I know it's not easy, but there's no other way up there. You've got to make this, or it's all over."

"No pressure, then?"

"You got this, man. You just need to focus. Talk to me when you've made it."

I sigh. I've got a bad feeling about this...

I look up at the roof. I find my balance and inch backward, allowing myself enough room for one step before I make the jump. I rub my hands on my legs to dry them and take one last deep breath.

I take the step and jump. With every ounce of strength left in me, I push off and reach to my full extent...

Shit! I'm not going to reach the ledge!

I miss and land awkwardly on the slanted roof. My back foot slips out from under me on the tiles and I topple backward, clutching at thin air for support.

Instinctively, I turn and drop to my front as quickly as I can, spreading my arms and legs out to stop me falling off the edge. My left foot and left arm find the guttering, and I cling tightly to the roof, burying my face in the tiles to make myself invisible.

"Adrian! What happened? Are you okay?"

The panic in his voice wasn't hard to miss.

"Fuck! I missed my jump and slipped as I landed. Anyone notice?"

"I'm looking at every heat signature on the property. No sudden movements. I think you're good."

"Christ, that sucked."

I steadily get back to my feet and line up for another crack at it. I take some deep breaths, focusing on nothing but the ledge I need to grab.

I'm capable of doing this... I can easily reach it... The roof's psyching me out, and it shouldn't. Come on, Adrian, you pussy! This is easy. Just get it done. No hesitation...

I take the step again and jump, stretching out as before.

My hands grab the ledge. I allow myself a split-second parade in my head to celebrate.

Uh-oh...

Whoa!

My left hand slips off and my body swings uncontrollably forward. I instinctively look to the side to protect my face. The side of my head smashes into the wall, crushing my Bluetooth earpiece in the process. I grit my teeth, trying to conceal the grunt of pain. I'm hanging on by my right hand, and I'm forced to watch the remains of my earpiece fall to the ground a good twenty-five feet below me.

Goddammit!

I use every ounce of strength I have to get my left hand back on the ledge. I eventually manage it, and I heave myself up using my feet on the wall to gain leverage. I roll over onto my back and drop down to the roof. I lie still for a moment, breathing heavily and waiting for the adrenaline to subside so I can think clearly.

My arms, my back, and my ribs are on fire. I've also got no way of communicating with Josh anymore, which means my advantage over everyone below me has gone. The only thing I have left is the fact they don't know I'm coming. But I won't know where they are beforehand now, so I need to be extra careful.

I push myself up to one knee and scan the rooftop. It's mostly flat, with the occasional air vent sticking up. Just off center is the large skylight Josh mentioned. It's a triangular glass prism with a metal frame. Both sides are around four feet high and maybe twelve feet long, joining at the top on an angle of forty-five degrees.

I stay low and make my way over to it, peering through from the side, so I don't cast any shadows on the room below. This is going to be tricky, and I have no margin for error. My plan is to attach the rappelling hook to the top of the metal frame and descend to the room below. However, I need to break the glass first in order to do that, so I need to jump through the glass and latch it on immediately as I start to fall. If I get it wrong, I'm a dead man.

I look down into what appears to be a huge drawing

room or library of some kind. In the middle is a large wooden table, with six men sitting along each side and one at each end. From my position, the guy at the end facing me has his back to the main doors. The guy opposite him, with his back to me, has a large fireplace behind him. From this angle, I can see his balding head with gray hair on the back and sides. His hands are flat on the table, with gold rings adorning almost every finger.

Roberto Pellaggio.

He's going to die last.

I can't see anyone in the room that isn't at the table, but I know they're there somewhere because of what Josh told me earlier. I'll need to keep my eyes open and act fast as I drop.

I unhook my two MP5s from around my neck and put one on each shoulder. I check the rappelling hook is secured to my belt at the back and pull a length of cable loose, ready. Finally, I reach into my pockets and pull out both smoke grenades.

I stand up straight and gaze down through the skylight. My breathing is slow and steady. I make myself forget everything—what I've just done to get here, the days before this, all the things I've been through and overcome... everything.

Finally, I can allow my anger to flow freely through me. I can let the unbridled rage and fury that lives just beneath the surface to rise and course through my veins. My Inner Satan takes control of my body. I smile, knowing that he only ever uses me for violence. This feeling, this... lack of control is what makes me so dangerous. I use it in short bursts to help me live the life I do. To do the things I do. But I rarely allow it to consume me completely. But as I look down at Pellaggio and his organization, I'm more than happy to make an exception.

I'm not really one for more modern rock music, unlike

Josh, who will happily listen to anything. I'm more stuck in my ways. But every now and then, he'll play me a song that isn't bad. The lyrics from one in particular have just sprung to mind.

It's called *Waking The Demon*.

I raise my right foot. "I hope you're watching, Josh, because this is gonna be somethin' pretty special..."

I smash my foot down and through the pane of glass. I pop the pins of both smoke grenades and drop them into the room below.

My Inner Satan is finally unleashed.

25

I lower my goggles and switch them from night vision to thermal imaging—similar to what Josh will be looking at via satellite. With the smoke grenades having gone off, night vision won't do anything except illuminate the dense fog that's rapidly filling the room below. But thermal imaging will pick up people's heat signatures through the smoke, making them visible to me. Albeit in a weird, glowing, red and yellow kind of way. But that's all I need. If I can see them, I can shoot them.

I grab the rappel hook and click it into place on the metal frame as I jump down. I descend fast, lying horizontally with an MP5 in each hand. I quickly scan the room and fire off a few bursts at the table. I take down four of the men sitting along the sides before anyone's had chance to even get out of their seat.

I've clearly retained the element of surprise—it's like

247

shooting fish in a barrel. They've got no idea what's happening and probably never will.

I cover the thirty-odd foot drop quickly, emptying both MP5s at the table. I'm not worrying too much about aiming —with a gun like this, the fire rate and the close proximity to the targets means that if I get the general direction right, the guns will do the hard work for me. I spray the bullets slowly back and forth, wiping out another seven men in the process, leaving just Pellaggio and the two men sitting nearest to him on either side.

I land heavily on the table and quickly detach the rappel rope from my belt. I throw down the empty MP5s and draw both Berettas. I scan the room. There are bodies slumped across the table, and a river of blood flowing steadily across the floor. Looking at them, I can just see large shapes, motionless, turning blue—the heat escaping their bodies, leaving nothing but a cold corpse.

I've got my back to Pellaggio. I turn to my right and put a bullet through the head of the guy in front of me. That's twelve out of fourteen down in less than thirty seconds by my count.

A door off to my left suddenly bursts open, and another five men run through, firing blindly in the smoke. Their muzzle flashes light up in the mist like fireworks on the Fourth of July. I figure they're the remains of the patrols from outside. I glance over at Pellaggio, who doesn't seem to have fully grasped what's happening or who I am. The look on his face is a mixture of confusion and sheer terror as he watches his empire crumbling around him.

The five men fan out as I jump off the table into a crouch. I fire at two of them, hitting one in the chest and narrowly missing the other.

I hear someone shout, "He's over there!" as the staccato roar of a thousand bullets fills the air.

I stand and run to my right, firing as I go. I hit another in the chest and head, and his red glow fades to blue through my goggles. I add him to the tally in my head. That's two out of the five down, leaving three, plus two at the table— including Pellaggio.

I holster the Beretta in my left hand and retrieve a frag grenade. I pull the pin and roll it over to the door. I dive away to my right as it explodes, splintering the wooden decor of the room and taking out one of the patrol guys standing near the entrance.

The guy at the table stands and attempts to drag Pellaggio to his feet. He must be getting over the initial shock of what's happening, focusing long enough to do his duty and get his boss to safety. I take aim and shoot him square in the chest three times. Pellaggio cries out with panic.

A burst of gunfire hits the wall just above my head. I duck and return fire, missing my target but causing them to dive to the floor for cover. I run around the far wall, making my way back to the table from the other side. The two remaining guys have spread out around the room. The smoke's starting to clear thanks to the hole I've made in the skylight, and they're able to make out my position.

I can see one of them in front of me to the left, trying to stay close to Pellaggio. The other's moving away to the right, trying to outflank me. He needs to go first. Once he's out of the way, I'll only have one target to aim for because the last man is standing next to Pellaggio, so they'll be easy pickings.

I drop to my knee and fire. I hit the guy on the right in the leg and again in the chest. He crashes to the floor with a thud.

I quickly turn back around and walk slowly over to the table. An unearthly silence falls in the room, giving me goosebumps. The one remaining guy walks over to meet me, cutting me off from the table. Unfortunately, he chose to walk toward me, *then* lift his gun to shoot. I, on the other hand, have had my gun raised the whole time, so as soon as he moves, I fire once and put a bullet between his eyes. The squelch of the round penetrating his skull, pushing through his brain, and forcing its way out the other side of his head echoes as he falls backward to the floor.

And then there was one.

I stand next to Pellaggio, who's rooted to his chair. His knuckles are white as he grips the arms. He's looking up at me, eyes wide and mouth open—the look of a man who hasn't yet realized he's lost everything and is about to die. I lift my goggles up, revealing my face.

His eyes bulge with fear. "Oh my God! You're a goddamn monster! P-please, I'm begging you!"

I raise my gun and place it against his forehead. "What's the matter, Roberto? Where's your anger? Where's your big mafia boss speech where you call me *kid* and insult me?"

"I'm... I'm sorry, okay! Please, just don't kill me. I'll give you whatever you want!"

I find it surprising and maybe even a little disappointing how easily he begs for his life, considering everything that's happened before. But it's too late. He's made his choice, and now he has to live with the consequences of it for the rest of his life.

All thirty seconds of it.

"You're pathetic. I told you, and I told you, and I *fucking* told you to drop this. To leave me alone and forget about that land and your money. I warned you quite clearly that if you didn't, this is how it would end. But still you wouldn't let it go, would you? You stubborn, arrogant, deluded little prick! And now... now you've got nothing. In less than an hour, I've single-handedly destroyed your entire world."

"Adrian, please... I'll give you anything you want! You want payment for the Jackson hit? No problem. What was it —a hundred grand? Let's call it two hundred! Just please, don't kill me!"

"Holy shit... really? After all the grief you've given me, you're *now* going to offer to pay me? You can shove your money straight up your ass!"

Pellaggio sighs. I can see it in his eyes. He knows now that he's beaten. I just hope for his sake that he chooses to go out like a man.

"You should've made sure you killed me with that car bomb. Now it's time to reap what you sow, you piece of shit."

He frowns. "Wha-what are you talking about? I don't know anything about—"

I fire once just to the left of his head to silence him. I'm not in the mood to listen to anything else he has to say.

"You know what? I told you and Manhattan that you're the only two people I've ever warned more than once. That you're in an exclusive club. Well, even more exclusive than that is the group of people who have seen exactly *why* I'm known as Adrian Hell and lived to tell the tale. Want to know how many of *them* there are?"

He nods nervously.

I fire again, putting a bullet through his brain. The spray of blood from the exit wound hits the fire behind him, causing the flames to dance and hiss momentarily. His head snaps back, and his lifeless body slumps forward to the right. He falls off his chair and sprawls face-down on the floor at my feet.

I shake my head. "None."

And just like that, it's all over.

I let out a heavy sigh and walk over to a chair that someone had knocked over in the initial panic during my descent. I stand it upright and sit down, looking around me at the bodies and blood everywhere. The place looks like a battlefield.

I allow myself a couple minutes to calm down. My heart rate slowly returns to normal. There's a deathly silence around me as I look at the carnage I've caused.

Is there something wrong with me?

I mean, no normal human being should be capable of this much violence, surely? And I feel absolutely nothing. It's like there's a black hole inside me. I don't feel bad, guilty, or upset. If anything, I feel relief because I know that I'm in the clear and Pellaggio won't try to come after me.

I guess that's the thing, isn't it? After everything I've been through in my life, I'm *not* a normal human being. Not anymore. And if I'm being honest with myself, I like it. I've made a living out of embracing that fact and seeking comfort in it.

I'm Adrian Hell. This... *this* is what I do.

I take another deep breath and sit back, feeling the door close once again, trapping my Inner Satan behind it.

26

August 24, 2013 — 01:15 PDT

I left Pellaggio's estate as soon as I heard the sirens in the distance. I walked for an hour or so, clearing my head and relaxing myself, allowing the adrenaline to subside. I'd left all my equipment there, except my Berettas, obviously. It was all clean and untraceable, so I wasn't worried about them being found.

I did a quick sweep of the grounds to make sure there were no stragglers and to retrieve my Bluetooth earpiece, which was sadly broken beyond repair. I took it with me anyway. The less evidence I was ever there, the better. I'd taken off my black coveralls and ditched them in a trashcan a mile or so from the estate.

It feels like I've walked through most of Heaven's Valley, but I suppose I *am* taking the most indirect route I can find back to the bus terminal. I'm trying to clear my head, but there's something gnawing away at me. It's not really the lack of closure I feel having killed Pellaggio and all of his men. I've already dealt with how indifferent I feel toward that.

No, it's something else.

A sense of... I don't know—dissatisfaction? Restlessness, maybe?

I don't know what it is, but I know what's causing it.

Dark Rain.

Robert Clark said he's going to work with Josh and coordinate an assault on their base. I know Clara's doing some recon work to help out. I feel like I should be doing something too. Pellaggio was my personal battle, but Dark Rain is everyone's war.

I take out my phone and call Josh.

"Adrian!" He's shouting, and I'm not sure if it's from panic or excitement. "Where the hell have you been? What happened back there? Are you all right?"

I smile. "Hey, man. I'm all right. Don't worry. It's all over."

"I know. I watched via the satellite uplink. I've said it once, and I'll say it again—I'm glad you're on my side, Boss!"

"And I'm glad you're on mine."

We both laugh.

"So, how come you went dark?"

"I banged my head as I jumped up to the roof that second time. My earpiece fell out."

"Ah, fair enough. I'm just glad you're all right. Feels weird to admit this, but there was something almost magical about watching you on that satellite feed. Just seeing body after body drop and turn cold. Knowing it was just you and your guns. It was poetry in motion. You're one scary bastard, d'you know that?"

"I don't know about scary. I think it's more accurate to say I probably have some serious issues."

Josh laughs but doesn't disagree.

"Listen, I was thinking about Dark Rain…"

"I'm due to link up with GlobaTech in a few hours. They've scheduled their assault for later this morning. They have ground forces en route to the city as we speak. Air support is standing by."

"Sounds like you're all good to go. How are they managing to move so many armed troops in broad daylight on U.S. soil? Surely, it's not the most discreet thing to do. Hasn't anyone questioned it?"

"They're using the old *training exercise* line, which I suspect the media has grown accustomed to not questioning. Plus, they've got permission and support from the U.S. government, so they've got the freedom to do whatever they feel they need to."

"Unbelievable. I appreciate their help, but do you think it's wise granting a private contractor that much power?"

"I know what you mean, but right now isn't the time to ask questions like that. They're the only people who have fought on our side since you got there. You know what they say about a gift horse and its mouth."

"Fair enough, I guess. You heard anything from Clara yet?"

"Not a thing. She might just be having communication issues, though. We've found out Dark Rain has taken over a disused military base out in the desert, a few miles outside the city limits. The phone signal out there will be patchy at best."

"Do we know what this base is like?"

"The place is an abandoned military compound from what I've seen of it. It's got its own airstrip, hangars, bunkers —you name it. Not to mention access to an old under-ground lab. According to the intel that Jackson fed Clara and GlobaTech before he died, they have everything they need there, including a few thousand soldiers and enough weaponry to seize control of a small country. Although, there's been no movement in the last few hours. No sign of anyone, in fact."

"Huh, that's odd. What are GlobaTech bringing to the party?"

"Well, you saw the level of tech they're working with from the care package they gave you. They don't just provide private security—they also manufacture weapons for the military. Their R&D budget is frightening. They've got the manpower, all ex-military, highly trained in combat and used to conditions like desert warfare. They've been running contracts in Afghanistan for the past five years. The standard of operative is high. You're not going to want these guys coming after you."

I laugh. "Sounds like they have a new addition to their fan club as well."

"Hey, I'm just saying! These guys are the market leaders in every area. They're what everyone else tries to be, and you can see why."

"Might be an idea to stay friends with them, then, eh? You never know when we might need to call in a favor."

"Absolutely! So, what do you intend to do now?"

"I need to swing by the bus terminal and pick up my bag from the locker. Figure I'll get some rest, grab a bite when the sun comes up, then get a ticket for the next bus out of here. I might head north to Minnesota and lie low for a few days. Give you chance to finish up here before finding me another job."

"Sounds good. I'll give you a shout when the operation's underway."

"Thanks. And if you hear from Clara in the meantime, tell her to give me a call, okay?"

"I will." I can tell he's smiling, and I know why. "It's not like that, Josh."

"Whatever, man."

I hang up and walk on toward the city center. It's not long before I reach the bus terminal. The place is empty, despite being open twenty-four hours. I see an empty bench at one of the stands. I'm all alone and in no great hurry. I might as well get some rest here. I sit down, stretch my legs out, and cross my ankles. I clasp my hands together across my chest and close my eyes.

08:01 PDT

I snap awake at the sound of footsteps nearby. I immediately squint as the morning sun blinds me. I sit up straight, giving my eyes time to adjust. People around me are giving me strange looks. I guess I do kind of resemble a tramp, sleeping on a bench in a bus terminal.

Looking around, it's a lot busier now. Buses will have been running for a couple hours, and people are dashing around, going about their day without a care in the world.

I stand and walk over to the lockers, retrieve my bag, and sling it over my shoulder. I feel a twinge in my stomach and realize how hungry I am.

When was the last time I had something to eat?

Jesus... it was that cheeseburger about thirty-six hours ago!

After everything that's happened in the last few days, I'll be glad to get back to what resembles normality in my life— eating and sleeping at regular intervals and not worrying about so many people trying to kill me.

I walk for a good fifteen minutes and find a diner that's offering a full breakfast and a pot of coffee for eight dollars. At this stage, it isn't going to take much to entice me into somewhere for food, but that sounds like a good deal to me.

I go inside and sit in an empty booth in the far left corner, looking out at the rest of the diner. It's busy, going through the morning rush before everyone starts work. There are three waitresses working the floor and two more manning the counter. Guys are going back and forth through the doors leading to the kitchen, picking up the latest orders and leaving a plate of food behind for the previous ones.

Most seats and tables are occupied. The booths are pretty standard—red leather two-seaters, one either side of a table that stinks of disinfectant. There are bar stools lined up at counters on either side of the entrance that offer a view of the street outside while you're eating breakfast.

A waitress walks over after a couple of minutes, so I order the full breakfast and a pot of coffee—black, no sugar. The coffee appears a minute later, followed almost immediately by the first course—a stack of six pancakes with a small jar of maple syrup. I remember Josh telling me once about what British people refer to as a full breakfast, or a full English, as they call it. Along with the usual bacon and eggs, they have sausages, tomatoes, beans... and something called black pudding. He did tell me what it was, but I've forgotten. I don't recall it sounding all that appetizing. Give me a waffle, some bacon, sausage, and my eggs over easy any day of the week. And a pot of steaming hot black coffee, obviously.

You know what? When all this is over, I'm going to take Josh on vacation. Take him on a trip across the pond and see *his* homeland for a change. It must be years since he's been back there.

Not long after we first met, which seems a lifetime ago, I was briefly stationed over in the U.K. for a training exercise. He never used to shut up about all the ways he thought they did things better over there than we did here.

I smile in fond recollection at one night in particular, when Josh, a couple of the boys from our unit, and I went for a few drinks at a bar in London. It took maybe twenty minutes for us to get into a bar fight. Despite Josh being happy nowadays sitting behind a desk, playing with his computers, back then, you couldn't ask for a better man to back you up in a fight. But after the first few years running black ops, it became clear we functioned better as a unit under his guidance, so we agreed to take him out of the field and put him in charge of our operations center. We had a damn good run with him working the intel.

I refocus on my breakfast and tuck into the pancakes—which are excellent—and wash them down with coffee. I check my watch. Speaking of Josh, I imagine he'll be linking up with GlobaTech any time now, planning the attack. I still feel like I should be doing something to help. But at the same time, like Robert Clark said, I know I couldn't take on an army by myself. And GlobaTech won't need my help at this stage. Probably best to just leave it to them.

I find my mind wandering to Ketranovich and his psycho soldier, Natalia Salikov, thinking about how they're likely going to be dead in a few hours.

Serves them right.

I glance up at the TV on the wall opposite. It's showing the news. A woman in a red suit jacket and white blouse is sitting behind a desk, with a picture of a large house behind her. The headline at the bottom of the screen says MANSION MASSACRE. I raise an eyebrow.

A waitress walks past my table. I attract her attention and point to the TV. "Excuse me? Can you turn that up a bit, please?"

She smiles and kindly does so. The woman behind the desk is in the middle of her report.

"...in the early hours of this morning. It's been confirmed that the deceased include local businessman and suspected crime boss Roberto Pellaggio. His body, along with several others, was found inside the mansion. Police have no suspects at this time, but sources close to the investigation have said that, based on early forensic evidence and details found at the scene of the crime, it's thought the mass slaying was a mafia hit carried out by a team of professional killers. Detectives are waiting to question the one survivor of this horrific event, twenty-seven-year-old Daniel Pellaggio—Roberto Pellaggio's youngest son. He was found with bullet wounds in his leg and chest and is currently in critical condition. More on this story as it develops. In other news, a local man has found..."

Holy shit! Someone *survived*? That's unexpected. He's a lucky bastard. No doubt about that. I should probably go and kill him to tie up the loose ends.

But having said that, the hospital is going to be a media circus and impossible to get inside unseen. Plus, like the reporter just said, everyone thinks it was a team of killers. Even if the guy talks, he doesn't know what I look like, and no one will believe just one person did all that.

With Jimmy Manhattan in police custody for the foreseeable future as well, it's probably not worth worrying about. Pellaggio's business will have imploded within hours of me killing him, given I slaughtered most of the people involved in its day-to-day running.

No, it'll be fine. It's all over now.

The waitress comes over and takes my plate away, replacing it with a plate of bacon and eggs. She tops off my coffee and leaves me to enjoy the food. I figure I'll finish up here and head back to the bus terminal. I'll get a ticket for the next Greyhound out of here and head north.

I manage one mouthful of bacon before my phone rings. I look at the caller ID. It's Josh. I put the phone down on the table. I'll let it go through to voicemail. I need to eat.

It keeps ringing.

I look at it and sigh, slightly frustrated.

I'm trying to eat... but he never rings me unless he needs to.

I put my fork down and answer the phone. "Hey. I'm just eating breakfast. What's up?"

"Adrian, we have a serious problem."

I grimace at the words. I was *this* close. Josh does sound uncharacteristically flustered, though.

"What happened?"

"Okay, let me explain."

"Take your time."

He's worked up, which isn't like him at all. He's normally pretty calm, given how logical he is in his approach to, well, anything. He's borderline unflappable, so for him to get so stressed to the point where he can't even think straight enough to get his words out, it must be pretty bad.

But seriously, after this week, how bad can it really be?

"Right, so you know GlobaTech are planning a strike today, yeah?"

I finish chewing some bacon. "Yeah, you said so this morning, didn't you?"

"Yeah, well I'm working with their analysts right now. We've re-established an uplink and have access to the satellite imagery from the area for the first time. We've detected a massive heat signature coming from within the compound, somewhere underground. It wasn't there the last time they looked, which was yesterday. There's always a signal blackout for a few hours due to the satellite's orbit around Earth, but when it—"

"Josh, spare me the technicalities. Do they know what it is?"

"They've got a pretty good idea, yeah."

"So, what is it?"

"Adrian, by the looks of it, and judging by the size, the gut feeling here is that it's an armory of missiles."

I sit up straight and push my plate out in front of me, resting my left elbow on the table and my head in my left hand. "What kind of missiles, Josh?"

He doesn't say anything. Surely, he can't think...

"Nuclear?"

I hear Josh take a very deep breath.

"Jesus fucking Christ, Josh!" I'm trying to shout and whisper at the same time, given I'm in a crowded restaurant. "Are you saying Ketranovich has a fucking nuclear warhead?"

"It's the worst-case scenario, granted, but they're considering it a viable option."

I just *had* to say it, didn't I? *How bad can it really be?* For fuck's sake.

"How?"

"We don't know. Clark's on the line with the secretary of defense now, working on a strategy."

"I'm definitely on the first bus out of here. Josh, leave this to the military and get out now. You hear me?"

Another pause.

"Adrian, there's something else."

"Of course, there is. Please, enlighten me. Tell me how this ten-story clusterfuck can get any worse."

"I'm sending you a photo. The image was taken via satellite thirty minutes ago."

"Hang on."

I take the phone away from my ear and look at the screen. I click on the attachment as it arrives and open the image file. It's black and white and a little grainy—clearly edited to zoom in slightly, then cropped down. But it's still a good quality photo nonetheless, and the scene it depicts is unmistakable.

It's Clara. Her hands are behind her back, and she's got an armed man on either side of her, escorting her somewhere.

Dark Rain must've caught her, and now they're holding her captive in their compound.

I put the phone back to my ear but say nothing. I don't have any words. My mind feels numb, like it's racing to focus on a million different things but can't find any of them.

"Adrian, I'm sorry, man."

"We have to get her back."

"I've already told Clark about her. He says he's going to give the order for the ground forces to retrieve her if they can. But he warned me that the priority is neutralizing Ketranovich and seizing whatever weapons systems they have."

I bang my fist hard on the table, causing a few customers to turn and stare at me. "That's not good enough, Josh! We have to get her out of there!"

"Adrian, I know! I don't like this anymore than you do.

Okay, wait—I've got a call coming through from GlobaTech. Give me a minute, okay?"

He puts me on hold. I sit with the phone to my ear, staring into space. My appetite has disappeared, and my anger has returned with a vengeance. I take some deep breaths and close my eyes, trying to calm myself, but it's not working.

I can't believe Clara's been captured. Whatever happens next, she's as good as dead. There's no way someone like Ketranovich will allow her to live when he's branded her a traitor to his cause. He'll be looking to make an example out of her. I figure the way he sees it, he's close to victory. He'll parade her body in front of his troops to send a message. He's going to—

"Adrian, you still there?"

"Yeah, I'm here."

"We've got another problem."

"Josh, the novelty of you saying that is rapidly wearing off. Do you know that? What is it now?"

"That was Clark, confirming the new plan following his discussion with the secretary of defense. Schultz has been in a meeting with the president and the joint chiefs for the last hour, assessing the situation. They've just made their decision."

How the hell have I managed to stumble into something that the president's ended up getting stressed over? If anyone ever asks me to work in Nevada again, remind me to shoot myself.

Or them.

Yeah, I'll shoot them.

"Okay, so, what's the master plan?"

"The U.S. government is going to get involved but take a back seat and only offer military support to GlobaTech.

Given that GlobaTech already has a presence in the area and existing involvement in the situation, they're going to let them take point on the ground. However, to support them, they've ordered the U.S. Air Force to launch a pre-emptive airstrike within the hour. Three F-22s are going to take off from Holloman Air Force Base in New Mexico and carpet bomb the holy hell out of the entire compound. The intention is to bury whatever arsenal of missiles they have there and kill everyone before any kind of launch can be attempted."

"Christ! That's an aggressive play. They must be convinced the nuclear theory is a real threat. So, presumably, GlobaTech will then move in on the ground, storm through the front door, and clean up whatever's left?"

"Basically, yeah."

Which is all well and good, but...

"What about Clara? What's their stance on any civilian casualties?"

Josh sighs loudly. "Acceptable."

27

I drop a twenty on the table, pick up my bag, and leave the restaurant. I walk fast down the street and around the back of the building to the parking lot. Josh is still on the phone.

"Tell me where I can find Dark Rain's compound and the fastest route to get there."

"Adrian, I know exactly what you're thinking, and I'm not going to let you do it. It's suicide!"

"I'm not asking, Josh."

"And what are you going to do when you get there? Huh? You won't even get in the front gate before you're gunned down. I'm not sending you to your death, Adrian. I'm sorry. I understand how you feel. Believe me, I feel the same way. Clara's worked well with us, and I know you like her, despite your protests. But this is the U.S. government, okay? Those F-22 fighter jets are already being mobilized. In a little under an hour, they're gonna come screaming across the skies, sweep over that compound, and reduce the whole place to dust. It's a done deal. Game over, Adrian. Nothing positive will come from you going there all pissed off and guns blazing. I wanna get Clara back too, but we have to let GlobaTech handle that and hope that she survives the airstrike."

I'm silent for a moment, so I can compose myself before speaking again. I don't want to say the wrong thing.

"The address, Josh."

He sighs, no doubt realizing after years of experience that it's pointless arguing with me.

"Ah, bollocks. Fine! I'm texting you the details now. Should take you just over fifteen minutes from where you are in current traffic."

"Thank you."

"Adrian, try not to get yourself killed, all right? If you're not bothered about coming out of this in one piece, fine. But do it for me, okay?"

I hang up without replying and scan the parking lot. I quickly look over all the cars before resting my gaze on a black Audi, which looks reasonably new, durable, and most importantly, fast. I walk over to it, take out one of my Berettas, and use the butt to smash the driver's side window. I set the alarm off. I open the door and duck inside, place my bag on the passenger seat, and reach beneath the steering wheel. I pull the wires out and work quickly to stop the alarm and start the car.

Eleven seconds start to finish.

I close the door and drive off. The tires screech as the rear of the vehicle drifts out to the side from the reckless acceleration.

I'm driving as fast as I dare, weaving in and out of traffic. I have absolutely no plan. I've not got around to thinking past the anger yet. Ideally, I'm going to drive straight through the front gate and get out shooting, taking out every single one of the bastards until I find Clara.

That's what I *want* to do.

However, despite how I'm feeling, even *I* realize that if I actually do that, it's unlikely I'll make it within fifty feet of the front gate, let alone out of the car with a gun in my hand.

I'll think of something. I check my watch. I'm running out of time.

I turn onto the main highway and leave the city limits behind me. I follow it for a couple of miles until it meets the state road, then I head left, out toward the mountains that border Heaven's Valley to the West.

As I'm driving along the road, pushing ninety, I can't help but look around at the scenery—the mountain backdrop and the desert, stretching out to the horizon in all directions. Despite everything, I find myself smiling as I realize this is the same road I walked down when I first arrived here a few days ago. I marvel at the irony that things are seemingly going to end exactly where they started.

I just hope I'll be able to walk back down this road again someday...

I'm following the directions Josh texted me. After a few miles along the state road, there's a right turn leading down an unmarked dirt track. I make my way down it, feeling the suspension of the car wrestling with the uneven surface underneath. A couple of minutes later, I see a dusty, damaged signpost at the side of the track, attached to a telegraph pole. It says that there's a military-controlled testing site a mile ahead. Someone's spray painted *Welcome to Paradise* across it.

I carry on slowly for another minute before pulling over. It's probably best I make the final approach on foot to minimize visibility. No point in announcing my arrival any earlier than I need to.

Keeping low, I move cautiously in a wide arc to my left— the intention being to approach out of sight of any guard posts on the main gate.

I check my watch again. I reckon I've got maybe thirty-five minutes before the airstrike hits.

I make my way up a gentle incline and navigate a cluster of rocks before coming to the edge of a small rise. I crouch down and take a look around.

Laid out in front of me is the base. It's much bigger than I thought it'd be, sprawling out across the landscape behind a huge fence. I've brought the scope from my sniper rifle with me. I put it to my eye and adjust the focus, then scan the vast compound.

It's large and impressive, with a razor wire fence surrounding the perimeter. On either side of the main gates are two guard towers. From my position, I'm looking down at it from a slight angle. Behind the fencing is an array of buildings that vary in shape and size. There are barracks, a hangar, a vehicle depot, and a large concrete building with a huge metal door in the center of it.

I can also see a camouflaged tent at the far end of the compound, which has tarpaulin covering two large rectangular objects that look like massive boxes.

I study the entire area. I look over every inch twice. My spider sense is going haywire. Something definitely isn't right.

The place is deserted.

There are no vehicles parked anywhere. There are no soldiers stationed at any of the lookout posts. In fact, there's no troop movement within the grounds of any kind. You'd be forgiven for assuming that there would be at least *some* activity, given the fact they're meant to be a large militia planning an imminent attack on American soil.

I put my scope away and sigh with a mixture of confusion and concern.

Where the hell is everyone?

08:57 PDT

I scramble down the slope and land almost level with the corner of the fence. I crouch and look around, but I still can't see anyone. I slowly approach the main gate, instinctively reaching behind me and grabbing a Beretta.

Even though it's still early, the sun is blasting down at a ridiculous temperature. There's no shade out here—there aren't even any clouds. The sky is blue and clear, and on any other day, this place would look stunning. The western mountain range looms ominously in the distance. I look over to my right, away from the compound, and see the other range of mountains with a reservoir at the foot of it. But today, this place looks like a graveyard.

Hopefully, not mine.

The main gate is padlocked shut. I look through the fence, squinting in the sun's glare. The light breeze swirls dust and sand across the open yard. But there's still no sign of life.

If Josh's intel is correct—and there's no reason to think it wouldn't be—then somewhere underneath this base is an armory of missiles with suspected nuclear capabilities. Also, somewhere within this seemingly abandoned compound is Clara.

I take out my phone to call Josh, but there's no signal. I

remember him saying Clara likely would've had the same problem when she was out here earlier, which is why we never heard from her.

It looks like I'm on my own.

In the interest of saving time, I take aim and shoot the padlock off the gate. The sound of bullet on metal at close range pings loudly and echoes for miles around.

Well, if this place *isn't* deserted, they sure know I'm here now.

I unravel the chain and push open one of the gates, making my way inside. With gun in hand, I walk cautiously across the courtyard, constantly checking around in a full three-sixty, trying to cover every angle by myself. On my left is a large mess hall, with two even larger buildings on either side that both look like living quarters. Beyond them, at the far end, is a helipad, which is currently unoccupied.

To my right is a large garage with at least eight black Humvees parked inside that I can see, in two rows of four. Next to that is the large concrete structure with the metal door, which has a keypad just to the right of it. This must be the entrance to the underground labs where they're storing whatever missiles they have.

Next to that, farther along, is a large hangar. The doors are closed. There must be a runway of some kind leading out the other side. In the center of the courtyard is a flag-pole, but there's no banner flying.

I walk down to the far end, toward the camouflage tent. The two rectangles covered with tarpaulin are huge—easily twenty feet long and maybe ten feet high. I've no idea what they are, but they look out of place here and are clearly newer than the rest of the installation. I approach them and reach out to remove one of the tarpaulin sheets, curious to see what's underneath. Just as I grab the material, I hear a loud metallic bang off to my right, followed by a motor of some kind kicking in. I look over and see the hangar doors rolling open.

Shit!

I duck in the narrow gap between the two rectangles, just out of sight. My hand clenches tight around the butt of my Beretta. I peek around the corner and watch as the doors fully open. Five people emerge from within, walking purposefully in my direction.

Ketranovich is in the middle.

On either side of him are two soldiers, dressed in black and carrying AK-47s. On the far right is Natalia Salikov. On the far left is her brother, Gene. Both are armed.

Do they know I'm here?

I close my eyes and shake my head, cursing my own stupidity.

Of *course,* they know I'm here!

The question is what's going to happen next? Natalia's the wildcard. There's every chance she'll ignore any order given to her and start firing at me as soon as she lays eyes on me.

I quickly try to play out every possible outcome in my head to find something I can work with.

The group stops in a line, but Ketranovich takes a couple more paces toward me. "Adrian Hell!"

Well, it looks as if the outcome's just been decided for me.

His voice sounds louder than I remember, although the vast emptiness of the compound is probably emphasizing it. It also sounds angrier.

"We know you're there. Just come out and throw down your weapons. You will not be harmed. Well, not immediately!"

He laughs at his own sense of humor, prompting everyone else to laugh with him.

What a dick.

Only Natalia remains silent. She's looking at me like I've just killed her favorite puppy.

Well, things aren't going all that well so far…

I check my watch again. I've only got fifteen minutes left until the airstrike, and I don't fancy being here when that starts.

I've not got a choice.

I stand up and walk out from under the tent, my gun trained on Ketranovich. I hear the multiple crunching sounds as everyone else immediately cocks their rifles and takes aim at me. I keep one eye on Natalia the whole time.

"I'm here for Clara. Let her go and take me in her place."

He laughs. "You're as predictable as I thought."

I take a step forward. "If you've hurt her, I'll kill you."

"Now, now, Adrian Hell, there is no need for such hostility. Put your gun down, so we can talk properly, one soldier to another."

I shake my head. "Not happening."

Ketranovich regards me for a moment and smiles. He looks over at Gene Salikov and nods. Salikov turns and walks back into the hangar.

He looks back at me, still smiling. "I was hoping to avoid all this. We could've enjoyed the show together, like civilized people. But this… you made me do this, Adrian Hell."

I keep my gun trained on Ketranovich during the few moments of tense silence. My aim falters for a split-second when I see Salikov reappear from inside the hangar.

He's got Clara with him.

I squint in the bright, relentless sun to get a look at her. She seems unharmed but looks tired. Her arms are behind her back. Salikov's pushing her forward, holding her arm. They stop next to Ketranovich.

"Clara, are you okay? Are you hurt?"

She shakes her head. "Adrian! I'm fine. They've not hurt me, but you shouldn't have come. It's a trap!"

"Forget about all that. Clara, listen to me. We have to get out of here right now."

"And why's that?" Ketranovich interrupts. "What's your hurry?"

I check my watch. Ten minutes left. I sigh and shrug to myself. There's nothing to lose by being honest, is there?

"Because in just under ten minutes, three F-22 fighter jets are going to rain down fire from the sky and destroy every inch of this place."

Ketranovich looks at everyone and suddenly bursts out laughing. Again, everyone with him follows suit, including Natalia this time. I look at Clara, who's staring at the ground like she's ashamed.

I'm confused. Normally, the threat of being blown up doesn't prompt laughter and amusement.

Natalia places her gun on the ground and walks over toward me. I move my gun slightly, adjusting my aim to cover her. She's walking casually, almost sauntering, like she has all the time in world. She pauses momentarily in front of me and fixes me with a curious look that feels slightly flirtatious but mostly threatening. Then she walks on past me, toward the large, covered rectangles.

I sigh with frustration. I'm past the point where anything I do will impact the outcome of this situation, at least for now. I lower my gun and turn to see where she's going.

She stops in between the two large boxes and turns to face me. She smiles a smile of pure evil. And coming from me, that's bordering on complimentary...

She grabs both pieces of tarpaulin, one in each hand, and walks forward again, taking the covers with her in a wholly unnecessary, almost theatrical gesture. By the time she reaches where I'm standing, the boxes are completely uncovered. She drops the tarpaulin on the ground next to me and walks back over to stand with Ketranovich. She picks up her gun without giving me a second glance.

I'm genuinely stunned. I can feel my jaw physically drop open in surprise, but I've not got the awareness right now to close my mouth and stop myself from looking like an idiot.

Ketranovich is laughing arrogantly. "As you can see, Adrian Hell, your military does not concern me. In fact, I'm rather looking forward to their attempted intervention."

Underneath the tarpaulin, hidden from satellites by the camouflage tent, are two MIM-23 mobile surface-to-air missile launchers.

They're more commonly referred to as SAM sites. They're mobile launchers primarily used for defense against airstrikes. The MIM-23's payload is three mounted Hawk missiles, each around five meters in length and weighing a hundred and twenty pounds. They travel at two thousand meters per second, using radar-assisted tracking to target and destroy enemy aircraft up to sixteen miles away.

The airstrike isn't going to get anywhere near us.

Shit. I knew Dark Rain was well funded, but this kind of hardware is on a whole other level.

I turn to face Ketranovich. "You know about the airstrike…"

It's more of a statement than a question. I'm thinking out loud, piecing it all together, as the full gravity of the predicament I'm in begins to dawn on me.

He smiles back, smugly. "We got a lot of useful information from our Clara." He turns to her. "Didn't we, my dear?"

He grabs her chin between his thumb and index finger in a condescending gesture, like he's addressing a small child or a pet. She snatches her face away from him and spits at his feet.

He laughs and turns back to me. He holds his arms out to the side, gesturing to the entire compound. "We are Dark Rain, and soon the world will know what we're capable of."

I raise my gun again, aiming at him. "You're just like every other crazy ex-soldier with delusions of grandeur. You think you're the next big thing, that your idea of a new world order is so much better than the one the last fucking idiot thought of. But the truth of the matter is, you're nothing. And you'll never be more than that. You'll get squashed like everyone else does, and the world will go on having never heard of you. You'll die and take your hollow legacy with you."

"You have it all figured out, don't you, Adrian Hell? Well, you know nothing! You think you're this smart, unstoppable killer. But the truth is, *you're* just like everyone else. You're small, and you fight battles you have no hope of winning, fueled by nothing but pride and a misplaced sense of right and wrong. I know everything about you... your little computer friend... those cowardly, treacherous, backstabbing bastards at GlobaTech Industries... and your government, with all their plans for saving the day!"

He turns to Clara, who's still staring at the floor. He puts his hand on her arm and shoves her forward. As she stumbles front and center, she looks up at me. Her eyes are full of apology, full of regret. I feel so sorry for her. She wouldn't have had any choice but to tell them what she knows, and in a way, I'm glad she did. At least she spared herself any torture.

I look at her. "Clara, it's okay. As long as you're not hurt, that's all that matters, all right? But I need to know, how much did you tell them?"

She takes a deep breath.

She moves her arms from behind her to her sides.

Huh? I thought she was tied up?

There's a gun in her right hand. She raises it slowly and takes aim at me.

I don't... I don't understand what's happening...

None of this is making any sense.

I look into her eyes, searching for answers, but I see a void—a black hole where humanity had once been. A smile creeps across her face. I just saw the same smile on Natalia's face a moment ago.

She says something to me in Russian. I don't know what it was, but it sounded derogatory and insulting. Her voice sounds more Russian than it had previously too. More full of hatred.

I frown and shake my head.

I don't understand.

Clara laughs. "I told them *everything*."

28

I feel like someone's punched me in the stomach.

I'm genuinely speechless. And that *never* happens to me. Ask Josh. I have an answer for everything. But not right now. Even after the mother of all shitty weeks, which left me feeling incapable of experiencing shock ever again, this is one helluva curveball.

My head's spinning, and I feel sick. My body gives up, and I drop my gun, sinking to my knees. I'm unable to take my eyes off Clara, much in the way you can't drive past a car crash without slowing down to look at the carnage with sick fascination.

I stare at the ground, unblinking, shocked. "I... I don't understand. I don't... I just... What the fuck is going on?"

Clara walks slowly over to me. "Poor Adrian. Finally lost for words?"

Behind her, Ketranovich and the Salikovs start laughing. She stops next to me and places her gun against my head, unwavering in her hand. I look up at her. My eyes flick between the barrel of her gun and her venomous green eyes. I have no words.

She practically snarls at me. "This has been the *longest* week of my life! Having to listen to you go *on* and *on* with yourself. Watching you skate around what's going on right in front of you, too stupid to figure anything out yourself. I almost *wanted* you to work out our plans sooner—at least then I'd have an ounce of respect for you as I watch you die."

I can't honestly describe how I feel right now.

Heartbroken? Maybe.

Betrayed? Definitely.

An idiot? Arguably.

My mind's working overtime, not just playing out every outcome ahead of me, but also piecing together everything that's led me to this moment.

Clara's been playing me right from the start... That much is now clear. But how? And why? I grimace at my own ignorance. I hate not knowing everything.

I see her watching me struggle to put it all together in my head.

She laughs condescendingly. "Get up, you pathetic little man. The *mighty* Adrian Hell, helpless in front of me."

I slowly get to my feet and brush the dust off my knees. I bend down to retrieve my gun, but I don't get chance to pick it up.

"Ah, ah, ah. Don't even think about it, asshole. In fact, you can toss the other one down as well."

I don't move.

She takes a step closer, re-emphasizing the gun she has pointed at my head. "Now."

I sigh and reach behind me to un-holster my other Beretta. I look at it in my hand for a moment. I reckon I could get three shots off before she fires. I wouldn't be able to move as accuracy would be the priority, so it's almost certain that she'll shoot me. But... I could put one between her eyes and two in Ketranovich before I hit the ground. That would be enough.

But what use am I dead? The Salikovs could potentially carry out their endgame on their own, in which case I'll have died for nothing.

Fuck.

I'm not happy.

I throw it to the ground, and it lands next to its counterpart.

We stand in silence for a moment, regarding one another. Her eyes show no sign of the person I believed I knew pretty well only a few hours ago. A gust of wind picks up and swirls dust around us. It feels like there's nothing except her and me. My gaze shifts from her eyes to her gun, then back again. My anger is rising quickly, bubbling away at the surface.

When I look back on this in years to come, I'll know it was this moment right here, right now, when I decided Clara was going to die. She was going to suffer, and she was going to know that death would be a welcome, sweet reprieve compared to the pain I'd make her experience.

She pushes the gun against the side of my head. "Walk."

We make our way over to Ketranovich, who's smiling from ear to ear. A smug look of triumph on his face that says he knew all along it would end like this, and I was a fool for not realizing it.

Maybe he's right.

Bastard.

He turns and nods to Salikov, who runs over to the MIM-23s and starts the activation process. The loud whirring of machinery sounds throughout the deserted compound as the SAM sites configure themselves and move into position, preparing to take aim.

The airstrike will be close. The squadron of jets will be zooming toward us right now at nearly sixteen hundred miles per hour, which means in less than ten minutes, those F-22s will be going down in flames. I have to find a way of warning Josh. But as things stand, like Clara pointed out, I'm helpless.

I look at Ketranovich. "How are your SAM sites going to target the F-22s? They're stealth fighters."

He chuckles. "Adrian Hell, you worry too much and know too little. Our low-frequency radar easily bypasses the stealth capabilities of your fighter jets. Now come—we have much to discuss and such little time."

He laughs out loud at nothing in particular and walks off toward the concrete bunker with the metal door. Natalia turns to follow him but stops in her tracks. She looks back at me, then turns and walks toward me. She stops mere inches from me, fixing me with her trademark evil death gaze of hatred and contempt. I figure I should say something to antagonize her. Something to—

Ah!

Shit!

She just planted a straight right fist squarely on my jaw. She's only a slight little thing, but she has some force behind her punches! Fuck! I rock backward, momentarily losing my balance and eventually dropping to one knee. I shake my head in an effort to clear the cobwebs and look up at her. She has a wicked smile on her face. She holds my gaze for a moment longer, then turns back and follows Ketranovich.

I stand up and look at Clara. "So, everything was a lie? You were playing me from day one?"

She smiles and shrugs dismissively. "Don't take it too personally. You're not the first person I've manipulated, and you won't be the last. Everything was going exactly to plan until that idiot Pellaggio brought you in to kill Jackson. Once we knew of your involvement, our plans had to change drastically. We needed to keep a close eye on you, so you didn't screw things up any more than you already had."

She prods me in the back with her gun, and we both set off after the others. I can still hear Salikov behind me, fiddling with the controls for the SAM sites.

I sigh. I've been played. Spectacularly. I'm angry with myself for not realizing it earlier. I should've spotted it days ago, but my emotions blinded me. Something I've spent half my life training not to do...

Goddammit!

I push those thoughts out of my head. The only thing that matters now is stopping Dark Rain from doing whatever they're planning to do. Then I'll look at getting my revenge.

We enter the main bunker. Inside is a large, open-plan maze of walkways and pipe work and containers, all dimly lit by the lights overhead. Ahead of us is a narrow metal stairwell that descends down into the bowels of the bunker. We walk down six flights of stairs before emerging into a long, much brighter corridor. The walls are old brick, mottled with damp patches—the result of years of neglect. Cobwebs and piping line the top of the walls, running up to the ceiling. Fluorescent lights hang from rusted fittings, flickering and buzzing all the way along.

At the far end is a set of doors, which look a lot newer than their surroundings. Ketranovich and Natalia have just gone through them as Clara and I approach.

I glance over my shoulder. "So, is this your little command center?"

She smirks. "You'll see."

With her gun in my back, I push open the doors and walk into a large, circular room full of computers and large monitors. It seems to act as a hub for the entire underground facility. There are three doors leading off to other rooms—one across from where I'm standing and one on either side, like points on a compass.

There are two men sitting at a bank of computers in the middle of the room, typing feverishly on their keyboards. Ketranovich is standing over one of them, looking at his screen. Natalia is a short distance away, staring daggers at me.

Or is she staring at Clara?

Hmmm, I can't be sure, but it looked for a brief moment like she flicked her evil gaze over to Clara...

Interesting. And duly noted.

Ketranovich looks over at me as I enter and gestures to the large, empty room. "Welcome to Dark Rain, Adrian Hell."

I gaze around. "Ooh, I'm impressed."

Josh would be proud of my sarcasm skills.

Ow!

Clara just hit me on the back of my head with her elbow. It wasn't too hard—just a little tap to get me to shut up, I think.

Ketranovich smiles humorlessly. "Everything will soon become painfully clear."

He turns back to the two men at the computers and starts chattering away to them in Russian.

I turn to face Clara. "Okay, so, forgive me if this is a

stupid question, but where is everyone? I thought you guys numbered in the thousands?"

She smiles like she knows something I don't and want to rub my face in it. "Patience, Adrian. All shall be revealed."

I *really* don't like not knowing what's going on, and this entire situation is getting weirder by the second. I also don't like being helpless, and right now I can't do anything besides stand with my thumb up my ass and watch as three fighter jets are about to get blown to pieces.

Behind me, the doors open. Salikov walks in and heads straight over to Ketranovich. He whispers something to him, and the colonel smiles. "Excellent news! You have done well, comrade." He turns to me. "We are ready."

He gestures to a huge monitor on the right-hand wall. It suddenly flickers to life, revealing a radar screen and a topographical view of the compound and surrounding area.

"As you can see, we've just picked up your F-22s on radar, about twenty-five miles away. As you know, they're on their way here to drop many bombs on us, to wipe the nasty terrorists off the face of the earth!"

He bursts out laughing, prompting Clara and the Salikovs to do the same.

My God, this is excruciating! Not just because of how smug these Russian bastards are but because they're forcing me to watch innocent soldiers die in someone else's war.

One of the men looks up at Ketranovich. "Sir, missiles are primed and ready for launch. Targets will be in range in thirty seconds."

I turn to Clara. "How did you even know about the airstrike?"

She shrugs. "I spoke to Robert Clark just before he spoke to your annoying British friend. He told me."

I shake my head in disbelief. She managed to get

everyone believing she wasn't a deceptive piece of shit, not just me. That's a small comfort, I guess.

"Arm the SAMs," booms Ketranovich. "Let the American death machines work their ironic magic!"

The other man taps away on his keyboard for a moment. "Missiles armed and locking on, sir. Firing in ten seconds."

I instinctively move to take a step toward them, but I feel the barrel of Clara's gun on the back of my head, and I restrain myself. I raise my hands slightly in frustrated resignation.

I look up as I hear the faint *whoosh* of the first Hawk missile launching, quickly followed by the second and third.

Shit, I'm too late!

On the radar screen, I see the small red objects on the left gradually approaching the three small green images of aircraft coming over from the right.

I feel the anger rising inside me. "You bastards! Call them off!"

Ketranovich shakes his head. "Don't you see, Adrian Hell? You caused this! Those men will die in flames because of *you*!"

I stand paralyzed by anger, watching the screen as the missiles creep on toward the F-22s—closer and closer with each blip of the radar.

I have to do something. But what? They've got me at gunpoint, trapped underground, fifteen miles away with no means of communication. I'm desperate, and I hate myself for resorting to begging, but I have no other choice.

"Please, just call off the missiles! If you're pissed at me, take it out on *me*. Don't kill innocent people just to prove a point!"

I've never wanted anything more in my life than I want those missiles to explode right now, sparing the lives of the pilots of those fighter jets. I stare at the screen, horrified and seething at my own uselessness. The methodical beeps of the images on the radar sound out in the deathly silence.

Beep...

Beep...

Beep...

The images collide, and the screen is empty once more.

Silence descends on the large room. I hold my breath as I stare at the blank screen, overcome with emotion.

Suddenly, the Salikovs cheer loudly and touch foreheads in celebration. Ketranovich smiles at Clara, who looks both relieved and satisfied.

I'm desperately trying to think of a way out of here, so I can warn Josh, but I've got nothing.

I keep staring at the large screen, willing the blips of the aircraft to re-appear. But they don't. I look over at Ketranovich, who's smiling at me, seemingly savoring my torment.

He pulls a gun from behind him, takes a step away from the men at the computers, and fires twice, putting a bullet in the back of their heads.

I shout out in surprise. "What the hell are you doing? Are you insane?"

He shrugs casually. "They've served their purpose, Adrian Hell. As have you."

He nods at Clara behind me.

I frown. "What the—"

29

Ah, shit.

I open my eyes, which sends a stabbing pain coursing through the base of my skull. I roll my head slowly around in circles to loosen some of the tension in my head and neck.

I'm sitting on the floor, leaning against the wall in a dark room. The first thing I notice is how hot it is. I'm soaked in sweat. I blink rapidly, trying to adjust to the gloom, but it's too dark to make anything out clearly. I don't know where I am, but it feels like I'm sitting in a goddamn oven.

I try to move, but my arms are tied behind my back. My legs are free, but I don't want to move around too much in the dark without first knowing where I am and who, if anyone, is nearby.

I slowly start to regain my senses. I move my limbs and quickly assess whether I'm injured. Aside from the pre-existing pain in my chest and head, I think I'm intact.

I frown as an eye-watering stench hits my nostrils. What the hell is *that*? It smells like dead animals.

I see an eerie orange glow coming from something in front of me. I squint and can just about make out a large shape ahead of me. It's huge—easily three meters across, leaving a gap of about two meters at either side to walk around. That means the room itself is about seven meters across... maybe the same lengthways.

I struggle to my feet and stagger around to my left. The farther around I get, the hotter it becomes, to the point where the heat is making it hard to breathe. The room is a large square with a smaller square in the middle, which seems to be giving off the heat. I turn right at the end and notice a door on the left wall. I see the orange glow intensify and realize that the huge square in the center of the room is actually an enormous furnace.

Christ!

Well, that explains the heat. It's almost unbearable standing this close to it.

I hear keys in the lock outside, so I back away around the corner and sit back down against the wall. The door opens, and Natalia walks in with another soldier dressed in black. They're dragging with them the bodies of the two men Ketranovich shot in the control room. They drop the corpses and work together to pick up one at a time and throw them in the furnace, like they're disposing of trash at the city dump.

Natalia turns toward me. Her face is illuminated from the right-hand side by the hellish blaze of the fire, giving her evil smile an almost supernatural appearance. She winks at me, then in the blink of an eye, she turns, draws a gun from the holster on her right thigh, and shoots the man she came in with in the side of the head. A brief cloud of blood appears in the air, lingering for a moment like mist before dripping to the floor.

The gunshot startles me. "Jesus! What is it with you people killing each other?"

She says something in Russian that I assume, judging by the tone of her voice, is derogatory. Then she walks out, slamming the door behind her. I hear her locking it from the outside.

What the hell is going on?

It seems that everyone who works for Dark Rain is expendable. The airstrike has failed dramatically, which I can only assume will force GlobaTech to bring forward their ground assault.

I have to admit, Dark Rain's countermeasures for the aerial assault completely surprised me. They clearly spent their funding wisely, prior to having their allowance cut off. But I can't see how they'd survive a ground attack. They keep killing their own troops, for God's sake! What's their next move?

I hear the door unlock again, and a moment later, it opens. This time, Clara walks in and points her gun at me. "Get up."

I raise an eyebrow. "What, no foreplay?"

She takes a step forward, smiling, bringing the gun closer to me. "Give me a reason, Adrian. Please."

I look at the gun, then at her. Hmmm... maybe right now isn't the best time to antagonize her.

Without another word, I stand up, never taking my eyes off her. She gestures toward the door with her head, signaling for me to walk out in front of her. I do so without further comment.

As I step outside, I immediately feel the welcoming cool breeze of the air conditioning unit. I stand, look up to the ceiling, and close my eyes, letting the refreshingly cool air hit my face.

I look around and see I'm in a mid-sized circular room with a metal grid floor and old brick walls. Ahead of me is a long corridor, leading into another room at the end. There are two more doors on either side of me, similar to the one I've just walked through and presumably containing the same sort of massive furnace that my room does. There's nothing else but the buzz of the fluorescent lights overhead.

The doors at the end of the corridor slide open, and Ketranovich walks through. He strides toward me with an almost arrogant swagger.

I watch him approach. He stops a few paces away from me. "Your guest quarters suck."

He shrugs. "Typically, our guests do not remain here long, Adrian Hell. The quality of where they stay does not concern me."

"Fair enough. So, when are you gonna tell me what the hell's going on?"

He steps closer to me. Clara's behind me to my left. My hands are still tied behind my back.

He smiles. "What do you want to know?"

"Where are your nukes?"

He looks at Clara, then back at me, seemingly confused. Then he laughs out loud and pats my shoulder like we're old friends sharing a joke.

I frown. "Okay, what have I missed?"

He chuckles. "Adrian, there are no nukes."

"What? But GlobaTech said they've detected a massive underground heat signature that they think is..."

I trail off, frowning as more pieces of the puzzle fall painfully into place.

I look around. Five rooms. Five humongous, three-meter-square furnaces on full blast. That's what the heat signature was!

"Holy shit. You've laid a trap for GlobaTech, and they're going to send their troops to walk right into it..."

Clara slaps the back of my head almost playfully. "Finally, he starts to use his brain."

"But I don't understand what you're going to do to them when you've lured them all here. There's what? Four of you now? GlobaTech are going to roll up to your front door with a few hundred heavily armed soldiers from their own private army."

Ketranovich walks past me, then turns and gestures for me to follow him back into the room I woke up in. "This entire compound is a network of underground chambers. Think of this place as a wheel. The control room back there is the center, and each spoke that branches off it brings you to its own little hub, like this one. Right now we're directly under the main yard of the compound. There are five mega-furnaces here, originally used to dispose of chemical weapons in the fifties and sixties. Your government says they never existed; they used them for trials and tests that they say never took place."

"Hey, *I'm* not responsible for what the government did or didn't do fifty years ago, all right? Don't take your little temper tantrum out on me."

"Whatever. The point is, when GlobaTech turned its back on us after your intervention, denying us access to the uranium we had planned on using, we had to quickly change our plans. Instead of launching an attack on America, we had to start off with something... slightly smaller."

He points to the ceiling. I look up, struggling to make out what he's looking at in the gloom. It takes a moment for my eyes to adjust, but I eventually see it...

Stuck to almost every inch of the ceiling is enough C4 explosive to blast the world out of its orbit.

My voice is shocked to little more than a whisper. "Fuck me..."

I'm struggling to get my head around seeing *this* much explosive in one place. There has to be close to a hundred bricks of C4, all with detonators in them, attached to the ceiling. If the furnace room is directly under the main courtyard, the explosion would blast up and through the ground, causing the compound to sink in on itself.

I suddenly see what he's planning. I look over my shoulder at the other doors, then back at Ketranovich.

He smiles, seeing me reach the frightening conclusion. "Yes, Adrian Hell. All the other furnace rooms are exactly the same."

"Holy shit!"

They're going to lure all the GlobaTech soldiers into the compound and then blow it to hell. The explosion will be catastrophic. The entire area for miles will become a crater, taking out a large chunk of both GlobaTech's and the U.S. military's forces in the process.

I shake my head with disbelief. "You're insane."

He laughs. "Sanity is simply a matter of opinion."

I turn and walk out of the furnace room, back into the cooler central hub. I turn to face them both and look at Clara. "So, where do you fit in, then? You were being shot at just as much as me."

"No one in our organization knew about my role in this except the colonel. I told you that he only tells people what they need to know. Loyalty and trust have been issues for us in the past, which is why we like to keep our numbers small."

"But I thought there were thousands of you?"

She smiles. "And who told you that?"

"Ted Jackson, and then you..."

I trail off again as I realize she clearly lied from the beginning about something else too.

She's practically gloating. "We told GlobaTech what they needed to hear to secure the deal for the uranium. A bit of inventive marketing goes a long way."

"Unbelievable. Jackson had no idea you were playing him?"

"Of course not! He was an idiot, blinded by his own greed. He would've believed anything if he thought he could get rich from it."

"I still don't get why Natalia was shooting at you..."

"I recognized you when I saw you tailing us days ago. I knew about the Pellaggio deal that Jackson had recently cancelled, so I put two and two together and figured you were in town to take him out. When you knocked on our hotel room door, I just let you and Jackson form your own conclusions and leapt on the opportunity to play the victim. I spoke to the colonel, who agreed we would play it out in secret to keep up appearances with you. It was difficult fighting against Natalia but necessary."

I shake my head. Unbelievable. "You guys are ruthless bastards. I'll give you that."

"Once GlobaTech turned their backs on us and you gave up the deeds to the uranium mine, we had to change our plans and simply go after the people who screwed us. It was easy cleaning up after we'd abandoned our original plan. I was able to take out the soldiers we no longer needed when Natalia found us in the bar. I got you to take out Marcus Jones, and I was able to get rid of Webster moments before you arrived at the safe house."

"Wait, *you* killed Webster?"

"Yes. The men at the safe house had passed the time torturing him once they'd learned he was no longer necessary. I went there to clean up. Again, you helped me with that. I was just about able to shoot him before you walked in, assuming I was the victim, as always."

I start pacing back and forth, trying to process the fact that everything I've gone through in the past few days has been a lie. I stop and look at Clara and Ketranovich, who has moved to stand next to her.

"You've been using me to clear up your mess and position everything to exact your revenge on GlobaTech this whole time?"

Ketranovich claps slowly. "And you played your part beautifully. Once everything was in order, we tried to kill you, but you somehow managed to survive the blast."

I frown. Damn it! "The car bomb... that was *you*?"

I remember when I was face-to-face with Pellaggio. Right before I killed him, he began to say something. It didn't register until just now, but he must've been trying to say he didn't know anything about the car bomb.

"Yes, but you assumed it was the mafia man, so we let you run with that idea, and it led to you wiping out his entire empire!" He pauses to laugh. "Very impressive, by the way. I've been saying it since the first time we met—we could use a man like you in our cause."

I stare at him, feeling the anger and the hatred boiling to the surface. "That's nothing compared to what I'm gonna do to you." I turn to Clara. "Both of you."

"I'm afraid you won't have chance to try, Adrian Hell. The next stage of our plan is beginning now, and soon you will be nothing but a stain on the graveyard that will replace Nevada."

I have one last card to play to buy me some time. And it's

a long shot. I look at Clara again. "And what did Natalia think of this master plan? I'm assuming she was kept in the dark as much as everyone else?"

She shrugs. "Of course. I'm the only one who knew what the big picture was. Our colonel keeps his plans to himself, remember?"

"Are you sure she's okay with not being the number one girl around here?"

Ketranovich brushes a piece of hair from Clara's face before kissing her on both cheeks. He turns to me. "Natalia is one of my finest soldiers. But who else could I trust with such a delicate plan, if not my own daughter?"

Ha!

Do you know what? I'm not even remotely surprised...

I obviously had no idea Clara is Ketranovich's daughter, but at this stage, nothing else can shock me.

"Your daughter? Of course, she is..."

Ketranovich smiles and turns back to Clara. "We must begin the next phase of the plan. See that our guest is comfortable, then join me in the control room."

She nods. "Yes, sir."

He gives me one last look before walking off back down the long corridor.

I turn to her. "*Yes, sir.* You make me sick."

"And soon I'll make you dead."

She looks past me, toward the long corridor. I turn to follow her gaze and see Natalia walking toward us. She has a pistol in one hand and a knife in the other. And she looks massively pissed off.

Well... *this* isn't going to end well, is it?

Clara signals to the furnace room with her gun as Natalia approaches. "Get in."

I walk in and turn right. The intense heat hits me instantly. The two of them follow me inside.

I suppose this would be the moment where she aims her gun at the back of my head and pulls the trigger. Game over.

Well, I have no intention of dying in this furnace.

I turn around to face Clara. The darkness closes in around us, broken only by the orange glow from the fire behind her. It gives her a demonic aura, making her look all the more monstrous.

Natalia walks in and stands next to her. She turns to Clara and says something in Russian. Clara responds and then turns to me, giving me a mischievous smile. "Have fun, you two!"

I smile. "I'm sure we will. She's gotta be more entertaining than you were."

Clara rolls her eyes at my apparently wasted attempt at a hateful remark and walks out of the room, closing the door behind her.

I watch her go, then turn to Natalia. "So... how are you?"

Like lightning, she raises her gun and aims directly between my eyes.

Shit, that was fast!

Small talk clearly isn't going to help. Time to try plan B.

"Okay. Do you speak any English?"

No response.

"Y'know, you strike me as someone who has some unaddressed anger issues. Would that be a fair assessment?"

Lowering the gun slightly, she swings a left hook from her hip and connects with the side of my face. I see it coming a mile away, but with my hands behind my back, there's little I can do to avoid it.

Ah!

Goddammit! That hurt!

But at least I know she can understand me.

"I'm gonna take that as a yes. Ketranovich was complimentary about your abilities as a soldier. A person could be forgiven for thinking you were his favorite, the way he was talking."

She pauses momentarily, presumably to think about what I'm saying, then throws another left hook.

Ah, shit!

Yeah, that one's going to swell up like a bitch...

I haven't really thought this through, have I?

Well, too late now to worry about minor details like a few bruises.

"I only mention it because, as a fellow soldier, I thought it was strange he would choose Clara instead of you for the mission to manipulate me..."

She goes to hit me a third time, but I back away slightly, causing her to hold back and look at me quizzically.

"I'm just saying. I mean, I was close to her all this time. She didn't strike me as being capable in the field. She was almost weak when it came down to it. Whereas you, Natalia, are a stone-cold professional. No hesitation, no doubt—you just carry out your orders with lethal efficiency. Not to mention, better-looking. If I were Ketranovich, there's no way I'd have cut you out of my plans like he did."

It looks like she's going to swing for me again, but instead, she steps in closer, lowering her gun more. She's no more than a foot away from me. In the poor light of the furnace room, this is the first time I've been able to properly see her eyes. They burn brighter than any fire could ever hope to. The anger that lies just beneath the surface is palpable. I keep my demons locked behind a big door. By comparison, I think little Natalia here keeps hers stored in a wet paper bag...

"I am twice the woman *she* is." She spits out the words in a strong Russian accent. "I would never have let you get away with what you have."

For a moment, I see a flash of that anger surface. I'll be honest—it genuinely worries me. Given my hands are still tied behind my back, I absolutely believe that, right now, she's close to and capable of killing me.

Which is all the incentive I need.

Do you know what the best thing about a headbutt is? No one ever expects them. More often than not, you hurt yourself more than the person you're hitting, so it's just assumed that nobody will ever bother to try one. But if you do it right, they're lethal.

I stand up straight and bring my head back slightly, then lurch my shoulders and neck forward, relaxing so that my skull becomes like a dead weight. Natalia's smaller than me, so I have to aim it right to compensate for the height difference. As my forehead comes arching down, I bend my knees slightly and connect with the bridge of the nose, right between the eyes.

I hear the bone shatter and feel the warm blood spray across my face. Her entire body visibly stiffens as consciousness leaves her, and she falls to the floor, rigid. As she lands, I hear her head crack against the concrete. She's down for the count.

Straight away, I crouch beside her, turning my body slightly so that I can reach her knife with my hands, which are still bound behind me. I get it and adjust it in my grip, so it's at the right angle to slice through the ties around my wrists.

I make short work of it and bring my hands up, rubbing each wrist in turn, trying to stimulate the blood flow once again. I stretch my arms and shoulders, feeling them crack. I pick up her gun and pocket the knife. I stand and look down at her, unconscious at my feet.

It would be so simple to just put a bullet in her head and move on. But after what these bastards have put me through, she deserves to suffer—at least a little bit.

I take aim and shoot her in her right kneecap. Her leg almost blows apart, and her body jolts violently as she flashes in and out of consciousness. Blood pools around her, as she lies motionless once again.

"See you in hell, bitch."

I leave the room, locking the door behind me.

When this place goes up in flames, it'll be taking her with it.

30

With Natalia out of the picture, I've just got Gene, Ketranovich, and Clara left to take care of. I'm not too worried about bumping into any other personnel, given everyone seems to be murdered the moment they've served their purpose. If there *is* anyone else left, I'll simply recommend they walk away while they still have the chance.

Armed with Natalia's gun and knife, I make my way down the long corridor, away from the furnace rooms and back toward the main control center. My priority is contacting Josh to warn him about the trap waiting for all the GlobaTech and U.S troops.

As I approach, I drop to one knee and sneak a peek through the window of the left-hand door. The room looks empty. The large screen that displayed the radar battle between missile and plane is off. The main computer hub isn't manned.

I nudge the door gently and wait to see if it provokes a

reaction. I wait a minute but get nothing. Happy the coast is clear, I stand and walk into the control room.

God knows where those three are or what they're doing...

I'll deal with them later. I run over to the control panel and look for a means of communication. There are consoles and screens everywhere but nothing that resembles a phone. I look around the room in desperation, but I can't see anything. I check my phone again, and there's still no signal.

Damn it!

If Josh were here, he'd have sorted this by now.

I glance around again one last time. In the corner along the north wall, I notice something flashing on one of the screens. Clutching at straws, I head over and look at the computer terminal. It looks like a communications system of some kind. The screen says satellites are offline and that there's an active signal emanating from the compound.

That must be why there's no cell phone signal in the area—they're manually jamming it!

I look around the room at all the doors to make sure I'm still alone before I sit at the console. I'm not a complete beginner with computers, but I'm not Josh either. I click through the various menus, and after a couple of minutes and a bit of luck, I manage to find a way of disabling the jamming signal. I check my phone and see that it's re-established contact with the cell phone network. I'm getting a signal again.

Jackpot!

I quickly call Josh.

He answers before it's barely had chance to ring. "Adrian! Where the hell have you been? It's all gone to shit up here!"

"I don't have time to explain right now. Just listen to me.

We've been played from day one. This whole thing is a set-up for GlobaTech, and we're playing right into their hands."

"Yeah, we figured something was up when the airstrike failed. What the hell happened?"

"They had SAM sites armed with Hawk missiles."

"Jesus! Where did they get that kind of hardware?"

"I'm guessing with the funds they got from GlobaTech before Clark cut off their allowance."

"But how did they know about it in the first place?"

I pause and take a deep breath, knowing that saying it out loud for the first time is going to hurt. "It was Clara. She's been with Dark Rain this whole time."

Josh falls silent. I make a note of the time and date. This doesn't happen often.

"Well... what a fucking bitch!"

"My thoughts exactly. But listen, you *have* to get Globa-Tech to call off the ground assault. If they come in here, they're all going to die!"

"No can do, Boss. It's already underway. In addition to Clark's little army, Secretary Schultz has brought in more official troop support too. Because the assault on the F-22s took place on U.S. soil, it's being treated as an act of domestic terrorism. Gives them just cause to intervene and make this more than just a private matter."

"Shit. How many soldiers?"

"Almost three hundred, plus another hundred and fifty GlobaTech operatives backing them up."

"Holy mother of God..."

"What?"

"Josh, they don't have any nukes here. They don't have missiles of any kind. They don't even have any soldiers. Everything you know about Dark Rain is a lie. It's just Ketranovich, Clara, and the Salikov twins. Everyone else, they kill after they've served their purpose."

"So, what exactly *do* they have, besides themselves?"

"What they have are five rooms, each of which contains a furnace the size of a house, which were apparently used for disposing of chemical weapons fifty years ago. Each room also has about three hundred pounds of C4 attached to the ceiling. The section of the compound that's rigged is directly under the main yard. You can probably see where this is going..."

"Christ almighty!"

"I know!"

He starts thinking out loud, piecing things together as I did earlier. I let him come to it on his own.

"Blowing the entire compound like that would leave a crater a mile wide and eviscerate everyone who was in the area—no question! But when it was just GlobaTech troops, it would all be looked at as a minor conflict that could be explained away by the media spin-doctors with no problems. But if the U.S. Army is sending men in and *they* die, then we have a much a bigger problem than that. Adrian, this could cause a war!"

"You need to do something—anything. Just stop them coming in here, Josh. Whatever it takes."

"I'll get on the line to Clark right away."

As he says that, the main entrance door opens. Gene Salikov walks in.

I turn and our eyes meet. He stops in his tracks, clearly confused. I can see him working it all out in his head. His sister, Natalia, was sent to kill me, yet here I am, and she's nowhere to be seen. He's staring at me, free as a bird, talking on the phone. Logic would therefore dictate that his sister is injured—or worse—and that it's my doing.

After a few seconds of silence and confusion, he screams something incomprehensible at me in Russian and reaches for his gun.

"Josh, I gotta go."

I duck behind the desk as the first bullet whizzes past my head. I throw my phone down and pull Natalia's gun out, instinctively checking the magazine. It's practically full, which is helpful. I reach up and blind-fire one round in the direction of the main door, just to get an idea of where he is.

There's a moment's silence before he stands and resumes screaming, squeezing off round after round in my direction. He walks toward me, firing and yelling. I stick my head around the corner of the desk and catch a glimpse of him. His eyes are wide with rage. He isn't thinking about anything other than putting a bullet in me, which I can understand, given what I've just done to his sister...

However, he has me pinned down, and I can't stay here without increasing the risk of getting shot. I fire another round blindly, trying to make him hesitate, buying me some valuable seconds. I look around the room at my options.

None present themselves.

Shit.

His gun clicks on an empty chamber.

I breathe a small sigh of relief. I don't know how many spare magazines he has, but I have no desire to find out. I stand and walk toward him with my gun aimed squarely at his chest.

"Put your gun down, Salikov. It's over."

I have him dead to rights, and he knows it. He stops where he is, on the other side of the center console about thirty feet from me. He tosses his gun to the floor, seething with rage and staring at me with an unblinking gaze of hatred on his face.

He stands casually, seemingly oblivious to the fact I have a gun pointing at him. "Why don't you throw your weapon down too? Fight me like a real soldier!"

His voice is similar to Natalia's, albeit a little deeper—a thick Russian accent and a minimal grasp of the English language.

He cracks his knuckles and smiles before switching into a fighting stance, similar to that of a boxer. Left foot forward, up on the balls of his feet. Hands high, guarding his face.

Despite my occupation, the concept of honor and tradition isn't lost on me. I understand that sometimes you just have to prove who's best. Anyone can pull a trigger, but it takes a true warrior to fight it out with someone, unarmed, to the death.

I look him up and down. He has a good, solid stance. He's light on his feet for a guy as muscular as he is. He seems to subconsciously put more weight on his front leg. That makes me think he has an old injury of some kind on his other, which could be useful. He's right-handed and holds his back hand slightly lower than his front—that means he favors a strong knockout blow. Easily avoided but deadly if it found the mark.

I look into his eyes. That rage is still burning bright. Ultimately, I all but killed his sister about ten minutes ago, and he knows it. Someone in a fight to the death, with hate as their fuel and revenge as their motive, would be capable of immense things.

Then I assess my own personal situation. I have some pretty severe bruising on my ribs and back, plus I've suffered two significant concussions in as many days. I've also been on the business end of a car bomb less than twenty-four hours ago, so it's safe to say I'm not exactly firing on all cylinders physically.

I consider his proposal a moment longer. "Nah, I'm good."

I pull the trigger twice. I aim at his chest, but because he's standing slightly side-on in his boxing stance, the first bullet grazes across him and hits his shoulder, making him stagger backward a little.

The second bullet, however, hits him in the face. His head disappears in a cloud of pink mist that sprays across the floor behind him. His body drops with a dull thud. I tuck the gun into my waistband and pick up the phone, dialing Josh again.

"Sorry about that," I say as he answers.

"What happened? Have you been making friends again?"

"Gene Salikov just started shooting at me. He figured out I'd killed his sister."

"You've taken out Natalia? How?"

"I knocked her out, shot her in the leg, and locked her in one of the furnace rooms. I'd like to think that's game over."

"And I'm assuming Gene's beef with you has now been resolved amicably?"

"Gene no longer has a head."

There's a moment's silence.

"Yeah... that'll do it."

I make my way out of the control room and down the main corridor, toward the stairs that lead up to the court-yard outside.

"You had any luck with Clark or Schultz?"

"I got in touch with Clark, but he's not convinced. He says their intel can't be that wrong."

"It is. Trust me. If they send the cavalry in here, everyone will die, Josh. Tell him to swallow his pride, reprimand his intelligence division, and pull all the ground forces way back."

I climb the last flight of stairs, push open the metal door, and step outside into the yard. The glare of the sun stings my eyes after being underground for so long. I squint until they adjust to the light. I look around, but I can't see any sign of Ketranovich or Clara.

I pace a slow circle, checking everywhere. "Josh, how long until everyone gets here?"

"Just under... twenty minutes."

"Shit. I've lost the mad colonel and his bitch of a daughter. I'm assuming he has the detonator with him."

"Hold up. Daughter?"

"Oh, yeah. Forgot to mention that, didn't I? Clara is Ketranovich's daughter."

"Jesus Christ. I officially fucking hate her."

"Join the club."

I hear the mechanical groan of the hangar doors opening again to my right.

"Scratch that—I've found them. Do what you can to buy me some time."

I hang up and run over to where my Berettas are still lying on the ground, near the SAM sites. I pick them up just in time to see Clara emerge from the darkness on a motorcycle. Ketranovich walks out behind her. They both stop to look at me, then at each other, clearly panicked.

Ketranovich points to the main gate and looks at Clara. "Go!"

I aim one of my guns and fire at the front tire of the motorcycle, causing her to slam her brakes on and slide to a halt.

I aim a Beretta at each of them. "Don't even think about it, either of you!"

Ketranovich looks pissed but seems composed. "You've lost, Adrian Hell. You can't stop this!"

"You've said that already. And now you're two Salikovs down, and I'm still standing here, so I'd say I'm doing a good job of winning so far."

Clara revs her engine.

I look at her. "Clara, I swear to God, I would give vital parts of my anatomy right now if it meant I could shoot you dead, so be a good girl and get off the fucking bike!"

Ketranovich raises his right hand into the air. He's holding something in it. "I don't think so, Adrian Hell." He looks at Clara. "Get out of here. I will see this through to the end."

After a split-second's hesitation, she nods and revs her engine again.

I'm looking at his hand.

"That's right, Adrian. This is the detonator."

I lower my guns.

Ah, shit.

The detonator looks like a gun but without the barrel. It resembles just the butt—a small silver handle with the trigger inside a small, circular guard. It fits nicely in the palm of his hand. His finger hovers over the trigger, ready to squeeze.

I look back and forth between Ketranovich and Clara. I definitely don't want to get blown to bits, but there's no way I'm letting Clara escape either. Not after everything she's done.

My hands tighten around the Berettas. I know I need to end things quickly. If GlobaTech and the U.S. Army come marching in through the front door, I have no doubt Ketranovich would gladly kamikaze himself to take them all out. Such an attack on domestic soil against U.S. troops would require a proportionate response by the government. Their logical target would be Russia, given that's where Ketranovich is from.

And we all know how a conflict between America and Russia would turn out.

So, here I stand. The sun's beating down on me relentlessly. The light breeze swirls sand and dust around us that occasionally stings my eyes. My mind is working overtime to find an outcome that doesn't involve a third World War. If Clara manages to get out of here on that bike, I'll never see her again. If Ketranovich moves his finger two millimeters, bits of me are going to land in Montana.

I sigh, seeing only one option.

As a wise man once said: fuck it.

Time slows down as I raise both Berettas, aiming one at Clara's head and the other at Ketranovich's right hand. Everything I've been through, everything I've endured, every bullet fired, and every drop of blood spilt... It all comes down to this.

For some reason, Ennio Morricone's theme from *The Good, The Bad, and The Ugly* starts playing through my mind.

"Ketranovich, drop the detonator, or I'll kill your daughter."

He shrugs and laughs. "Drop your guns, or I'll kill us all right here, right now."

Well, *that* worked.

I check my aim on both guns and take a deep breath, keeping my poker face on as best as I can. This is either the smartest or the dumbest thing I've ever done. If I get it right, you could argue I'll have saved the world from war, which is good to have on your résumé. However, if I get it wrong, well... I'll most likely be dead, so people can think whatever the fuck they want.

I take one last deep breath and hold it. My heart rate is nice and steady. The adrenaline is at bay—for the time being.

I slowly breathe out as I squeeze the trigger in my left hand. The bullet covers the distance between Ketranovich and me in a fraction of a second and hits his forearm roughly two inches above his wrist. A thin stream of blood erupts from the impact, and the gunshot almost completely severs his hand. The detonator flies out of his grip and lands a few feet away from him, off to his right.

A split-second later, I squeeze the trigger in my right hand. I aim a couple of feet in front of the motorcycle, anticipating Clara's sharp exit. The bullet strikes just above the front wheel as she hammers on the gas, pushing the bike out to the left. She loses control and topples over the handlebars, landing awkwardly on her back and neck. She rolls over a couple of times and comes to stop a few feet away from the bike, face-down in the dust. She makes a low, muffled, groan from inside her helmet.

I breathe an audible sigh of relief and rush over to Ketranovich, who's on all fours, screaming. I kick him hard and flush in the ribcage. He rolls over on his back, clutching at his forearm, which is leaking blood at a steadily increasing rate.

"That's for making the last week of my life as shitty as it was, you sonofabitch!"

I holster my guns and look over to the detonator. I'll get it in a minute. He's not going anywhere, and I want to deal with Clara first.

She's managed to get up on one knee and remove her helmet. She's shaking her head and holding her neck, trying to get her bearings. It reminds me of the first time we met, in Ted Jackson's hotel suite. I walk up behind her, and when

I'm a couple of feet away, I launch a kick to the side of her head. I turn my hip over as I swing my leg round, making sure I follow through for maximum effect. Her body lurches to the side, and she's out cold before she hits the ground.

"And *that's* for betraying me, bitch!"

I'm breathing harder and faster as my adrenaline starts to flow. The anger gradually rises inside me. I want revenge. I want to make them both pay for everything they've done and everyone they've hurt. My door is opening, and I can feel my self-control leaving me once again, so that nothing remains but my Inner Satan.

They're going to suffer for what they've done here...

I hear shuffling behind me, and I turn to see Ketranovich on his feet, slowly moving toward me. His eyes are wide, and he has a crazed look on his face. He's screaming, half in English, half in Russian. He has his arms raised, ready to attack. I walk over to meet him head-on, ready to fight. He can barely stand. Half his right arm has been blown apart, and he'll likely have a few cracked ribs to go with it.

There is only a few feet between us. I raise my arms to meet his, grabbing his good arm with my left hand and launching a right hook to his kidneys. I catch him clean, and he bends over to the side, letting out a grunt of pain.

As he doubles over, I move in for the kill. My plan is to bring my elbow down on the back of his head, near the top of his spine. I can hear him coughing, and he drops to one knee in front of me, spitting some blood on the sand. I raise my elbow. I'm going to finish this once and for—

My breath catches in my throat. My eyes go wide involuntarily as I feel the impact of a blow against the right side of my stomach. An icy cold washes over me, and I stumble backward a few steps, staring at him in shock.

What the hell was that?

I look at Ketranovich, who's reaching up with his left hand, his eyes manic with rage. I see the knife in his hand. I see the blood on the blade.

Oh, don't tell me…

I look down and see an expanding, dark red stain on my T-shirt.

Shit.

I never saw it coming. I never expected him to have enough left in his tank to even lift a knife, let alone use one. I stagger back a few more steps and drop to my knees. The shock wears off, and the pain erupts throughout my entire body. The shiver I feel up and down my spine counters the warmth from the blood pumping freely from the wound. I instinctively clasp at it with my hands, but it's too late. The damage has been done.

I can feel myself falling forward. The dust on the ground is rushing toward me. I can't get my breath… I can't—

31

I'm not religious in any way.

You could put my atheism down to losing my family, but even before that, I didn't buy into it. I just think it would be in poor taste to say I believe in God, then go around killing people for a living.

Plus, I've simply never needed the comfort that religion seems to give to so many. As a result, I've never been very spiritual either. I believe what I can see with my own eyes. Anything else is fiction until proven otherwise.

Which is why whatever's happening to me right now is so bizarre. I swear, it's like I'm floating above the compound. I'm looking down at myself, lying motionless and barely breathing on dark, bloodstained sand. Ketranovich is struggling to his feet, searching for the detonator. Clara's still lying there, not moving after the kick to the head.

I look around. There's nothing else. The world outside the compound is a flat, barren desert, decorated only by

313

mountains in the distance and the odd rock or bush dotted here and there for effect.

There's no sign of the cavalry charging over the hill to the rescue. No sound of trumpets as the soldiers approach, guns raised and ready for war.

What the hell is going on?

Am I dead? Is that what this is?

Have I been rejected by both God and Lucifer? Have I been left to roam around in my own personal Purgatory for eternity? Am I being forced to relive my death over and over as penance for my lifetime of sin?

I look at my body again. The blood is still pooling around me, but I can see my right leg moving slightly...

Well, if my leg's moving, and the blood is still being pumped out of me, then I can't be dead, can I?

And if I don't believe in God or the Devil, how can they possibly exist to kick me out of their respective domains anyway?

This is just a dream, isn't it?

This is my subconscious giving me a massive kick up the ass to show me that it's not over. Not by a long shot.

I'm Adrian fucking Hell, goddammit! You think stabbing me is going to stop me?

I'll tell you when the fight's over. *I'll* tell you when I'm done.

If there's breath in my body...

Whoa, the ground's rushing up at me really fast!

32

My eyes snap open. My vision struggles to focus, clouding the world around me in a light fog. My mind feels just as hazy. My entire body is screaming at me, begging me not to move. But I have to. I lift my head slightly and turn to look the other way. I can just about make out a figure ahead of me, staggering across the courtyard.

Ketranovich.

Everything suddenly comes flooding back.

Oh, shit—the detonator!

I bend my arms, preparing to push myself up. I bring my knees slowly up to my chest, then in one colossal, excruciating effort, I lift my body from the ground and stand up. I can't straighten my back—I have to hunch forward to relieve the pressure from the knife wound in my stomach. But I'm up.

I rub my eyes, trying to clear the haze in front of them. I

look ahead and see Ketranovich slowly making his way over to the detonator. He drags himself to his feet.

I try to walk, which is harder than I would've liked. Everything is unfolding in painfully slow motion.

"Hey!"

Ketranovich looks back at me, almost losing his balance. His face is a mixture of shock and anger.

I try to laugh but end up coughing. I spit some blood on the ground next to me. "Is that all you got?"

He turns away from me, more concerned with getting the detonator than he is with any potential threat I may pose. I have to distract him.

"Hey! Don't walk away from me, you fucking coward!"

He stops in his tracks and turns to look at me once more. He's barely able to stand up straight either, probably thanks to the damage my kick did to his ribs. He's holding what remains of his right forearm in his left hand.

I continue toward him, stopping a few feet away. We look the same—hunched over, covered in blood, barely able to move, hurting more and more with each breath we take.

"I... am... no... coward, Adrian Hell! I am... a hero! I am a great... warrior... fighting for my country... since you were just... a child."

I grimace at the effort this is taking. "You're a maniac. You're prepared to kill hundreds of good men and women in the blink of an eye. And for what? Some self-righteous cause you use as an excuse for the fact you're pissed because your country screwed you over? You're just an angry old ex-grunt who wants to stomp his feet and relive the old days of killing without consequence, and you try to justify it by calling it revenge."

He laughs and coughs through a bloodstained smile. "You think your... opinion matters to me? You're an insect...

A parasite… A product of western capitalism who thinks… they're superior to the rest of the world. You sit… and you talk… and you offer an opinion on others' problems. You know nothing… of real war. Of real struggle. Of real… values. Time and again, people like you use warriors… like me, for your own battles, then cast us to one side the moment… we're no longer of any use. Well, no more! Today, I will send a message… to the entire world, showing them that *everyone* is expendable—not just the men and women who… choose to fight for their people!"

"Roman, you're certifiable. Do you know that? This ends now."

I leap forward as much as I can under the circumstances, leading with my left elbow. He's not expecting it, and I connect hard with his face. We both fall to the ground —him flat on his back, dazed, and me on my hands and knees.

I can't afford to let him get an advantage. I don't have much energy left. I've lost a lot of blood, and it's getting harder to stay conscious than it is to fight him. I crawl forward so that I'm level with him and hammer my fist down into his face. Once. Twice. His lip splits and blood runs slowly down his chin.

I go to stand, intending to kick him a couple of times, but as I get to my feet, I feel Ketranovich's hand grab my ankle. I can see what's going to happen, but I'm moving too slow to stop it. He rolls over and slams his right elbow into my left knee. It immediately gives way, and my borderline dead weight loses what little support it had left. I crash heavily to the ground.

Oh my God…

I grit my teeth and fight to ignore the pain. I roll over on my back, bringing both legs up to my side. I quickly rub my knee to get the blood flowing again, as well as trying to take some pressure off my knife wound—which doesn't look or feel good.

I look over, preparing to defend the inevitable onslaught from Ketranovich. But nothing comes. He simply struggles slowly to his feet and stubbornly sets off once more for the detonator.

I roll onto my front and reach behind me for a Beretta. I'm lying on the ground, as straight as I can, with my right arm outstretched. It's pulling at my stab wound, but I try to ignore it. I close one eye and take aim. I can see a dark blur with a lighter blur on either side, dancing around. I blink rapidly to clear my vision. It doesn't work. I relax my arm a moment, closing my eyes tightly.

I could just as easily never open them again, but that's the easy way out... I can't allow myself to stop. Not yet.

I take a few deep, agonizing breaths and take aim again. The dancing blurs slowly merge together, and I can finally see Ketranovich. He bends down for a moment, then stands up slowly and turns toward me. He has the detonator in his left hand.

Ah, shit!

This is it. Bottom of the ninth. Do or die. I only have time for one shot. If I miss, he'll hit the switch, and it'll be game over. I don't think or hesitate.

I fire once. The gunshot echoes around the compound.

The split-second it takes for the bullet to reach Ketranovich feels like a lifetime. I hold my breath and wait.

The bullet hits him in the chest, dead center. He lets out a scream of pain as he flings his arms into the air and staggers backward. The detonator once again flies out of his grip. He takes a couple of steps back and falls to the ground.

Goodnight, sweetheart.

I let out a long breath and let go of my gun.

It's over.

11:37 PDT

I roll over on my back and close my eyes. I want to take a nice, deep, relaxing breath, but I'm in far too much pain for such luxuries.

God, I feel like I've been stabbed in the stomach or something.

Oh, wait...

I prop myself up on my elbows and look down at the wound.

I huff dismissively. I've had worse.

I roll onto my side and push myself up into a sitting position. I hug my knees up to my chest and sit squinting in the afternoon sun, listening to the eerie silence that's descended around me.

What a shitty day.

I check my watch.

Christ, it's not even lunchtime!

I look over my shoulder and see Ketranovich lying on the ground, not moving. I breathe a sigh of relief.

That's a good sign at least.

I reach for my gun and painfully try to stand up. I stagger over to his body, one hand clutching my stomach, the other clutching my Beretta. I need to make sure he's dead. And Dark Rain along with him.

I approach him and tap his leg with my foot. There's no reaction. I raise my gun and take aim at his head. I look at him for a moment and fire three times. Each gunshot echoes around the deserted base. His skull all but disappears, dissolving into a dark red puddle on the sand, slowly expanding around him.

Better safe than sorry.

I quickly find the detonator. I holster my gun and look behind me, over at the main gate. No sign of the cavalry just yet.

Sadly, there's no sign of Clara either.

I've got a bullet with her fucking name on it.

I pick up the detonator and hold it in my hand, regarding it for a moment. It's hard to believe that such a small device can control such devastating power. I put it in my pocket and take out my phone. I sit back down on the dirt and call Josh.

"Adrian, thank God!" he says as he answers. "Are you all right?"

"Yeah... I'm good." I wince as I try to get comfortable. "It's all over. Ketranovich is dead and I have the detonator. I just wish I could've stopped them shooting down the airstrike."

"Adrian, don't blame yourself for that, okay? It was a tragedy, but forget about it now—it'll be handled by all those government types. You've done enough. I'm just glad you're alive."

"Me too. I just wanna get out of here, Josh. I need a holiday."

He laughs. "I'll book the flights right now, Boss." He falls silent a moment. "What... ah... what happened to Clara?"

I look around again, but I know it won't change anything. Her bike's still there, resting on its side from earlier. The hangar door's still open. I want so badly to go after her and put a bullet right between her eyes. But right now I need all my energy just to stay conscious.

"No idea. She disappeared while I was fighting Ketranovich. I don't know if she's still on site or not, and if I'm completely honest, I don't really care. If she's alive, I'll find her and kill her. But... not now."

Josh laughs again. "That's the smartest thing you've said all week. Get outta there, Adrian."

I glance over at Clara's motorcycle and smile. "Way ahead of you, my friend."

I hang up and walk over to the bike. I take one last look around to make sure Clara isn't lying in wait somewhere, planning to shoot me when I least expect it. I use what strength I have left to lift the motorcycle up and climb on. I start it up, take one last look at Ketranovich's body, then speed off across the courtyard, through the main gate, and out to the desert track.

I blast down the dirt road, past the Audi I stole to get here, past the warning sign about the compound, heading for the main highway. After a couple of miles, I spot the first helicopter in the air. It's quickly followed by two more. Ahead of me, I see a convoy of vehicles speeding toward me, leaving a thin trail of dust behind them in the distance.

The helicopters approach and hover above me as I turn off the track and hit the highway. I immediately slow down, coming to a stop a moment or two later. I sit with the engine idling, one foot on the ground, my arms folded across my chest. My right hand is resting on top of my stab wound. The convoy reaches me a minute later and slows to a stop.

As the truck in front pulls over, the passenger door opens, and Robert Clark jumps out. He walks over to me hurriedly. He's wearing a dark gray suit with the jacket open, flapping in the wind. "I took your advice and stayed out of your way..." He has to shout over the noise of the choppers overhead. "Definitely one of the better decisions I've made in the last few days. You're a resourceful individual. Do you know that?"

He's smiling. I still don't completely trust the guy, but I'll concede that I'm starting to like him.

I shrug. "I just don't like people who go out of their way to do bad things." I gesture to the troops behind him with a small nod as he stops next to me. "Impressive."

"Thanks. They're not all mine, though. Most of the men here are on Uncle Sam's dime, not mine. But I've got a hundred and fifty of my best guys watching our backs."

"You're late for the party. I already ate the good stuff."

"We mobilized as fast as we could. It was a short-notice joint operation and not the easiest thing to arrange, unfortunately." He gestures to my stomach. "You all right? You look like shit."

"Thanks. I got stabbed a little bit, but I'll be fine. It's all over, Bob."

"So I heard. Your British friend is one hell of an asset, Adrian. You're lucky I don't try to poach him from you." He laughs at his comment, which was probably half-serious.

I simply smile. "You can't afford him."

He nods and smiles back. "Fair enough. Can you give us any information about Dark Rain's operation?"

I shrug. "Not much to tell, really. Despite what Clara told us, it was mostly smoke and mirrors, combined with some clever bullshit. But their hardware was top-notch... Well done funding all that, by the way."

Clark holds his hands up in resignation, acknowledging my sarcasm. "Hey, you're preaching to the choir about that. I'm *still* trying to clear up the shit-storm that Jackson left me."

We fall silent for a moment. I look at Clark as he scans the horizons all around, looking across the vast expanse of unforgiving desert, as I have done on occasion this past week. He looks back at me. "So, where you heading?"

I shake my head. "Honestly? I have no idea. Somewhere away from *here*."

He nods to my stomach wound. "Please tell me you're going to a hospital first?"

"Why, Bob, I never knew you cared."

He smiles. "I don't. I just want you to move, so I can get these guys into that compound and clean up the mess you've made."

We both share a laugh.

"Take care, Adrian. We're going to gut this place and gather everything we can on Dark Rain." He turns to walk away but looks back. "I'll let you know if we turn anything up about Clara, okay?"

I smile but say nothing. He walks off back to his truck.

I sit there for a moment and think about everything Dark Rain has done. Everything they put me through. All the times I came close to death. I even think of all the members of Dark Rain that Ketranovich used, lied to, and killed in the name of his pathetic little cause. Then I think of all the innocent people who were caught in the crossfire. The pilots of those F-22s that I couldn't save...

I realize that every single shred of data on Dark Rain is inside that old military base. They don't exist anywhere else in the world except here, on the outskirts of Heaven's Valley.

I reach into my pocket and pull out the detonator, looking at it in my hand for a moment. There's nothing to think about. I know what I need to do. I know what's right.

"Bob..."

He stops at the side of the truck, one hand on the door, and looks over. I hold the detonator in my hand, high in the air, for him to see.

"I can't let you go in there. I'm sorry."

"What do you mean?" I hear panic in his voice, and he starts slowly walking back over to me. "What are you doing?"

"After everything they've done, I'm not interested in their assets or their secrets. I want them erased from history. It's the least Ketranovich deserves—for his legacy to disappear in smoke."

Realizing what I'm going to do, he sets off running toward me, his right arm outstretched in a futile attempt to reach for something he's nowhere near.

"Adrian, no!"

But he isn't going to stop me. No one is. I think of Clara, hoping she's still in the compound somewhere. I think of Natalia, whom I *know* is still in there. Finally, I picture Ketranovich, lying dead on the floor, beaten.

With that image in my mind, I squeeze the trigger.

33

September 17, 2013 — 16:06 MDT

I'm sitting on a worn, brown leather stool, resting on the bar of a quiet little place in Colorado Springs. I'm wearing a black T-shirt and jeans with my brown boots. My shoulder bag is by my feet, resting against the bar stool. In front of me is an ice-cold bottle of Budweiser, and next to that is a shot of whiskey.

The bar isn't exactly busy. There are a few small groups of two or three people dotted around. The bar has the obligatory pool table in the corner, with three lights hanging low above it. There's a jukebox attached to the back wall, next to a door that leads to the restrooms.

I take a long drink of my beer. It's been over three weeks since I left Heaven's Valley. I was in a hospital for a few days, courtesy of GlobaTech. My knife wound didn't cause any permanent damage. The blood I lost had caused the most trouble, and it didn't take long to recover from that. Globa-Tech spared no expense on my medical treatment, which

325

was nice of them. Robert Clark was pretty pissed at me for pressing the button and destroying Dark Rain's military base, though.

Well, *destroyed* doesn't sufficiently describe what happened to that compound. Every square inch was completely obliterated, and there's now a crater there a quarter-mile wide and about the same deep. I spoke to Josh when I left the hospital, and he said he saw the explosion via the satellite feed he was linked up to. He said it was one of the most spectacular things he'd ever seen.

I still have no idea whether Clara was in there when it blew up. I know the bodies of Ketranovich and the two Salikovs were. Three out of four isn't bad, I guess.

I reduced Dark Rain to nothing but dust and myth. Pellaggio was dead and buried. The government was protecting the uranium mine, and despite recent events, I can now count one of the biggest private military contractors in the country as an ally.

Aside from the uncertainty about Clara, I'd say I've come out of that whole situation in a good position.

After leaving the hospital, I took the first Greyhound bus out of Heaven's Valley. I told Josh to leave me be for a week or two. I need the rest and the peace and quiet. I made my way down through Phoenix before heading over here to Colorado Springs, where I've been for the last four days. It's a nice place. Been here almost a week, and no one's tried to kill me yet, which is a marked improvement on Heaven's Valley.

I walk over to the jukebox and feed some quarters into it. I cycle through the playlists and choose some songs that catch my eye. My phone rings. It's Josh.

I answer as I'm selecting my last song. "Hey. You all right?"

"I'm doing fine, Boss. You all rested up?"

"I'm getting there. I'm just enjoying the downtime, to be honest. How are things with you?"

"Not too bad. I've been speaking with Clark on and off since you left town. Figured it couldn't hurt to keep in touch and maybe whore ourselves out to them every now and then."

I walk back to my stool and sit down, smiling. "No, I guess not."

"Other than that, I've got a few jobs you can look at when you're ready to get back to it."

"Maybe in a few days. Listen, has there been any..." I stop mid-sentence. "Never mind."

"Any sign of Clara?"

I sigh. "Yeah. Anything at all?"

"Nothing. But she'll forever be on our own little Most Wanted list."

"You better believe it."

The music starts playing in the background—the first of my song choices. I figure I'll start off with something mellow.

"Is that *Carry On, Wayward Son* by Kansas I hear in the background?"

I smile. "Certainly is, my friend."

"Then I shall leave you to enjoy what I imagine is a bottle of Bud and a shot of whiskey in peace."

I laugh. "There's a lot to be said for predictability."

"Take care, Boss."

He hangs up, leaving me to my bar stool, my drink, and my music. I take another pull of my beer and signal to the barman to open me another.

I forget myself for a moment, enjoying the song, the beer, and the welcome return to anonymity.

I figure I'll have another couple of drinks, head to a motel for some sleep, and move on in the morning. I'm thinking of heading back to my hometown of Omaha for a day or two. It's only a half-day's travel from here, and it'll be nice to see the old stomping ground again.

Another minute goes by, and the song finishes, fading into my second choice. I went for something a little heavier with this one.

The opening riff of *Cowboys From Hell* sounds out across the bar. One of my all-time favorites, this one. It's real whiskey drinking music. I grab my shot and swill it around the glass for a moment before knocking it back in one.

As the barman places a fresh bottle of Bud in front of me, a man appears at my side and signals to him. He's a tall, broad guy with an unkempt beard and long hair. He's wearing a red, checked shirt and jeans. "Hey, which asshole put this crap on the jukebox?"

The barman looks uneasy, and his eyes betray him by flicking over to me. The guy turns and looks at me. "This is a nice, peaceful bar, *asshole*. We don't appreciate devil music blasting out disturbing folks."

Devil music?

Okay, I'll bite...

I turn on my stool to face him. "We?"

He nods to the corner of the bar. I look over to his table and see two more guys of similar build and wearing similar clothes. They're just getting out of their seats, watching us intently.

I sigh. It's a loud, long, heavy sigh.

I reach into my pocket, pull out a twenty-dollar bill, and throw it on the bar. The barman looks at me apologetically, but I wave my hand dismissively. It's not *his* fault this guy's an asshole.

I stand up. "That's for the drinks. I might owe you some more in a minute for the damage." I turn and casually square up to the guy in the checked shirt, tilting my head slightly. "Man, you're abusing the right to be ugly. Do you know that?"

He looks confused—probably too stupid to realize he's being insulted.

"Seriously, it's like you fell out of the ugly tree and hit every branch on the way down."

The barman hides a small smile as he steps away.

The guy in the checked shirt holds his ground, still more confused than angry, it seems. His two friends from the table join him.

"Okay, I've had my fun. Are you and your boyfriends ready?"

He frowns and sneers. "Ready for what? Who do you think you are, asshole?"

I smile, moving my head slightly to crack my neck.

What a good question.

Who do I think I am?

I take a deep breath, stepping back into a loose fighting stance.

I'm Adrian Hell.

THE END

A MESSAGE

Dear Reader,

Thank you for purchasing my book. I hope you enjoyed reading it as much as I enjoyed writing it!

If you did, it would mean a lot to me if you could spare thirty seconds to leave an honest review on your preferred online store. For independent authors like me, one review makes a world of difference.

If you want to get in touch, please visit my website, where you can contact me directly, either via e-mail or social media.

Until next time...

James P. Sumner

CLAIM YOUR FREE GIFT!

By subscribing to James P. Sumner's mailing list, you can get your hands on a free and exclusive reading companion, not available anywhere else.

It contains an extended preview of Book 1 in each thriller series from the author, as well as character bios, and official reading orders that will enhance your overall experience.

If you wish to claim your free gift, just visit the website below:

linktr.ee/jamespsumner

You will receive infrequent, spam-free emails from the author, containing exclusive news about his books. You can unsubscribe at any time.

Printed in Great Britain
by Amazon

24498813R00199